A Killer Who Bakes the Cake

I saw no one and nothing seemed out of place in the anteroom with its trendy black-and-white patterned wallpaper, upholstered chairs, and shabby chic painted tables topped with stacks of bridal magazines.

Then I heard the mournful wail repeated.

"No, no, no," a voice sobbed in a tone that broke my heart.

I dropped the borrowed dress and shoes, hurrying as fast as I could through the waiting area. Without further preamble, I burst into Olivia's office.

"Millie, are you o—" I started to say, and then my tongue lodged in my throat. "Dear God," I breathed, taking in the frightening tableau before me.

Millie kneeled on the rug not six feet away, looking anything but okay. She turned her wide eyes upon me, her time-worn face stricken.

"Oh, Andy! This is bad," she choked out and shook her head, "very bad."

Very bad?

That had to be the understatement of the year.

For Millie held a silver cake knife in her hand, its blade slick with blood. And lying on the rug before her was Olivia La Belle, her body still and her eyes rolled to the heavens, her throat slick with blood as well.

Also by Susan McBride

The Debutante Dropout Series
Say Yes to the Death
Too Pretty to Die
Night of the Living Deb
The Lone Star Lonely Hearts Club
The Good Girl's Guide to Murder
Blue Blood

The River Road Series
Not a Chance in Helen
Mad as Helen
To Helen Back

Published by William Morrow Paperbacks
The Truth about Love and Lightning
Little Black Dress
The Cougar Club

SAY YES
TO THE
DEATH

A DEBUTANTE DROPOUT MYSTERY

SUSAN
MᶜBRIDE

WITNESS
An Imprint of HarperCollinsPublishers

WITNESS

An Imprint of HarperCollins*Publishers*
195 Broadway
New York, NY 10007

Copyright © 2015 by Susan McBride
ISBN 978-0-06-235860-8
www.witnessimpulse.com

First Witness mass market printing: October 2015

HarperCollins® is a registered trademark of HarperCollins Publishers.

Printed in the United States of America

10 9 8 7 6 5 4 3 2 1

*To all the wonderful folks who kept asking,
"When will we see Andy and Cissy again?"
This one's for you!*

SAY YES
TO THE
DEATH

Prologue

Millicent Draper yawned and nudged her owl-like glasses back up the bridge of her nose, leaving a smudge of ivory fondant on the tortoiseshell frames. Her plastic-gloved fingers were smeared with the stuff. Her knuckles felt stiff, and she could barely keep her eyes open. She'd worked through the night on a wedding cake for Senator Vernon Ryan's daughter, Penny, and she hadn't slept a wink.

Olivia La Belle, the bride's wedding planner, had phoned at six o'clock the night before—just as Millie was closing up shop—demanding an early delivery. "Sorry, Millie, but the ceremony's been pushed up a wee bit," Olivia had said in a honey-sweet twang that implied softness when Olivia was anything but.

Four whole months was "a wee bit"? Millie thought with a groan.

"We must have the cake by three o'clock tomorrow sharp," Olivia had insisted, her sugared drawl turning hard. "The ceremony's at five with a sit-down dinner reception to follow. If you don't get this done, it will make me very unhappy. Do you understand what I'm sayin', sugar?"

Oh, yeah, *sugar*, Millie understood. Ticking off Big D's premier event planner was a big no-no. Olivia might as well have said, "If you don't get this done, you're as good as dead in this town."

Ever since Olivia had done weddings for an Oscar winner and the spawn of a former president, her head had blown up as big as Texas. She'd become society's go-to girl and, not only for Dallas royalty, but honest-to-God foreign royalty and Hollywood's A-List. She'd even finagled her own reality TV show on a cheesy cable network and used it to promote herself and to punish those who displeased her. Anyone who dared defy *The Wedding Belle* risked hanging a "Going Out of Business" sign on the front door.

Millie had seen it happen most recently to Jasper Pippin, a floral designer in Big D for decades. Fed up with Olivia's lies and demands, he'd finally drawn a line in the sand. "She lied her tight little ass off and said the tulips I had flown in from Amsterdam for the mayor's wife's birthday party were wilted," Jasper had told Millie, moaning. "She threatened a drubbing on her TV show if I didn't eat the cost. I'm going to lose my shirt if she keeps pulling these dirty tricks."

"What will you do?" Millie asked him.

Jasper had drawn in a deep breath and said,

"I'm going to let her have it. I am *not* going to give in."

So the always civil Jasper had finally squared his thin shoulders and stood up to Olivia, sure that other vendors who'd been jerked around would follow suit. Only no one dared, and Olivia had bad-mouthed him on her reality show. His orders dried up one by one until Jasper had to shutter his doors, claiming early retirement, though Millie knew better. He'd withdrawn, refusing to return her calls. She had no clue what he was up to, but she knew he wouldn't give up so easily. Millie hoped he would rise like the phoenix and stick it to Olivia somehow.

That evil woman had her French-manicured fingers in so many pies around Dallas that everyone who worked with her was scared to death. Even Olivia's current assistant seemed skittish, and with good reason since the job seemed to involve a revolving door. The gangly twenty-something, Terra, followed her everywhere, taking notes. She never seemed to say anything but "Yes, Olivia" and "Of course, Olivia," like a well-trained parrot.

Millie wished she'd had the gumption to tell Olivia that she could take this impossible cake deadline and stuff it, but she couldn't risk losing everything she'd worked so hard for. She'd started Millie's Cakes in her own kitchen thirty-five years ago and had built her impressive client list from scratch. She wasn't ready to give it all up because she'd ticked off the very fickle Ms. La Belle. Unlike Jasper, she had no intention of being forced into early retirement.

Millie swallowed, glancing at the clock on the wall. With a noisy *tick-tick*, its hands crept toward seven.

She only had eight hours left and still had to attach the two hundred handmade sugar orchids she'd painted a delicate shade of purple. Her feet ached from standing, and her arthritis was acting up so badly that her fingers felt like unbendable sticks. If the shop wasn't so busy, she would have turned the whole shebang over to her staff, but they had other orders to fill, cakes that had been on the docket for months and were equally important.

No, this monkey was squarely on her back.

If she blew this job for Senator Ryan's daughter, it would be on her head, no one else's. She tried to convince herself that she couldn't blame the bumped-up time frame entirely on Olivia. It was Penelope Ryan who was truly at fault.

"Silly girl got herself knocked up," Millie muttered, having heard the gossip that the bride's belly had begun to pop and that the senator—a button-down conservative if ever there was one—wanted his daughter legally wed ASAP. He couldn't afford to have the nineteen-year-old college sophomore he'd painted as pure as the driven snow during his campaign get photographed walking down the aisle in a maternity gown.

"You can put her in a big white dress and marry her off but that doesn't change anything," Millie murmured, and she pushed at her glasses again.

Was the senator going to pull one of those "the baby came prematurely" routines when his grandchild popped out in another five months or so? People didn't seem to have a whole lot of sense these days, but most of them could count, so long as they had enough fingers and toes.

Ah, well, Millie mused, there would always be brides who got knocked up before their vows. There would always be disappointed fathers who wanted to pretend their darling daughters stayed virginal until their honeymoons. And there would always be bitches like Olivia La Belle behind the scenes, wielding a phone in one hand and cracking a whip with the other, either telling everyone off or telling them what to do.

Millie sighed.

"Enjoy your moment while it lasts, Queen Olivia, because it won't be forever," she whispered, thinking of Marie Antoinette and her date with the guillotine. "As for me, I will let them eat cake," she added, knowing that Olivia would get her comeuppance one of these days. Women like her always did. She just hoped she'd be around when it happened. Heck, she'd pay good money for a front row seat.

But for now Millie blinked her bleary eyes and tried to keep her hand from shaking as she delicately affixed the edible orchids to the seven-layered concoction she'd created overnight.

She would get this damned cake done or die trying.

Chapter 1

"If we're too late, we'll get stuck in back and we won't be able to see a thing," Cissy complained as she drove with one manicured hand on the wheel and the other madly gesticulating. "For heaven's sake, Andrea, how long does it take to brush your hair and put on a dress?"

"Longer than the five minutes you gave me," I replied, wondering how I'd gotten roped into this cockamamie date with my mother when she had a perfectly good fiancé who could have escorted her to the bumped-up wedding of a Texas senator's spoiled daughter. I had a perfectly good fiancé of my own who was sitting back at my condo, a bottle of Shiner Bock in his hand, watching the Stars take on the Blues in the Stanley Cup play-offs, which sounded a whole lot better than what I was doing at the moment.

"No, Stephen couldn't come," my mother said as though reading my mind—something she did far too often, and it freaked me out every time. "He's flown off to Augusta for a golf outing with some old IRS cronies."

"You mean he didn't dump his plans for you even though he'd rather be in his yoga pants watching a hockey game with Brian?" I threw out for good measure.

"His yoga pants," my mother sputtered, "watching a hockey game with Mr. Malone?" Her brow tried hard to wrinkle. Then she blinked and gave me a sideways glance. "You're talking about yourself, aren't you?"

"Of course I'm talking about myself," I growled, tempted to ask if Botox killed brain cells, but I refrained.

My mother sighed and did a very odd thing.

"You're right, I'm sorry, sweetie. I shouldn't have gotten huffy. I really am glad you could come to my rescue at the last minute. You are the most considerate child on God's green earth," she drawled, reaching over to pat my thigh, "and I appreciate that you're tagging along with your old mom."

I opened my mouth but nothing emerged. Yes, I, Andrea Blevins Kendricks—smart-ass extraordinaire—found myself speechless. My mother didn't often offer apologies, unsolicited or otherwise.

"Truly, I didn't intend to drag you out on such short notice, but I only got the call from Shelby Ryan just before I went to bed last night. I had no idea they were moving up Penny's wedding to today," my mother explained. "It was too late for Stephen to back out of his golf weekend, and I didn't want to pressure him."

No, I thought. No use making Stephen feel bad when it was all too easy to guilt me into going instead.

"What about Sandy?" I asked, referring to my mother's Girl Friday. Sandy Beck had been Cissy's personal assistant for as long as I could remember. She'd had as much a hand in raising me as my mother and couldn't have been more a part of our family if she'd been blood. "Why isn't she your date?"

"She's visiting her sister in Magnolia, Arkansas, and won't be back till next Sunday," Mother told me with a sigh. "Honestly, I tried."

"It's all right," I murmured, and added, "I can survive a few hours away from my yoga pants and Malone." *Two hours tops,* I told myself. That was all. Then my dress would turn into rags, my coach into a pumpkin, and I'd be all the happier for it.

Although I wasn't sure I would survive wearing Spanx. I could already feel them strangling my intestines. Unfortunately for me, my mother didn't consider jeans and T-shirt proper attire for a swanky wedding; unfortunately for Cissy, my closet was full of jeans and T-shirts and little else. I did have one little black dress that I'd kept around for a decade in case of emergencies, but Cissy had nixed it the moment I'd offered. "Who wears black to a wedding?" she'd remarked with a sniff. "Morticia Addams?"

Instead my mother had deemed herself my fairy god stylist, bringing over a new pair of Spanx along with a fresh-off-the-rack-at-Saks Carolina Herrera springy floral dress that was made for a skinny woman who survived on lettuce and water and/or had the meat sucked off her bones in seasonal liposuction sessions. It would have probably involved amputation or a bottle of Wesson oil to get me into the thing without the gut-strangling Lycra underpants. So for my mother's sake—and, boy, was she gonna owe me big-time—I wriggled into the killer girdle and the very fitted dress though I could barely breathe, let alone eat a piece of wedding cake without rupturing an organ.

"Why was the wedding moved up?" I dared to ask, something Mother hadn't yet explained, although I had a pretty good idea. When I'd last heard Cissy mention the invitation to Penny Ryan's knot-tying, it was set for late summer. It was currently the middle of April. There was only one reason I could fathom for such last minute maneuvering. I muttered, "The word 'shotgun' comes to mind."

Cissy sighed. "Well, I'm not one to gossip."

I laughed and replied, "Since when?"

My mother's Rouge Coco lips settled into a disappointed moue. She tossed her coiffed blond head and drawled, "Well, that was hardly very nice. I'm sure they taught you better in your Little Miss Manners classes all those years ago, or I should ask for a refund."

"Oh, for crud's sake," I said under my breath and rolled my eyes. There wasn't a Highland

Park matron who loved to gossip more than Cissy Blevins Kendricks, the Doyenne of Beverly Drive, and every socialite within a fifty-mile radius knew it.

"So how far along is the bride?" I asked point-blank.

"About four months as near as anyone can tell," Cissy blurted out, and a spark lit her eyes. "Shelby said Penny's starting to show, which is why they had to do the wedding stat. In another month she wouldn't fit in her dress."

Ha! I thought with a smirk, so much for detesting gossip.

"Shelby also said the latest scan showed that the baby's a boy," my mother rattled on, hardly able to stop herself. "They're all pleased as punch since Penny's an only child. She promised to name the boy after the senator." Cissy took her eyes off the road long enough to turn her head and give me a wicked smile. "Vernon Ignatius Ryan Tripplehorn," she said, adding, "Quite a mouthful isn't it? They want to call him Iggy."

"Oh, my God, the poor kid," I muttered. "That'll virtually guarantee a regular ass-whooping by junior high if not sooner."

And I should know. Being nicknamed "Andy" by my father early on—though my mother had always insisted on calling me Andrea—meant I'd heard plenty of playground cracks about being a girl with a boy's name.

"Well, Penny might not have gone about things the proper way but at least she's giving Shelby a grandchild before Shelby's too old and creaky to enjoy it," my mother went on, and I saw her squint behind her oversized sunglasses, peering at the signage overhead as she drove south toward Preston Hollow. "Some of us are still waiting," she said with a sideways glance before gliding toward the toll road exit.

Oh, joy, I thought, *here we go again.*

At least my mother was progressing in a forward direction when it came to guilt trips. Ever since Malone and I had gotten engaged the year before, she'd begun dropping less than subtle hints about wanting to become a grandmother. "Don't wait too long," she'd said most recently, "or that womb with a view will start looking like Miss Havisham's cobweb-filled abode." Somehow, the digs about my ticking clock were easier to take than the jibes that had come before Malone put a ring on my finger.

For years my mother had laid it on thick, reminding me of how I'd broken her heart by refusing to debut when I was eighteen, right after my dad's sudden death from a heart attack. As a reminder of her deep disappointment, Cissy kept my fancy white deb dress hanging in my old bedroom closet, and it surely would have had cobwebs on it by now save for the fact that she had a regular housekeeper tasked with banishing cobwebs.

Yes, I knew I'd wounded Mother deeply for being a debutante dropout, considering how much her world revolved around traditions. She had been a debutante, after all, as had all the Blevins women before her dating back to pre–

Civil War. But how long did I have to pay for it? Sure, I understood that since my conception, she'd envisioned my following in her footsteps: coming out to society, pledging Pi Phi at SMU, marrying a bona fide blue blood, and settling down in Highland Park. But I hadn't done any of those things. I wasn't Cissy. Wearing a white dress and kidskin gloves at cotillion had been *her* dream for me, not mine. Losing my father had made me realize that life was too short to live someone else's dream for them. So despite how hard my mother had tried to draw me back to the dark side, I'd fought just as hard to become my own person, whether she liked it or not.

Heck, I was still fighting.

". . . and they had to throw off the media, so he's letting them use the place since it's been sitting on the market for months anyway," I heard Cissy saying as I shook off my thoughts and realized we'd somehow gotten from the Tollway to Northwest Highway and exited, ultimately landing on Alva Court with its ginormous mansions tucked safely behind guard houses and privacy fences.

"What?" I said, since I'd obviously missed the most important part of her monologue. "Who let them borrow their place for the wedding?"

"Lester Dickens," Cissy announced and gave me a for-goodness'-sakes look when I appeared genuinely puzzled. "The oilman," she told me, as if that explained everything. "He's had the house on the market since he divorced his last wife. I think her name's Phoebe." My mother shook her blond head. "I don't even recall how many wives he's gone through since he was married to Adelaide. She was such a lovely woman. She used to play bridge with us at the Junior League before she died not a year after the divorce. He truly broke her heart."

"That's sad," I said, because it was, and not the kind of thing one usually discussed en route to a wedding.

"Les and Adelaide were high school sweethearts," Cissy blathered on, "and she gave him three sons before he traded her in for a younger model." She clicked tongue against teeth. "It's like his wives got younger as he got richer."

"Isn't that how it works?"

"Les told Vern and Shelby they could use the place for Penny's big day since no one's livin' in it at the moment," Mother informed me. "Lester's latest ex got the house in Vail, and he's been staying in a suite at The Mansion."

The Mansion being The Mansion on Turtle Creek, of course, one of Dallas's swankier hotels. It was a go-to spot for the very rich when they wanted to run away from home but not *too* far.

Click! A lightbulb went on in my brain, and I put two and two together. Lester Dickens wasn't just your run-of-the-mill rich-as-Croesus chauvinist cum oil baron: he was Senator Ryan's biggest supporter. He had put together a PAC and bought TV ads out the wazoo to help Vernon get elected in the first place. Word was that Dickens aimed to put Vernon Ryan in the White House come the next presidential election. It was no wonder he'd loaned the senator his mansion for a day. He was probably even more anxious than the Ryans to get the pregnant Penny married off.

"You know, it's a good thing you came with me, sweet pea," my mother said, changing the subject, "it'll give us some ideas for *your* wedding." She smiled as she pulled the Lexus up to a pair of gates and rolled down her window to give her name to a security guard. "Your old classmate from Hockaday, Olivia La Belle, will be here. She's Penny's wedding planner," Cissy informed me as the guard stepped back and the gates parted, revealing a sprawling Mediterranean villa sitting at the end of a very long driveway beyond palm trees and cascading fountains.

"Did you say Olivia La Belle?" I repeated, because I hadn't heard anything else my mother had said after the name. And all of a sudden I was flashing back to prep school and the athletic blonde who used to taunt me during Phys Ed. *You must be a boy, Andy Kendricks, 'cause you have no boobs at all! Andy's a boy, Andy's a boy!*

I flinched as though I'd been hit hard with one of Olivia's carefully aimed dodge balls, and I rubbed my arms. I could still feel the bruises.

"Yes, Olivia La Belle," mother repeated and wrinkled her nose. "Do you have wax in your ears, sugar plum?"

My mouth was too dry to tell her my ears weren't the problem. "I thought we'd chat her up and see if she's available any time soon," Cissy said, clearly ignoring the stricken look on my face. She steered the Lexus past a long line of shiny Caddies, Mercedes, Range Rovers, and Beemers that took up one side of the driveway and some of the expansive front yard. She finally turned into the circle around the fountain and pulled up to the valet. "You and Brian really need to firm up the date. Wouldn't it be the bee's knees, havin' your old schoolmate in charge of your wedding?"

Was Cissy insane?

La Belle from Hell planning my wedding?

I shuddered at the thought.

"Absolutely not," I said, plain and simple, and gave my mother the evil eye as we got out of the car; but she ignored me, smiling at the valet as she handed over her keys.

Hiring Olivia wouldn't be the bee's knees at all. It'd be more like being swarmed by an entire, very angry beehive.

Chapter 2

"If you'd follow me, please," an unsmiling man in a dark suit with a headset said politely, and he led Mother and me inside to the two-story foyer with dripping chandelier and curving staircase that had been set up like the security checkpoint at the airport.

Impeccably dressed guests were lifting their arms and being wanded, while others were opening purses for inspection and surrendering their cell phones to receive paper stubs in a modern-day version of a coat check.

"They're confiscating cell phones?" I murmured.

"Shelby said they were running a tight ship," my mother whispered. "They don't want anyone but the official wedding photographer snapping pictures."

What, no selfies with the pregnant bride and her proud papa?

"Spoilsports," I said, but Cissy didn't laugh.

I figured the Black Suits were hired guns, not Secret Service, since Senator Ryan wasn't yet a presidential nominee. We opened our bags so one could rifle through the contents and then another confiscated our phones and gave us numbered stubs in return.

"After you," my mother said and nudged me forward toward the guy with the wand.

"No, no, age before beauty," I cracked. But if Mother's frown was any indication, my attempt at humor once again fell flat.

At the Black Suit's prompting, I raised my arms, and he started scanning the length of me. I suddenly feared he'd do a pat-down and feel the Lycra binding my gut and butt. Would he then ask me to remove the Spanx to make sure I wasn't hiding anything? I wondered, although it was impossible to hide anything beneath Spanx but flesh.

I'd heard more than a few TSA horror stories involving strip searches, and I'd read about police arresting a teenage girl and finding a loaded gun hidden in her hoo-ha.

Big Brother wasn't just watching. He was doing body cavity checks.

"You're good to go," the Black Suit said, and I exhaled the breath I'd been holding.

I watched my mother take her turn next. She looked as anxious as a bull at a cattle auction, gearing up to have its hooves checked and its junk inspected. But she was done in a minute flat, and all was well.

"What, no three-D X-ray machine?" I remarked once Cissy had rejoined me. "That's disappointing."

"*Andrea*." She said my name in that way mothers had of issuing a warning with one mere word.

"Will we at least get one free beverage on this flight?" I asked and snapped my tiny clutch closed—a Judith Leiber bag of my mother's, also on loan like the dress—that contained little more than a wad of Kleenex, one Vanilla ChapStick, and a half-eaten roll of Wintergreen Life Savers.

"This way, please." A woman in a crisp white shirt, black vest, and bow tie approached us after we'd cleared security.

No way was she Secret Service. I don't think they ever dressed like cater-waiters.

"Thank you, dear," Cissy said to the woman and proceeded to follow, her Saint Laurent kitten heels tapping a beat on the polished marble floors.

We traveled a path from the foyer through a wide hallway into a richly appointed living area that seemed to be missing one wall entirely. A bank of folding doors had been opened wide, and we stepped onto a partially covered patio with balconies above supported by dramatic arches. Beyond lay a backyard that looked more like a ritzy resort than private property. Farther along the expansive patio area, the black-vested waitstaff appeared to be putting the finishing touches on tables for the reception.

"Oh, my," I heard my mother say, "this is lovely."

What Cissy considered "lovely" seemed like overkill to me. I tried to calculate in my brain how many rescued dogs and cats Lester Dickens could have saved by donating to Operation Kindness instead of putting in multiple freaking swimming pools, and I figured it was plenty. Yes, dead ahead were acres of limestone pavers surrounding not one, not two swimming pools, but *three*.

Beyond the centermost pool sat a cabana with its awnings drawn wide. The opening was framed by a thick arch of twigs twined with fairy lights and scads of purple orchids. In fact, there were twigs and orchids and fairy lights just about everywhere I looked. As we approached the cabana, I heard music and saw a string quartet off to the side playing Mozart. At least they weren't playing the "Wedding March," so we couldn't be *that* late.

When my mother realized where we were going, she hesitated.

"We're sittin' in the pool?" she drawled none too happily into my ear, noticing the rows of silver Chiavari chairs that appeared to be hovering atop the water.

"There's an acrylic floor," I told her and stepped onto the thick plastic. "See? We're fine. You'll stay as dry as toast."

"What if the weight's too much and we all fall in?" she asked, raising a hand to her freshly done hair as if getting it wet would be a fate worse than death.

"Then I guess I'll drown instead of being squeezed to death by my underwear," I replied and tried to take a deep breath but couldn't.

The woman in vest and bow tie cleared her throat.

"Would you prefer the groom's side or the

bride's?" she asked, and Mother told her, "We're with the bride."

The woman found us spots on the outside aisle closer to the back than the front, which made Cissy grimace.

"You can see from here just fine," I told her as we sat down, but that wasn't exactly the case.

Dallas women liked their hair big and—apparently where spring weddings were concerned—their hats, too. Well, the seating was outdoors without a canopy above. So maybe their chapeaus protected their helmet heads from bird droppings. As I was scoping out the headgear, which was worthy of the Kentucky Derby, Mother was craning her neck this way and that, trying to get a fix on the spot beneath the arch of twigs and orchids where the bride and groom would stand.

When I heard her sigh, I looked at my feet to avoid what I was sure would be a first-class glare. Pale blue water seemed to ebb and flow beneath my shoes. Though the clear acrylic floor sat at least six inches above the water line, I could still feel water sloshing. Maybe it was all in my head, but it had a most unfortunate result.

I leaned toward my mother and whispered, "I have to go."

"Go where?"

"To the bathroom," I said. I could feel the Spanx compressing my poor bladder. I suddenly wished I hadn't drunk half a gallon of green tea with lunch.

"Now?"

"Yes now."

"No." She grabbed my arm and held me still. Did she think I was purposefully trying to skip out on the ceremony? Or was she afraid I'd get into trouble if I didn't have proper adult supervision?

"Do you want me to pee in my pants?" I asked and crossed my legs. "You're free to chaperone if that'd make you happy."

For a moment she seemed to consider the option. Then she sighed and let me go. "I don't want to risk losing our seats," she said. "Just be quick about it, please."

"Don't worry," I told her. Quick was my intention.

Although I'd attended a few outdoor events in the past with Mother and/or Brian where the hosts had fancy portable potties stationed outdoors (they had sinks for hand washing, which was probably as fancy as portable potties got), I couldn't imagine Senator Ryan making a former president and his wife duck into plastic water closets to do their business. Yes, I'd seen the pair seated a few rows ahead of my mother. And, nope, I didn't spot a single Porta Potty anywhere around.

So I meandered back toward the faux Mediterranean manse, figuring a house that size had to have a bathroom or ten. I made a beeline for a cadre of folks in black vests and bow ties hurriedly setting up for the sit-down dinner, figuring one of them could point me in the right direction.

"Could you tell me where I'd find a powder room?" I tried to ask one and then another, but they scurried about like ants on a mission. Either they didn't know where the restrooms were or else they'd been told not to interact with the guests.

I dared to step inside the open doors leading into the kitchen, which not surprisingly looked like a granite and stainless steel vision from *Architectural Digest*. Voices shouted instructions, pots and pans clattered, people raced about, and steam rose from various burners on industrial-grade stoves.

One voice in particular sent a chill up my spine.

"Where the hell have you been?" I heard it snap.

Oh, no, I thought and swallowed hard, stopping in my tracks.

I would have recognized that derisive drawl anywhere even if it wasn't yelling, "Andy's got no boobs! Andy's a boy!" But I quickly realized the shouts weren't aimed at me. Instead the angry tone appeared to be directed at a woman in owlish glasses who stood near two young cater-waiters balancing a board between them that carried a seven—yes, I counted seven—layer wedding cake. The way the two guys were wincing, it must have weighed a hundred pounds.

"What in God's name took you so long, Millie? Did you walk all the way here from your shop on Mockingbird with the cake strapped to your back? You're an hour late!" Olivia La Belle, the bully from my prep school days, berated the baker, who I knew was Millicent Draper of Millie's Cakes. Mother had used her for all my birthday cakes starting from Year One, and I'd adored her. She'd forever be the Cake Lady to me. Yes, Millie was older and snowcapped—with a blob of ivory fondant stuck to her tortoiseshell glasses and a terrified expression on her face—but she still looked much as I remembered.

Unfortunately, the same could be said for my archenemy. I hadn't laid eyes on Olivia in over a decade, but she'd hardly changed a fig. She was still tall and broad-shouldered, just as she'd been when she captained the tennis team at Hockaday. The only difference I noted besides vague crow's-feet and frown lines was that she'd cropped her white-blond hair from the shoulder-length bob I remembered. Her head now sported a pixie cut framing a face that would have been pretty in that vacuous Texas pageant girl way if it hadn't been so viciously scowling.

"I'm sorry, Olivia," Millie apologized and wrung her hands. "I did my best, but it took every spare second to finish up. I did the whole cake myself, and it had to be absolutely perfect—"

"It had better be perfect," Olivia cut her off. "If I hear one guest complain that their slice is dry or the fondant's too thick, you won't get a penny."

Millie blanched. "But that's a ten thousand dollar cake!"

Ten grand for a cake?

My mouth fell wide-open.

"Go on now, boys, and set it down on the round table on the patio that's ringed with orchid petals. I'll bring the servin' pieces out," Olivia told the two waiters. Then she reached into a suitcase-size satchel and removed a robin's-egg-blue box. The recessed lights glinted off sterling silver as she plucked a long, sleek cake knife from within.

"Do you want me to stay and cut?" Millie asked, though her meek tone suggested she'd like to do anything but. "Once the bride and groom get their pictures, I mean. Because you'll need to be careful with—"

"Are you nuts?" Olivia cut her off with a little shriek. "Do I want you to stay and cut?" she repeated, her tone ugly. "Over my dead body," she hissed, and she waved the cake knife in the air for emphasis. "Now get out of my sight, you old bag, before I say somethin' I'll really regret!"

Poor Millie's hand went to her heart and she swayed.

That did it.

I was no longer a scrawny teenager with braces and an inferiority complex, and I wasn't about to let my old bully push around a nice woman like Millicent Draper. It was sort of like watching the devil make mincemeat out of a sainted grandmother.

My feet started moving, and I did a Texas two-step around the waiters hauling out the mile-high cake. My chin up, I strode toward the wedding planner with my hands clenched into fists.

"Back off, Olivia," I barked in Millie's defense— something I'd wanted to say for a very long time—nearly forgetting in my rush of anger that I seriously had to pee. "If you're in the mood to pick on someone, go ahead and pick on me. But be warned that I just might bite back."

"Okay, that's it," Olivia shouted at someone over her shoulder. "Turn it off, Pete," she ordered, and I realized there was someone standing not six feet behind her. He'd been so quiet back there in the shadows, stalking Olivia with a handheld camera. "Take ten while I put a cork in this nutcase."

Pete nodded but didn't speak. I noticed his beard and plain black T-shirt—and the tattoos of roses and thorns wrapped around his arms—as he lowered the camera and walked away.

Was Pete chronicling the wedding for the family or was Olivia taping for her silly reality show? I assumed it had to be the former. It was hard to believe the senator would allow Olivia to record private moments from Penny's wedding for a reality TV show when the security detail was confiscating cell phones at the door. Then again, I wouldn't put anything past Olivia La Belle. She'd never cared about other people's rules.

"Just who do you think you are in your bad shoes and ill-fittin' designer knockoff," she snapped, squinting hard at me.

Bad shoes?

My cheeks warmed, and I glanced down at my feet. I was wearing my best pair of J.Crew wedge espadrilles, which hadn't thrilled my mother either. But they were comfortable and they didn't even have a lick of paint on them, like every other pair of shoes I owned. As for the borrowed dress, yeah, it was a tad too tight. I'd give her that. But it *wasn't* a knockoff. My mother didn't buy knockoffs. I would know for sure that Armageddon was near if I ever caught Cissy shopping at Nordstrom Rack or TJ Maxx.

"I'm nobody," I told her, "and you're making a scene." Although no one else in the busy kitchen was paying any attention to us, and I wasn't sure that Olivia cared besides.

She continued to rant like she had a fatal case of PMS. "How dare you interrupt when I was right in the middle of—" Abruptly, she stopped screaming and blinked.

"Yelling," I finished for her and jerked my chin at Millicent Draper, who was vaguely trembling and appeared on the verge of tears. "You were reaming out Millie. Then you insulted me. Wow, it's like flashing back to prep school. Are you going to give us wedgies next, or push us into a gym locker?"

"Oh. My. God." She breathed each word.

The way she'd acted, I didn't think Olivia had recognized me. Then I watched something change in her face. Her pale blue eyes flickered, and the frown on her wide mouth twitched at the corners.

"Is it possible?" she drawled, and her finely plucked eyebrows arched. "Is it really Andy Kendricks in the flesh? Your mama must have hogtied you and hauled you here, didn't she? I know *your* name wasn't on the guest list."

"Brilliant deduction, Sherlock," I said dryly.

"Oh, I know more than that," she remarked with a smirk. "Like, I heard you design Web sites for charities. How quaint. Didn't you go to some dinky art school in Chicago? But then you never did aspire to much, did you?" Her gaze dropped to my chest and she added with a slow grin, "Some things never change. I can see that you're still lacking in the boobs department, too. You should've dug into your trust fund to have those puppies fixed."

She was right. Some things never changed.

Self-consciously, I crossed my arms. "And I can see that you're still acting like Attila the Blonde and pushing nice people around," I replied, about as witty a comeback as I could come up with on such short notice. Although I'd lain awake with tears in my eyes many nights during middle school, mulling over all the things I wanted to say to Olivia La Belle. But I didn't figure calling her a "big stinky poop face" was going to do the trick.

"Oh, Andy, darlin'," she said in such a honeyed tone you'd think I'd given her a compliment. "It's so sweet that you're holding a grudge after all these years. And I thought you'd forgotten me."

"Mean is hard to forget," I told her.

"You thought I was mean? C'mon, it was all just good-natured teasing," she replied, but there was a spark of malice in her eyes. Perhaps making fun of other people *was* funny to her.

"Good-natured teasing, right," I murmured, getting angrier by the minute.

She'd shoved me into the gym's equipment cage in my underwear and locked it so that I was left to be found by the next class. She'd covered a sculpture I'd made for a school art exhibition in maxipads doused in ketchup. She had pummeled me with volleyballs hard enough to leave marks. *That* was good-natured teasing? Was that how the CIA classified water-boarding, too?

My chest tightened, my heart aching in a way it hadn't since my school days, and all the angst and confusion I'd felt back then threatened to bubble to the surface. Did old pain never go away?

I opened my mouth, ready to tell her she was a sorry excuse for a human being and that I'd never hated anyone the way I'd hated her. But this wasn't about me. I glanced at Millicent Draper's exhausted face and what came out of my mouth was simply, "Leave Millie alone or else."

"Or else what, Kendricks?" Olivia smiled tightly. "Are you gonna sic your mama on me? At least *she* has a reputation as a steel magnolia. You're more like Silly Putty."

"Cissy doesn't fight my battles," I said firmly, incensed at her implication that I was weak because I'd never struck back. I'd never even told my mother about Olivia picking on me. I hadn't wanted her to know.

"What battles? We're grown-ups, right? I've got no beef with you," she said, and she tapped her open palm with the cake knife. "If you haven't noticed, Dorothy, we're not in prep school anymore."

Maybe we weren't, but Olivia La Belle was still the Wicked Witch as far as I was concerned.

"Could have fooled me," I said under my breath.

She waved the shiny knife toward the open kitchen doors. "Now click those ratty heels together and scoot. I've got a wedding to put on, and Millie here's already thrown me off schedule."

"I was just leaving," Millicent Draper said and touched my arm. "Thank you, Andy, for trying to help. You always were such a sweet girl." She gave me a sad little smile. Then she turned to Olivia. Her cheeks flushed, she raised a finger and shook it. "If you think you can do to me what you did to Jasper—" she began, then sucked in a breath and started over. "One day you'll get what's coming to you, and it won't be any too soon."

"Do I need to call security to have you thrown out?" Olivia snapped at her.

"No," Millie said, dropping her arm to her side. "I'm leaving already."

I watched her go, shuffling away with her head down, and I couldn't help but feel angry all over again.

"Wow, way to go, Olivia! You just beat up on a woman twice your age. I hope you're proud of yourself," I said, sticking out my chin and looking my old nemesis in the eye. "The cake looks stunning. Why give her so much crap for being a little late?"

"A little late?" Olivia balked. "She almost missed the whole damned wedding!"

I shook my head, too disgusted to speak.

"C'mon, Kendricks"—she sniffed—"cut me some slack." And suddenly, for a brief moment, her bravado slipped. Her face pinched, and I noticed the shadows around her eyes that even a good makeup job couldn't hide. "You don't know how it feels to have so much riding on your shoulders, so much at stake, and it's not just the business. It's—everything. One wrong step and—" She made a noise and drew the knife across her throat.

Oh, Lord, she was such a drama queen.

"So you let out steam by screaming at people?"

"Don't be so naïve." She glanced around as if someone might overhear. "I scream because that's how I get things done. Do you know how lazy people are these days? Besides, I'd lose my TV show if there wasn't drama. Sometimes you have to ramp things up to keep it interesting. Why do you think Bravo's got those housewives throwing tables and prosthetic legs? It's so the public keeps watching, and I need them to watch and believe."

Did that mean Pete the Cameraman *was* filming for her stupid reality show? And that she'd reamed out Millie for the sake of ratings? Did she think blaming her rudeness on Nielsen numbers made her any less of a jerk?

"That doesn't make it okay," I said, not feeling sorry for her in the least.

Maybe I imagined it, but I thought Olivia almost looked contrite, like perhaps there was actually a half-decent human being hidden beneath all the makeup and shellacked pixie hair. Then the mask slipped back on, and her eyes turned hard as stone.

"Christ, you're still playing Joan of Arc, aren't you? Andy Kendricks, defender of strays!" she mocked. "At Hockaday, it was that scholarship girl, Molly, and now you're standing up for tired old pastry chefs who are past their prime. If I had anything to say about it, Millie would hang up her apron and retire."

"Luckily, it's not up to you," I told her.

"Isn't it?" she said with such arrogance that I had to bite the inside of my cheek to keep from cussing her out, which I knew wouldn't solve a danged thing.

It was sad, I thought, realizing some people never grew up. I had a theory that whoever people were in high school was who they were forever, at least at their core. Just because a body aged didn't mean a narrow mind opened or meanness morphed into kindness. I could envision Olivia bullying old ladies at the Shady Acres retirement center when she was ninety-five. Maybe I wasn't the epitome of maturity, but I'd grown up enough to know that I was done being her victim. There had been so many times I wished I'd had the last word with Olivia La Belle; but at that moment I had nothing more to say.

"Lovely seeing you again," I said, dripping sarcasm. It would be my pleasure if I didn't run into her for another dozen years, or ever again for that matter. "Excuse me," I murmured and brushed past her, heading toward the hallway. I wasn't about to ask Olivia for directions to the loo. I'd find it on my own.

"You're going the wrong way! The wedding's outside," she called after me. "But if you see a lost bridesmaid while you're wandering around, tell her I'm looking for her and I'm mighty pissed!"

I ignored her and kept walking.

I took more than a few deep breaths as I hurried along the hallway, stopping to open every closed door along my path, sure that one would be a guest bathroom. I stumbled upon what must have been Lester Dickens's den, as it had a massive desk and a wall filled with photographs of the oilman with various celebrities and presidents. I glimpsed a Black Suit patrolling outside the windows and he paused, looking in, so I made a beeline for the door.

A few more doors along the hallway revealed rooms filled with carefully staged Oriental rugs and gleaming antiques or closets stuffed with linens or cleaning equipment, like a house that wasn't actually lived in anymore.

Where in the world was the powder room? Surely Lester Dickens had to pee every now and then.

Farther up the hall, a patrolling Black Suit appeared out of nowhere, like he'd gotten wind that a wayward guest was bumbling around the house. He put a finger to his headpiece and started my way just as I opened a door and ducked inside.

A chandelier glowed above a massive four-poster bed. Across from the bed was a fireplace with a sitting area. There was an open door to what had to be an en suite. Ah, I thought, relief was near!

Only as I headed toward it, a terrified-looking young woman with a skunklike dye job and impossibly high heels raced out, screaming into a headset, "Olivia? Olivia, where are you? I've got an emergency here!"

"Olivia's in the kitchen," I said, because that was where I'd left her. "The cake just arrived, and she's looking for a missing bridesmaid—"

"Oh, please, you have to help," she cried, cutting me off, and rushed toward where I stood in the doorway. "Penny's in serious trouble!"

Before I had a chance to speak, she grabbed my arm and dragged me in.

Chapter 3

"Whoever you are, can you give me a hand?" the girl asked. Her heavily lined eyes looked frantic. "I can't do this by myself, and the bridesmaids are upstairs getting final touch-ups on their hair and makeup."

"Um, okay," I said hesitantly, because I had no earthly idea what I was getting myself into, and I was afraid that if I didn't find a potty soon, I'd be in deep doo-doo. "I'm Andy, by the way."

"I'm Terra," she told me. Her hand on my elbow, she pulled me through the room. "Olivia La Belle's assistant."

"So what's wrong with Penny?" I asked, scurrying alongside her. A few things came instantly to mind. "Does she have morning sickness? Did she get cold feet?"

"I wish it was that simple!" Terra said and paused, out of breath. "I managed to lace her up in her corset—which was a feat in itself—and then wedged her into the hoop skirt. But when I got her into her gown she suddenly had to pee."

There was a lot of that going around apparently.

When I didn't remark, Terra went on, "That's what happens when you're pregnant." She nudged my arm and ushered me into a marble bath fit for a king. "You have to go a lot," she added, tugging me toward what had to be the water closet, separated by a door from the rest of the bath.

My heart—and bladder—leapt at knowing there was a toilet within reach.

Terra released me to throw the door wide, and I stopped in my tracks.

"Oh, my," I breathed, staring at the scene within.

"Help," a disembodied voice said, sounding totally panicked. "I can't move. You've got to get me out of here!"

"Penny?" I said and glanced at Terra.

Terra nodded, biting her lip.

I couldn't even see the senator's daughter through the mountains of crinoline. Her gown and hoop skirt looked like an upended umbrella.

"She's stuck?" I asked, pretty much stating the obvious and thinking all the while that surely this couldn't be the only potty in the whole mansion. If so, it was no wonder the place had been sitting on the market for months. It was, like, eight thousand square feet, ten bedrooms, and one crapper.

"Olivia's going to kill me!" Terra said under her breath, and all the blood drained from her face, so that her frosty blue eye shadow and pink blush stood out like clown makeup. "Olivia told me to use a wastebasket and make Penny squat, but Penny wouldn't do it! Now I don't know how to get her out!"

I heard a noise that sounded like an old furnace wheezing. At first I thought it was Penny having a panic attack. Then I realized Olivia's assistant was hyperventilating. All I needed was for her to pass out on me.

"Deep breaths, Terra," I told her very calmly. "This is doable."

"It's doable," she repeated and gulped in air. The color came back to her cheeks. "Okay, yeah, sure."

"She walked in forward, right?" I asked, because that was the general rule of thumb. Before I'd dropped out of my debut, I'd made it through plenty of lessons on everything from how to do the Texas Dip—the ultra-deep curtsy that Dallas debs must execute—to how to pee in a bathroom stall with your gown on, so I wasn't completely ill-prepared for this emergency.

"For God's sake, yes, I'm on the john ass-backward!" Penny barked less than delicately, having overheard the conversation.

"That is the standard procedure," Terra replied with a nod, her skunk-hair bobbing. At least the color had reappeared in her face like the blood was flowing again.

"Good," I told her. That meant one of us could gather up as much of the gown and oversized petticoat as possible and the other could get a grip around Penny's waist and start hauling her out rear end first. There was just one more question

I needed to ask before we got rolling. "Is she, um, done?"

"Yes, I'm done, although I might have to go again soon if you don't get me out of here!" Penny said shrilly from somewhere within the cloud of silk and crinoline. "So somebody *do* something!"

"Stand up slowly," I advised her while Terra gathered up the yards of material so I could see what I was dealing with. "Terra's going to hold your gown overhead while I guide you out, okay?"

"Please, just hurry," Penny said with her voice catching. "I can't be late for my own wedding. My mother will be madder than a hornet's nest."

"Which isn't half as mad as Olivia will be when she hears about this," Terra murmured as she edged past me, taking charge of corralling the exploding hooped petticoat, although it seemed to fight her every inch of the way.

"You'll be out in a flash," I told Penny as she whimpered, and I meant it. I had a serious ulterior motive. I felt a twinge in my bladder, and I reminded myself of all the childhood road trips I'd taken with my father where I'd had to hold it for hundreds of miles. He'd never liked stopping until the car was nearly out of gas—he had a thing about public restrooms—and I wasn't about to use the coffee can with the plastic lid that he'd brought along "for emergencies."

"Brace yourself. I'm coming in," I said by way of warning. My Spanx threatened to cut off my circulation as I crouched, diving beneath the big skirt to blindly grab Penny around her belly. Well, more like her hip bones. I didn't want to hurt the baby when I yanked. "On the count of three, we're all taking a step backward."

I paused but heard no protests. So I began to count.

"One, two, three," I said and pulled at Penny while Terra wrestled the hoop skirt out of the tiny space.

I suddenly understood what it felt like to be the cork in a champagne bottle, jerked free and sailing through the air, as the rings on the hoop skirt popped out of the cramped space and the three of us stumbled backward, ending up in a pile of crinoline and silk and arms and limbs on the floor. I felt something snap around my middle and thought at first I'd pulled a muscle.

Penny burst into tears, and I worried that she'd been hurt.

"Don't cry," Terra told her as she struggled through the layers of fabric. "You'll smear your makeup!"

But I was more concerned about what was inside Penny than what was painted on her face. "Do you need a doctor?" I asked, sure there was at least one—or more likely a gaggle of them—sitting outside on a Chiavari chair positioned over the center pool, waiting for the ceremony to begin.

"No, I don't need a doctor," she said, sobs catching in her throat like hiccups. "But I think I broke a nail."

Oh, boy. I rolled my eyes.

"We'll fix it!" Terra reassured her. "The manicurist is still upstairs with your bridesmaids. Well, the ones that are here," Terra whispered as she extricated herself and set about tugging Penny up from where she'd landed on top of me. "We'll have Desiree repair that broken nail ASAP."

By the time Terra had Penny upright and had straightened out her gown and everything underneath, I'd managed to sit up. I sucked in a deep breath, amazed at how easy it was to breathe again.

I saw Terra pluck something from her big bag, and then she pushed a bit of paper in my hand. It was her business card—or rather, Olivia's—but I saw Terra had her cell number written on the back of it. Maybe Olivia went through so many assistants that she never bothered to give them cards of their own.

"If I can ever repay you," Terra said, "let me know, okay?"

"Sure," I told her, figuring there was little chance of that. But I folded the card into a tiny sliver and tucked it in my bra for want of a better place to put it.

She smiled nervously. Then her face took on a horrified look. "No, no, of course I wasn't avoiding you," she said, seemingly out of the blue. "I was busy with Penny. We, uh, had a situation."

"Yeah, I know," I told her, confused.

"Everything's fine, Olivia, I swear," Terra went on, and I realized she was talking into her headset to my old buddy from Hockaday. "One of the guests helped me out," she rattled on as she grabbed the big tote bag and led Penny out of the expansive bath. "A woman named Andy," I could hear her saying in the distance, "Yes, she's still here, but I'm taking Penny upstairs for an emergency nail repair."

And then the bedroom door slapped closed, and I was left blissfully alone.

Chapter 4

I struggled to my feet in the too-small dress that suddenly felt that much tighter, and I quickly realized why. I definitely hadn't pulled an ab getting Penny out of the toilet. My Spanx had popped off my belly and rolled down to my hips. Not a problem, as I needed out of them pronto. So I shimmied and pushed them past my thighs, finally getting them off entirely. I kicked them aside and hobbled into the water closet as fast as I could.

To say that I relieved myself was to put it mildly.

After I'd washed my hands, I bent to retrieve the Spanx and heard a tearing that sent a chill up my spine. It was the distinct sound of a zipper ripping apart. "Oh, fudge," I said, only I didn't say "fudge."

This could not be happening.

"No, no, no," I repeated, as if saying the word

over and over again would change the outcome.
But when I swiveled so I could see my back in the
mirror, my eyes took in a horrifying sight.

I swallowed hard, an anxious butterfly doing
tailspins in my stomach as I surveyed the damage
done. The whole back of the dress had split wide-
open. The zipper had torn clear out on one side. I
could see my bra strap and a lot of skin down to
my booty. If I'd had my phone, I could have called
Cissy so she might wave her magic wand and
produce a new dress (or at least call her personal
shopper at Saks to hand-deliver another).

But the Black Suits had taken my cell. What was
I supposed to do? Pretend like nothing had happened and sashay out of the house and back to
Cissy with my backside in full view? Maybe that
would work if I were attending the wedding of
one of those Kardashians where the dress code
was Clothing Optional. But my mother would die
a certain death—or at least be the butt of high society jokes, no pun intended—if I were to appear
in public half clothed.

I tried not to panic.

Think, Andy, think.

Had Penny left the clothes she'd had on before
she changed into her gown? I looked everywhere
but saw nothing but dust-free surfaces. No, Penny's things had probably been stuffed into Terra's
big bag.

Then another thought hit me: surely Lester
Dickens had left some of his button-down shirts
or tailored blazers around the house, if only to
show off the size of the closets to potential home

buyers. If I had either one, I could cover up well enough to get back to my chair without too much scrutiny from Mother's upper crust friends.

I threw open the double doors of what had to be a massive walk-in, only to find it completely and utterly empty. There was a bureau in the bedroom, and I checked all six of the drawers. Not even a balled-up pair of socks. The Chippendale tallboy had been cleared out as well. Er, except for a dusty-looking pack of condoms in the top drawer.

I didn't know what else to do and found myself on the verge of tears.

When I heard the bedroom door open, I nearly swooned. If it was a Black Suit, I'd at least be able to borrow his jacket, right?

"Oh, thank goodness you're here! I've never been so happy to see anyone," I said and rushed out from the bathroom suite only to stop cold.

Instead of Obi Wan Kenobi come to save me with the Force, I saw Darth Vader standing in the doorway. I could practically hear the noisy breathing and the black cloak swishing as Olivia La Belle sauntered forward on her strappy Louboutins.

Inwardly, I groaned. Really, could this get any worse?

"You're happy to see me? That's a good one, Kendricks. Are you dipping into Mommy's little white pills?" Olivia remarked in her patronizing drawl. She had one hand hanging over her shoulder, holding something behind her back.

Before I could come up with a pithy response, La Belle from Hell droned on.

"Terra told me you helped her out of a jam. Honestly, she's an incompetent twit and does her makeup like she went to clown school, but I can't seem to find a good assistant these days. I go through them like napkins."

What a shocker.

"So I guess I should thank you," she said, frowning.

Wow, that sounded so magnanimous. *Not.*

"It was no big deal," I replied with a shrug. Though my heart pounded, I tried to pretend that everything was fine. I just wanted her to go away.

"You're acting weirder than usual. What's going on?" She came closer and gave me a funny look. "Is that your underpants you're holdin'?" she asked with a smirk on her lips. "What's wrong with your dress? Before it was snug as a sausage casing, and now it's hanging off you kind of wonky."

Oh, how I wished there was another way out than to ask for help from my worst enemy! But I had no choice. I had to come clean. Besides, I told myself, she owed me big for saving her bride.

I swallowed hard and screwed up my nerve.

"Look, I need a small favor, Olivia," I said, because it was that or skulk back to Mother in a shredded dress. "My zipper ripped out."

"Why so it did," she said and walked around me. I heard the swish of nylon over her shoulder and caught a glimpse of a slim garment bag. "Well, wouldn't you know but I'm in a bit of a bind myself. Maybe we can help each other out."

I didn't like the sound of that. But beggars could hardly be choosers.

"Help each other how?"

She whipped the garment bag around and shoved it toward me. "Seems we're one bridesmaid short. I just got a call from Penny's cousin, Darlene. She has pink eye," Olivia said as she unzipped it and unveiled the most hideous chiffon dress with a giant bow that looked like a butterfly perched on one shoulder and a skirt comprised of tiny rosettes all stitched together. To add to its crazy-quilt quotient, the dress was a shade of purple somewhere between lavender and eggplant.

"Couldn't she just wear an eye patch?" I suggested.

Olivia looked at me like I'd lost my mind. "What is she, a pirate? Like that wouldn't ruin all the wedding pictures entirely," she said and shoved the chiffon monstrosity in my direction. "What do you think?"

"Wow," I said, for lack of anything nice.

"It was custom-made by a very hip designer named Draco," she replied defensively, as if that suddenly made it pretty. "Okay, so it's not his finest work. It was during his naturalist phase. But he couldn't get the dresses Penny wanted done in time when the wedding got moved up. Even still, it's not so bad"—Olivia gave the dress a loving pat—"they flew out of the store when Macy's sold them off the rack last season. Though I shouldn't expect someone like you to know anything about what's fashionable," she tacked on, and my back stiffened.

Maybe they "flew" out of the store because that

enormous butterfly on the shoulder needed to migrate to Mexico for the winter. Maybe my fashion sense was resigned to Gap T-shirts and Levi's; but I didn't require a degree in runway to see that the dress was completely overdone. Personally, I wouldn't want to be caught dead in it.

"Um, could you go get Cissy for me," I said, because Olivia didn't appear to grasp my situation. "I'm sure my mother can figure out how I can attend this wedding in something that's not in shreds, or else I guess we'll have to leave this lovely shindig you're throwing, and what a shame that would be."

But Olivia merely wiggled the dress in my face.

"It's a size eight," she said, giving me the once-over. "You should totally be able to get it on without blowing out the zipper." Then she looked at my feet. "There are shoes, too, in the bottom of the bag. Surely you can squeeze into seven and a half. So ditch the clodhoppers, will you and get changed."

Whoa. "What?"

"Hurry up," she said. "The natives are restless. We need to get this show on the road before anything else happens to derail the happy occasion. Penny Ryan needs to get married today! If she doesn't, pissy old Les is going to pitch a fit, and I'm already on his shit list."

Pissy old Les?

"Lester Dickens?" I said. "Why would he care?"

"He's the one who pushed up this wedding. Why do you think we're at his house? There was nothing else available on such short notice except church basements," Olivia said and swallowed. "If things don't go as planned and Penny doesn't tie the knot today, it'll be my fault. You'll see."

So Lester Dickens wasn't merely being generous by allowing the ceremony to take place at his house. He'd pressured the Ryans to move up the wedding date. It was probably his idea to confiscate the cell phones, too.

"You've got five minutes," Olivia barked, causing me to jump.

I had a sudden attack of déjà vu, since that was exactly what Cissy had said when she showed up at my condo with the Spanx and Carolina Herrera dress that still had its price tag dangling.

"Five minutes?" I repeated, and then the full impact of the situation hit me. "Oh, no, no, no," I said, shaking my head. "I'm not getting into that chiffon mess and playing Penny's bridesmaid!"

"You can't go outside this room lookin' like you were mauled by a coyote, now can you?" She gave me a triumphant smile. "And I can't have asymmetry in my wedding party. It would not play well in *D Magazine*."

"You're nuts," I breathed.

"At least you won't need a shoehorn to get into this puppy," she remarked and eyed the crumpled Spanx in my hand. "Penny's cousin isn't skinny either."

Wow, was that a slam about my weight? If I'd had another option, I would have told her to take that dress and shove it.

I started to say, "My mother will wonder where I am—"

"I'll take care of Cissy," Olivia cut me off. "I

promise to tell her what's up so she won't send out a posse of Texas Rangers looking for you."

"I barely know the bride, so playing her bridesmaid seems almost sacrilegious," I protested, only to have Olivia wave a hand to shush me.

"Oh, honey, I've had to hire bridesmaids for society weddings so the spread looks good in *Town & Country*," she said dismissively. "Some of these girls can't drum up a real friend to save their lives and others have bridesmaids too ugly to photograph through cheesecloth."

I wondered if Olivia was speaking from personal experience about not having a real friend to save her life. I couldn't imagine anyone wanting to be buddies with her. That would entail having an eye in the back of your head to avoid being stabbed in the back.

I wet my lips and made sure to properly enunciate every word, for all the good it would do me. "No," I told her, "I will not replace Penny's cousin in her wedding party. *Capisce?*"

"Oh, yes, you can, and you will," Olivia insisted and pushed the garment bag at my chest. "Now shake a leg, Kendricks. I'm going upstairs to grab the others then I'll be back for you in"—she checked the glittery watch on her wrist—"four minutes and thirty seconds. And you'd better be ready or I'll post a pic of you in your undies in the equipment cage on Facebook for Throwback Thursday this week. How does that sound?"

It sounded like a threat.

What could I do? Besides strangle her, I mean, which was pretty tempting.

"Swell," I murmured.

I hadn't even wanted to come to this wedding and suddenly I was standing in for a bridesmaid? I wasn't sure if Olivia was doing a favor for me or if I was doing the favor for her. But I took the dress from her because I didn't have a choice.

Ugh.

"Oh, hey, and run a brush through that tangled nest on your head," my nemesis added as she sashayed toward the door and paused. Her grin disappeared, so she just looked plain irritated. She raised a fist in the air like Scarlett O'Hara and declared, "As God is my witness this ceremony's starting in ten minutes."

She left me to change, and I glared at her retreating back. It was all I could do not to scream out loud. So I simply screamed in my head.

Worst. Wedding. EVER.

Yet another reason I didn't want Olivia La Belle coming anywhere near mine.

Chapter 5

If there was one good thing about standing in for Penny's cousin with pink eye—and standing on my feet in borrowed heels for half an hour—it was that I actually *did* fit into the ugly purple dress without the Spanx. Breathing felt natural again, and I realized I'd be able to eat every bite of the catered dinner and a piece of Millie's seven-tiered wedding cake to boot.

So instead of wallowing in self-pity, which I'd gotten pretty good at in my thirty-plus years on the planet, I focused on the positive and tried to smile for Penny's sake, ignoring the quizzical looks from her family and from my own mother as well.

". . . your love is like the sunrise, so pink and soft and promising sunny skies and calm winds . . . ," the groom said tearfully, reading from a crib sheet tucked into his sweaty palm.

I tried not to cross my eyes.

Truly, I made my best effort to focus on the happy couple as they wept and stumbled their way through their handwritten vows, but my gaze kept straying to the rows of guests; in particular, to the way-back row on the bride's side where my mother sat.

If I peered between two large hats, I could see her blond hair styled à la Grace Kelly in *Rear Window*. She sat as ramrod straight as ever, her chin up and shoulders squared. Her posture was always perfect, I thought; her composure cooler than a cucumber. So cool, in fact, that just the sight of Cissy had intimidated me for years, until my adulthood when I'd unearthed the gooey center buried beneath the Ice Queen exterior.

Somehow, in the intervening stretch since losing Daddy, my relationship with Cissy had gone from adversarial to grudging respect. And it hadn't been easy. After disappointing my mother with my failure to debut, I'd left Dallas for college in Chicago and tried to keep my distance for a while; but Mother was a riptide and I inevitably found myself caught in her current. It had taken a lot of growing up for me to understand that wasn't necessarily a horrible thing. Call me a slow learner, but I'd finally figured out that sometimes it paid to go with the flow when it came to my mom. In the past, we'd often fought about stuff that didn't matter—because that stuff wasn't really what we'd been fighting about. I loved Cissy, no question. Still, she could vex me like nobody else. Maybe that was the nature of all mother-daughter relationships. If you didn't rebel, how would you know how to be yourself?

Cissy must have *felt* me thinking about her, because her gaze fastened on me and she returned my stare. Then she cocked her head and wrinkled her nose. I couldn't tell if she thought my performance as a substitute bridesmaid stunk or just the giant butterfly on the one-shouldered dress. It was probably a bit of both.

I quickly disconnected, glancing at my feet—the shoes were starting to rub my pinky toes in a bad way—and then I looked at the bride and groom again, trying hard to pay attention.

". . . when I'm with you, your love wraps me up like my favorite Snuggy, warm and cuddly as microfleece," the bride rambled on through her tears.

And my mind wandered again.

Thankfully, I stood well off to the side, the ninth of nine bridesmaids, so I didn't have to do anything important like perform a reading or hold the bride's bouquet. I tightened my hold on the nosegay of dripping purple orchids, and I smiled, thinking I'd have a good story to tell Malone when I got home.

I could already picture him shaking his head and saying, "Geez, Andy, how do you always manage to get yourself into such messes? You're like a magnet for trouble." Then we'd both laugh, and I'd swear that I'd never go anywhere alone with my mother again because we both knew that always ended up in disaster.

". . . you may now kiss the bride," the minister said, his voice interrupting my thoughts.

Wait, what? Kiss the bride? We were there already?

Yay, I thought, hoping I could ditch the borrowed shoes soon. My pinky toes ached like blisters were brewing.

"Thank you, Jesus, now the baby's legit!" bridesmaid number eight muttered beside me. "Penny's mom and dad can stop having a cow."

I smiled and leaned forward, glancing past the other eight bridesmaids to catch Penny and her brand-new husband Jeff leaning in for a kiss, which took some doing considering the width of her hoopskirt.

Their lips finally locked, and I heard more than a few guests from the groom's side whoop and holler from their Chiavari chairs. Those on the bride's side merely clapped politely. Despite how cynical I often felt about old-fashioned traditions—pretty much meaning anything Cissy saw as "doing things right," like debuting into society or wearing a chastity belt until marriage—my heart twanged as I watched Penny and Jeff beam at each other before dashing up the acrylic aisle hand in hand.

They certainly looked like a couple in love. They were young, yes, and maybe they should have waited until after college to get engaged, much less to get pregnant with baby Iggy. But whose life wasn't full of ill-timed moments? Just because you didn't take the same path as everyone else didn't mean your trek wasn't worthwhile.

If an old friend of mine hadn't been wrongly accused of murder, I never would have met Brian.

I'd still be living alone in my Prestonwood condo, designing Web sites for nonprofits, painting abstracts in my spare time, and wondering if I should get a cat. Not that it would have been a horrible existence by any means, but having Malone in my life amplified all the good, downplayed the bad, and somehow made dealing with my overzealous mother more bearable.

"Hey, y'all better get moving. We still have pictures to do before we're allowed to chow," bridesmaid number eight drawled, shaking her nosegay of orchids in my face.

I limped after her up the aisle as the groomsmen and bridesmaids paired up and pursued the blissful newlyweds through the sea of guests and toward the expansive patio where dinner would be served. I could see the cater-waiters wandering about with trays of hors d'oeuvres, and my stomach grumbled.

Forget the pictures! I was ready to chow *now*.

My radar homed in on a bow-tied young woman describing the lobster corn dogs with tarragon mustard sauce on her sterling silver tray. I was nearly there and practically drooling when Cissy snagged my elbow.

"What in heaven's name is going on?" she said as guests detoured around us, snatching up the lobster pops and the ever-circulating champagne. "You left me to use the powder room. So how'd you end up in a bridesmaid's dress and high heels?"

I wanted to tell her that it was all her fault. If she hadn't roped me into accompanying her to this wedding—and forced me into the too-tight Carolina Herrera dress—I wouldn't have ended up in such a pickle.

Instead, I said, "I had a fashion emergency, and Olivia offered me a way out."

"A fashion emergency? *You?*" Mother sputtered and attempted to furrow her brow, but it remained smooth as glass. "Olivia told me you'd volunteered to fill in for a bridesmaid with pink eye. Why on earth would you do that when you didn't even want to come? You hardly know Penny besides, although you did babysit her once when Shelby's nanny quit abruptly. I think you were fourteen—"

"Mother," I cut her off and opened my mouth to explain.

Did I really want to confess that while helping extricate the bride from the toilet, my Spanx had snapped and rolled off and then I'd split my dress up the back?

It was far easier to reply, "Olivia was right. She was in a bind, and I offered to stand in so the wedding wouldn't be asymmetrical."

Cissy blinked. Then she put a finger to her chin and nodded thoughtfully. "I see. Now that makes perfect sense."

It did?

Well, it probably made as much sense as the truth.

My mother's perfectly powdered face broke into a grin. "Oh, Andrea, how sweet of you to be so helpful to Olivia when I was getting the impression you didn't like her. We really should snag her as your wedding planner before she's all booked up," she said and steered me toward the table with the placeholders.

Had she inhaled chlorine fumes while sitting over the pool?

"Oh, gosh, Mother, that's so generous of you," I replied, biting my cheek. "But Malone and I want to figure out the wedding stuff ourselves."

"Um-hmm," she breathed, and I could tell she'd already tuned me out. My mother squinted at the alphabetically arranged place cards written in swirly calligraphy. "Yes, here we are!" she said, triumphant, and plucked up two folded bits of fancy paper—with her name and Stephen's, I noted—that had our seating assignments.

I was hoping we were at a table near the fringes, somewhere that would make it easy to escape after I'd stuffed my face with free grub.

"Looks like we're at the table next to Vern and Shelby," Cissy remarked, glancing in the direction of Table #3. "Oh, my word! We're with the former president and first lady. Shelby said she had a surprise for me, and I guess this is it!" Though she tried to speak in a hushed tone, her voice quivered ever so slightly. Then she frowned and hissed, "Shoot! We're with that smarmy old Lester Dickens, too. I swear, if he tries to grab my bottom again, I'll stab the man with my steak knife."

The big-time oilman had grabbed Cissy's ass? No wonder he couldn't keep a wife to save his life. Was this a recent offense or one that had happened when Les was married to the bridge-playing Adelaide? I wanted to ask that very question but what came out of my mouth instead was, "We're sitting with the former president?"

Would he know I hadn't voted for him?

"Well, if you'd rather sit with the wedding party, I'm sure you can take Penny's cousin's seat instead," my mother said dryly.

I glanced toward the cluster of bridesmaids and groomsmen, who giggled and flirted as Olivia and her sidekick Terra corralled them for pictures. I found my mind flashing back to the kids' table at Christmas dinners when my grandparents were alive. Back then there had been dozens of relatives who'd come out of the woodwork to kiss up to Grandma and Paw Paw; relatives I'd never seen again once my grandparents had passed. Was it horrible of me to confess that I hadn't missed them a bit?

I sighed loudly without meaning to. The table with the wedding party did look like a kids' table complete with hair-tugging and jostling.

"Well?" my mother prodded.

"I'll sit with you," I said and swallowed. Maybe the fact that I would rather break bread with Cissy meant I was actually maturing. Or else I didn't want to risk being caught in the middle of a food fight again. (It had taken two days to get the cranberry mold out of my hair after the unfortunate Christmas dinner incident of '95.)

Unfortunately, Olivia saw me looking over and made a jerking gesture with her arm. Since we weren't in the middle of Manhattan and she wasn't hailing a taxi, I figured she wanted me to mosey over in my ugly dress pronto.

Phooey, I thought with a frown, so much for sitting down, kicking off my heels, and eating hors d'oeuvres, which was all I wanted to do.

"I'll be back as soon as I can," I remarked to my mother, whose expression turned sour.

"You said that before and it wasn't true."

"Well, this time I mean it," I said and patted her hand. "How long can it take to snap a few pictures?"

Ah, famous last words.

Olivia, the evil taskmaster, had us trailing up and down the spiral staircase in the foyer and encircling the fountain in front (a quick grab from the best man kept the maid-of-honor from falling in). We bookended the bride and groom beneath the orchid and twig canopy out back and all but hung by our heels from Lester Dickens's dining room chandeliers (there were three, and they were BIG). All the while, Penny's bridesmaids kept glancing at me and whispering, "Who is she? She looks too *old* to be a friend of Pen's!" I wanted to tell them that in ten years they'd all be in my (borrowed) shoes so they should stop with the tanning booths and start moisturizing posthaste. But luckily I held my tongue.

And finally we were done.

"I need some shots of just the bride and groom with their parents," Olivia said, her eyes on Senator Ryan, who stood patiently nearby while his wife fussed with the boutonniere on his lapel.

I was off the hook, I realized, and sighed loudly with relief.

But before she let me get away, Olivia instructed, "Drop the dress and shoes at my office tomorrow morning, would you? I'll be in at eight so why don't we make it eight-fifteen?"

"Why the hurry?" I asked.

She paused for so long that I wondered if there was something she wanted to get off her chest. "I don't like leaving loose ends," she finally said, instead of confessing some deep, dark secret.

"So you don't take Sundays off? Event planners don't get a day of rest?" I said, because it sounded nicer than *the devil doesn't get a day of rest*?

Olivia made a noise of disgust. "People get married on Sundays, you know. They have birthday parties and anniversaries and fund-raisers on Sundays, too. It's just another day in my book."

Okey-dokey.

"Besides, Terra Haute doesn't do Sunday mornings," she went on. "So if I get in early enough, I have a few hours to myself."

"Her name is Terra Haute?" I repeated, "As in Terra Haute, Indiana?"

"No, it's Terra Smith." Olivia waved a hand. "But she *is* a Hoosier," she drawled and rolled her eyes. "I'm not sure I can keep her much longer. She's been with me for, like, three months, and it's already wearing thin." She gnawed her lip. "Although letting her go could get very messy."

"But wouldn't that be good for ratings?" I said, a remark that Olivia ignored.

Poor Terra, I thought, feeling sorry for the girl. She seemed hardworking and earnest. I pondered talking to her and suggesting she start looking for another gig.

"So you'll bring the dress in the morning or do you want me to show up on your doorstep bright and early to retrieve it?" Olivia pressed, like it was life or death.

"I'll come to your office," I agreed, because I didn't want to drag things out with her, not with regard to the bridesmaid's dress or the conversation. I turned on a heel, ready to head back to Mother, when Olivia grabbed my arm.

"Wait, Andy, I just wanted to say that I"—she glanced toward the waiting senator and his wife again—"that I can't always do what's right and I can't always please everyone, can I? I have to look out for myself and sometimes that makes me a little too—" She stopped abruptly and pushed her lips together as if reconsidering.

Too *what*?

Bitchy? Annoying? Rude? Selfish?

Pick one, I mused, wondering if La Belle from Hell was about to say she was sorry.

I looked around to see if she was being dramatic for the camera, but I didn't spot the tattooed camera guy—Pete, she'd called him—who'd been hanging over her shoulder when she'd yelled at Millie earlier.

Finally, I prodded, "You've been a little too what, Olivia?"

She glanced around her and muttered, "Forget it. Go back to Cissy and put on your feed bag. Just don't get anything on the dress, or I'll bill you for the dry-cleaning."

The annoying smirk returned to her lips, and she let go of me, walking toward Senator and Mrs. Ryan.

For a long moment I stared after her, wondering if perhaps Olivia La Belle's heart wasn't two sizes too small after all. Had the guilt at her bad behavior finally gotten to her—or almost gotten to her? Did she want to turn a new leaf and start making amends?

But then I shook away the thought.

I had no doubts she could play nice when it suited her. I would bet even Attila the Hun had his moments. But Olivia was a Mean Girl to the bone and, as any Hockaday grad worth her trust fund knew, that kind of mean was forever.

Chapter 6

 By the time I made it back to Cissy, who'd taken her seat at Table #3, my stomach noisily groaned. I slid into the empty chair between my mother and an elderly man whose much younger blond and bejeweled wife kept nudging him awake. The cater-waiters had begun serving the salad—oh, yum, spinach with crumbled feta, cranberries, red onions, and raspberry vinaigrette!—and I dug into my plate as fast as I could pick up a fork. I'd barely digested the fact that Cissy was sitting next to the former president until their conversation invaded my brain.

"I heard that you've taken up painting," my mother was saying between nibbles of salad and sips of champagne. "Do you use those paint-by-number kits or just do it free-hand?"

Lord have mercy.

I tried hard to tune out their conversation and

was ever-so-grateful for the narcoleptic fellow on my left. No need to waste chitchat on him while he was snoring. Instead, I listened to the string quartet that had relocated to the patio. As they wrapped up a Beethoven sonata, they segued into a classy bit of fanfare, and I sat up straighter, seeing Olivia take center stage to introduce the bride and groom.

"It is my immense pleasure," she said into a wireless microphone, her voice booming from hidden speakers, "to introduce Mr. and Mrs. Jeff W. Tripplehorn, Junior!"

I shook my head, thinking of poor little Iggy Tripplehorn. His only hope for avoiding getting teased big-time was if Senator Ryan won the presidency and Iggy got Secret Service detail.

"Thank you so much for coming today," I heard the bride and groom saying right and left as they meandered through the twenty-odd tables, pausing now and then for hugs or air kisses.

Dusk had fallen, and the fairy lights winked around me like lightning bugs. Candelabra centerpieces had been lit upon the tables, and there was a soft golden glow all around. I found myself wishing Malone were with me instead of my mother. The atmosphere was rather romantic, and I got a flutter in my chest, imagining what my big day would be like. I wasn't a girl who'd spent her life cutting pictures of frothy white gowns or floral arrangements out of magazines. I didn't know what I wanted in terms of guests, food, or flowers. I wasn't my mother. I didn't have a detailed plan for everything. As I'd told Cissy earlier, Brian and

I hadn't made any decisions. Whatever we ended up doing, we'd figure out together.

"Hey, Andy, thanks for everything," Penny Ryan—er, Tripplehorn—said, bending low beside my chair. She squeezed my shoulder lightly. "You saved my ass today. Literally."

I smiled and told her, "Consider it a wedding gift."

As they walked away, my mother leaned over, pushing aside the giant butterfly on my shoulder to whisper, "I hope she's as over the moon about *my* gift. I got her the newest Dyson. Shelby said it's what she wanted most on her bridal registry, though God knows why. She could hire someone to sweep her rugs for her. I just don't understand kids these days."

"You got her a vacuum cleaner?" I said and grinned. "That sucks."

My mother frowned.

"It's a joke," I explained, though clearly one lost on Mother.

"Ha ha," Cissy replied stiffly and gave me a look that I interpreted as, *How on earth did I spawn you?*

Well, my father would have laughed, I thought, and I grabbed the glass of bubbly near my plate. He'd shared my sense of humor.

"Down the hatch," I murmured and took a long chug that ended up draining my flute. It was sweet and dry, and it hit the spot.

I glanced across the table at Lester Dickens, who smiled and winked.

Yuck. His grin caused the champagne to curdle in my stomach.

The newlyweds finished making the rounds, and I watched the groom escort his bride back to their private table, pulling out her chair. I saw his hand graze her belly as she settled down, and he planted a kiss on her head. What a sweet and gentle gesture. I felt a lump grow in my throat. As I cleared it away, I woke up the sleeping octogenarian to my left.

"Yes, dear, whatever you say, dear," he murmured before his eyes quickly closed again.

I glanced at the heavily made-up blonde on his other side, sure that her attraction to him had not been his sparkling personality. Did trophy wives marry for anything but money?

Senator Ryan detoured to our table, making a beeline toward the ex-president and former first lady. He was a nice-looking man with sandy-colored hair going gray at the temples, kept short to remind voters of his long-ago stint in the military. He had craggy features, wide-set blue eyes, and an "aw, shucks" grin. I knew my mother and the rest of the Highland Park matrons were totally smitten. Even the normally sensible Sandy Beck had remarked on more than one occasion before the last elections, "I don't care what the man's selling, I'm buying!"

I wasn't so convinced. Seemed to me that most elected officials these days said one thing and did another. Kind of like the social climbers I'd known at prep school. Come to think of it, more than a few of those girls had ended up as arm candy for politicians, and one had made a run for mayor of Highland Park.

"Shelby and I so appreciate ya'll coming to celebrate Penny's marriage with us," Vernon Ryan said to the rest of the table after making small-talk with the former president. But the senator's smile didn't reach his eyes. He looked flushed and dabbed at the sweat on his brow with a pressed handkerchief.

"Vernon, you must be relieved now that the knot is tied and you've got a legitimate grandbaby on the way," my mother said in her typical unabashed way.

Senator Ryan nodded as he shoved the hankie into his breast pocket. "Yes, we're thrilled," he murmured. "Good to see you again, Cissy."

But he didn't appear thrilled, more like wrung out, I mused, and I wondered if he was worried about the press getting wind of Penny's condition. I wasn't sure if his fans—er, his constituents—would care now that the knot was tied, as my mother had put it. People seemed to have greater tolerance for "mistakes" made by the children of public figures as opposed to the sins of their fathers.

Before Vernon Ryan retreated to join his wife—who was giving him a "hurry up" look—Lester Dickens reached out to catch his arm.

"Congratulations, Vern, old boy," Dickens said in his folksy twang. "Now you can put all this cockamamie wedding crap behind ya—and I mean *all* of it—and get your head back into the game. We'll talk soon, right? 'Cause we've got a lot of work to do before November."

"Sure thing, Les," the senator said, giving

Dickens a tight smile before he moseyed off to the missus and settled down beside her.

"Damned fool," I heard Lester Dickens mutter as he stared at the senator's retreating back. When he turned his head and caught me watching him, he reached for the bread basket, snatched up a roll, and viciously buttered it. "A man can't reach his full potential when he's distracted by women and babies," he said, shaking his head.

"Les, it was so kind of you to offer up your home for the wedding," the former first lady remarked to the oilman, clearly attempting to engage him. "The grounds are remarkable. Is it still on the market?"

Dickens set down the roll on his bread plate and dusted off his hands. "Yes, ma'am, it is, and I'd sure like to get her off my hands. You happen to know anyone interested in a prime piece of real estate?"

"Sorry." The first lady politely shook her head.

I was tempted to suggest to Mr. Dickens that adding a few bathrooms to his mansion might help speed up a sale, but I kept my trap shut.

Then out of the blue my mother declared, "Well, I know someone on the market for a family home."

I turned to her, wondering which of her friends was on a house hunt.

"Andrea and her fiancé need to find a place to live," she said, reaching over to pat my cheek. "And they'll need plenty of space to expand their family. Isn't that right, sweetie?"

My empty salad plate rattled as I dropped my fork.

"Mother," I said under my breath. She couldn't be serious. Had she mixed champagne and Xanax?

"Well, Cissy honey, if you want a tour of the place, I'll give you one myself," Dickens said with a wolfish grin. "Just give me a call whenever you want to see it."

"Oh, um, that's so thoughtful of you, Les," Cissy replied, giving him as fake a smile as I'd ever seen. "Although I think I'd like Andrea livin' in Highland Park so she can be close to me. I want to help out with my grandbabies."

"For Pete's sake," I muttered as the chatter at the table hushed and all eyes fell upon us. "You have no grandbabies," I reminded her. Like, I could ever imagine her changing a diaper or burping an infant.

"I don't have any yet, but I'm sure it won't be long now. Tick tock, tick tock," she said, doing her best clock impression.

"Brian and I are fine with my condo," I told her, wishing she'd knock it off.

But Mother was winding up, not down. "Honestly, Andrea, you can't live in that tiny condo forever or in Malone's ratty apartment. There's not room for a nursery, much less for the nanny."

"What nanny?" I said, hoping to God she hadn't already hired someone merely in anticipation of my producing offspring.

Cissy let out a weighty sigh. "Surely you don't intend to try to raise children without live-in help," she said as the cater-waiters reappeared to remove salad plates and set down the entrée. "I could hardly have handled you without Sandy full-time. It takes a village to raise a child, or at least a lot of hired help, don't you agree?" she asked, cocking her head and glancing pointedly toward the other women at our table.

I noticed the former first lady took that moment to pat her mouth with a napkin, though I hadn't seen her eat a bite from her plate.

The blonde with all the bangles chortled and wiggled bejeweled fingers in the air. "I would've loved to pop out a few rug rats of my own but Herbert already had five grown ones and grand-kids. So he bought me a pair of Pekinese pups and a live-in groomer to go with 'em. That's kind of like a nanny, wouldn't you say?" She nudged her cotton-haired husband awake. "Herb, come alive! We're at a party."

He snorted and opened his eyes. Nodding, he replied, "Whatever you say, dear." Then his chin dropped to his chest and the snoring resumed.

"Women and dogs," Lester Dickens remarked with a grunt, shaking his head.

The chatter at the table resumed, and I sighed with relief that no one was paying the least attention to us as my mother leaned over and loudly whispered, "Oh, yes, a pet groomer is *just* like a nanny."

When I shushed her, she rolled her eyes, putting a hand up to her mouth and hissing behind it, "She's wife number three and a half. One marriage was annulled so that only counts half as much."

"You don't say," I whispered back and leaned nearer so that Mother's hair brushed my cheek. I inhaled a familiar mix of Joy perfume and Aqua Net. "FYI, I am all weddinged out. So I'll stay for cake but then we're leaving."

She drew away. "But you're having fun."

"No, *you're* having fun."

"You don't want to stick around for dancing? Shelby said they flew in some big-name singer I've never heard of." Cissy tapped her chin. "I'm told his wife's a pop star, too, and they named their baby after a primary color."

Dear Lord.

Even if Shelby and Vern had booked Bon Jovi, I'm not sure I would have wanted to stick around, although I would have been tempted. I was a die-hard fan of '80s rock.

"No, thanks, I don't want to stay to hear the wedding singer," I told Mother. Who would I dance with, besides? The former president? Lester Dickens? Blondie's snoozing hubby?

"I heard the singer and his entourage are arriving by helicopter," Cissy added, as if that would change my mind. "Good thing there's a landing pad on the roof of the house. That's how Les gets around town. He doesn't like traffic."

I glanced across the table at the oilman and decided some people just had too much money and too little sense. So Lester Dickens's house for sale had a helipad and, like, two bathrooms? That was what I'd call having your priorities in disorder.

"Watch my lips," I told Mother. "I do not want to stay," I said, enunciating every word in case I'd been speaking in a tongue that she didn't understand.

"Spoilsport," Cissy replied and set her face in a sad little moue.

"I could take a cab," I told her, and she clicked tongue against teeth.

"And pay with what? Life Savers?"

She was right. I hadn't brought along any cash. Silly me.

"All right, we'll leave early," she said reluctantly, "but not until after the cake's cut."

"Deal," I replied. Once I had a piece of Millie's gorgeous seven-layer creation—and told Olivia how absolutely divine it was—I would be more than ready to escape. I had no intention of staying until the bride tossed her bouquet. I didn't need to catch it. I already had Malone.

I'd just finished devouring the herb-crusted Chilean sea bass with champagne sauce when I heard the chime of silverware tapping crystal. Then Olivia's voice boomed through the microphone again. "Ladies and gentleman, it's time for another sweet moment," she said in her honeyed drawl, and she waved her arm at the circular table that held Millie's towering, flower-encrusted seven-tiered confection. "The bride and groom will now cut the cake!"

I had to shift position to see around a few large hats. As I did, I spotted Pete in his dark garb with his shoulder-camera, lurking in the background.

The sleek silver knife that Olivia had brandished at Millie earlier now glinted in the glow of candlelight as the newlyweds raised it, hand in hand, to cut through the first and largest layer. Before they lowered the knife, I saw Olivia motion Pete closer. Penny and Jeff hesitated for a moment, as if they realized they were about to vandalize a piece of art. Truthfully, it was a crime they had to cut it up. Millie's cake was a thing of beauty.

"Go for it," I heard Olivia urge to nervous laughter.

After counting "one-two-three" aloud, the pair finally brought the knife down onto the bottom tier of ivory fondant ringed with lifelike orchids glistening with sugar. I found I was holding my breath, waiting. Others must have done the same as a collective sigh followed when the knife plunged into the cake. Only instead of sliding through, it got stuck like the sword in the stone. Though the newlyweds pushed, the knife resisted.

"What's the damned thing made of?" I heard Lester Dickens say with a snicker. "Concrete?"

Penny and Jeff both let go and glanced anxiously at Olivia, which is when La Belle from Hell marched toward the cake and bent down to take a closer look.

"My God, it's Styrofoam!" Olivia remarked quite loudly enough for everyone to hear. And then she pulled the knife from the cake, shook her fist to the heavens, and shouted, "Millllieeeee!"

I felt like I was watching a scene ripped from the Star Trek movie that Malone had made me watch last weekend where Captain Kirk screwed up his face and screamed, "Kaaaaahn!"

To say I was startled by the outburst was putting it mildly. It seemed so staged that I had a strong suspicion Olivia had rehearsed her reaction, although Penny and Jeff seemed earnestly surprised, and not in a good way. In fact, Penny's eyes welled up and a big sob escaped her throat.

And all the while Pete moved about with his camera, recording every tacky moment.

Chapter 7

"I'm free at last, and I'm heading home," I told Malone, speaking into the cell phone that I'd retrieved from the Black Suits with a coat-check stub. At least they hadn't frisked us on the way out to make sure we hadn't stolen pieces of silverware.

"So it was that bad?" Brian asked, and I could hear the noises of the hockey game on the TV in the background.

"Let me count the ways," I said and sighed.

"You'll have to tell me all about it."

"Only if you promise to give me a foot rub," I said, and my mother quietly snorted from behind the steering wheel of the Lexus.

I hung up and slumped back against the comfy leather seat, happy to be leaving Lester Dickens's House of Horrors. Although I still wore the ugly bridesmaid's dress, I had my own shoes on at least.

I couldn't wait to return the borrowed dress and heels to Olivia first thing in the morning. While I was there, I planned to give her another piece of my mind about her public bashing of Millie Draper. The bullying had to stop.

"Well, that was certainly something," my mother remarked, and I knew she didn't mean the ceremony. She'd also seemed stunned by Olivia's histrionics involving the cake. "I can't believe Olivia behaved so badly. Shelby looked horrified, and Penny burst into tears. Why on earth would she do that?"

"Because she's like a black hole bent on sucking happiness from the galaxy," I said, and my chest tightened. I had a feeling I knew exactly why Olivia had performed her *Wrath of Kahn* routine. I'd been an eyewitness to her threatening Millie with nonpayment if the cake wasn't perfect. What better way to carry out that threat than to point out an "imperfection" in front of two hundred guests.

But something didn't sit right with me—namely, why should Olivia care about a $10,000 bill for a cake if that's what Penny had ordered? Surely Senator Ryan—or Lester Dickens—would pay the tab, no matter how high. Olivia's actions made no more sense than the senator allowing Pete the Cameraman to selectively tape footage from the wedding for Olivia's show. What was up with that? Could it be that the senator didn't care because Pete was mostly focused on Olivia's take-down of Millie rather than on Penny and her burgeoning belly? Or maybe he'd given Olivia a pass because the show wouldn't air for months down the road, until after the election, so it wouldn't likely damage his campaign.

"Something smells fishy and it's not the Chilean bass," I said aloud, only to have my mother agree.

"You're darned tootin' something's fishy," she drawled, "because if Millie used foam, there was good reason, and Olivia has to be well aware of that. Millie's Cakes is not some fly-by-night operation."

I agreed.

"I've chaired enough fund-raisers and hosted enough galas to know that a cake with that many layers needs a strong foundation," she went on, flicking manicured fingers in the air. "If Millie hadn't used Styrofoam on the bottom, I'm sure it would have collapsed. Certainly Olivia understood that."

Oh, yes, I'm quite sure Olivia had understood. I'd bet my brand-new convection toaster oven that Millie had told her there would be a polystyrene foundation, or perhaps Olivia had even asked for it. Either way, it meant Olivia had acted like a jerk.

"They don't call her La Belle from Hell for nothing," I muttered.

"Who calls her that?" Mother asked.

Well, um, I did, and I was sure that I wasn't the only one.

"It's too bad no one will stand up to her," I said, changing the subject. "It would serve her right if someone would give her a taste of her own medicine."

"As the rumor mill has it, someone did stand up to her," Mother informed me. "Jasper Pippin used to do all the flowers for the White Glove Society's deb balls, but Dorothea Amherst quit using him. She said he didn't follow through as promised on last year's fete and then she saw the bit on Olivia's show about him overbilling the mayor for flowers that weren't fresh. Now he's out of business."

That had to be the Jasper I'd heard Millie mention. Yep, those dirty tricks sounded just like the Olivia La Belle I knew and detested.

"So if you don't play Olivia's game, she'll shut you down," I said, shaking my head. "Why does anyone want to work with her? Surely, there are other event planners in town that don't treat people like crap."

"She has exquisite taste," my mother explained, "and she's incredibly well-connected. She's on a first-name basis with everyone who's anyone. Her father was once an ambassador and traveled extensively. In fact, he and Jolene live in Monte Carlo now."

So what exactly did that mean? Had Ambassador La Belle taught his only child how to twist people's arms with a smile on her face? Olivia had always been great at kissing up at Hockaday. She knew how to get what she wanted by charming those who could help her most. The rest of us got kicked to the curb.

"I'm sure Millie won't suffer the same fate as Jasper," my mother offered with a lift of her chin. "I had heard friends complaining that Jasper's arrangements were too fuddy-duddy. Everyone wants organic, earthy arrangements now. But everyone *loves* Millie's cakes. They're exquisite. Anyone who's ever tasted Millie's Italian meringue butter cream icing knows that she doesn't skimp or take shortcuts. I said as much to Shelby, for all the good it did," she murmured, and her fingernails testily tapped the steering wheel. "Millie's a magician for even getting that cake done on such short notice, and she pulled it off beautifully. Olivia should have praised her to high heaven for that alone, and Shelby should have given her a generous tip."

"Amen to that."

Millie had looked positively exhausted when I'd stumbled upon her and Olivia in the kitchen before the ceremony. She'd undoubtedly stayed up all night, working her fingers to the bone, and for what? So that Olivia could bad-mouth her in front of two hundred very influential Dallasites?

"I certainly hope she doesn't lose business over this," my mother remarked. "But people do talk in this town."

"And how," I whispered. CNN had nothing on the real housewives of Highland Park.

Well, at least the Black Suits had separated the wedding guests from their cell phones, otherwise someone would have recorded Olivia's rant against Millie and it would have gone viral already. Then I remembered Pete and groaned. Even if the besmirching didn't happen overnight, it would happen as soon as the new season of *The Wedding Belle* premiered, since the tattooed camera guy had definitely caught Olivia's outburst.

Would word spread so quickly that Millie would instantly feel the repercussions? Were canceled orders already popping up? Though I'm sure the worst wouldn't come until after the scene aired on TV, whenever that would be. I'd have to check the local listings, as Olivia's televised train wreck wasn't exactly on my "must watch" list.

"Olivia admitted that she ramps up the drama for ratings," I said. "I wonder how many vendors she's skewered so that she can keep her show on the air. I'm surprised no one's sued her for defamation."

"Maybe they tried but it never got very far," Mother suggested. "Besides"—she clicked tongue against teeth—"I can't imagine anyone believes anything they see on TV these days. Even the news has gone tabloid. It's all sordid crimes and scandal." She sighed. "How I miss Walter Cronkite."

"The public is fickle, and the Internet's pretty much a web of misinformation," I said, because it was the truth. What seemed like real news on Monday could be exposed as a lie on Tuesday. I'd designed Web sites for hardworking nonprofits that reaped steady donations until one piece of bad press—often an unsubstantiated story, review, or tweet on the wonderful World Wide Web—could dry up the well in a snap.

"It's a shame," Cissy said, shaking her head. "It's as though there's no dignity in anything anymore."

Since I couldn't disagree with her there, we both got quiet. In fact, neither of us said another word as the Lexus rolled north. It wasn't until we'd exited the Tollway, driven along Preston Road for a spell, and Cissy had pulled into the parking lot of my condo complex, that she opened her mouth again.

"You know what, Andrea? You're right," she said, putting the car in park and letting the engine idle as I unhooked my seat belt.

"I am?" I hesitated before opening the door. "About what?"

She nudged the bridge of her Jackie O sunglasses and sucked in her cheeks before she replied, "I don't think I want to hire Olivia to plan your wedding after all. She's too unpredictable, and I don't want to risk her mucking up your big day. So after you return that god-awful dress tomorrow, we'll wash our hands of her."

Hallelujah! My mother had seen the light!

"Do come by the house in the morning once you've dispensed with the dress," she told me. "It's the perfect opportunity for some girl time with Stephen away. We'll have lots of time to chat."

"You want to hang out?" I asked, because my mother and I didn't usually chill together. There was generally an ulterior motive behind our get-togethers, like her calf-roping me into Penny's wedding. "But it's Sunday, won't you be at church?"

"I think God would forgive me for missing a sermon if it was for a good reason." She shot me a grin like she had something up her sleeve.

"Um, I'm not sure I can make it," I murmured, not wanting to miss pancakes with Malone. "Maybe another time?"

As I waited for her response, I grabbed the borrowed shoes from the floor mat. Before I slid out of the Lexus, I took my ChapStick and Life Savers out of Mother's sparkly Judith Leiber bag and left the bejeweled clutch on the seat along with the torn Carolina Herrera dress and the Spanx. The Underpants from Hell belonged to her, too, I figured, since she'd bought them, and I definitely didn't want to keep them. I would never wear them again. She could burn them both for all I cared.

"'Bye, Mother—" I started to say, but she wasn't finished.

"Andrea, please!" she begged. "Olivia's office is just around the corner. I insist you drop by when you're through with her." She had her chin up and her jaw firmly set like she wasn't going to take no for an answer. "I'll grab some bear claws at Starbucks and we can confab over coffee."

I didn't drink coffee. But that was beside the point.

"Why do we need to confab all of a sudden?" I asked as I planted my feet on the asphalt and stood up. "What's so important? Are you dying?" I asked facetiously, but suddenly I felt a bit worried. She had been acting pretty weird.

The window whirred as she opened it. I shut the door and ducked down to hear her answer.

"Am I dyin'?" she echoed, then cracked that Cheshire cat grin again. "I don't have that scheduled any time soon, pumpkin, not before I get you married with a house full of babies."

"Good," I said, "because that might be a while."

"No, no, it's not about *me*. It's about *you*. Since you're so dead-set against hiring a wedding planner, we'll need to get started *toot suite* on planning your wedding ourselves. Won't that be fun, sweet pea? Just you and me and my checkbook?" she asked, then added in a singsong voice, "Dum dum da dum, dum dum da dum!"

My mouth fell open.

"*Hasta la vista*, pumpkin!" Cissy wiggled her fingers in a wave as she rolled the window up.

Then she backed up the car and drove off.

Chapter 8

I was lucky Mother didn't roll the Lexus over my foot because I couldn't move. I'd gone catatonic at the idea of Cissy taking charge of my wedding. *Because that was exactly what would happen.* She would do what she wanted come hell or high water, taking over like that bossy Tabatha on Bravo who bulldozed bad beauty shops. I'd end up in a frothy frou-frou dress that made me look like a giant marshmallow for starters. She'd invite five hundred of her closest friends and have a staid and formal reception and sit-down dinner at the Dallas Country Club. It would be *her* dream wedding, not mine.

Suddenly, I felt the Chilean bass lurch in my stomach.

"Hey, Kendricks! What're you doing standing in the parking lot when there's a hockey game going on?"

At the sound of Malone's voice, I glanced up.

He must have spotted my arrival out the window as he stood on my tiny porch, wearing his St. Louis Blues T-shirt and waving his arm.

"If you hurry, you can catch the tail end. We're heading into triple overtime!" he said and waved again, clearly wanting me to move it. When I stepped onto the sidewalk and headed toward the porch steps, he cocked his head and let out a whistle. "What the heck are you wearing? That's not the dress you left in. So was it a theme wedding? Are you supposed to be some kind of mutant flower like the one that only blooms once a year and stinks?"

"You're getting warm," I said as I preceded him through the doorway and into the tiny condo that had been my sanctuary since I'd moved back to Dallas after college. "What happened was worse than being a stinky flower in a theme wedding. I ended up being a bridesmaid."

"Are you serious?"

"Sadly, yes."

He smothered a laugh. "I want to hear the whole gory story," he remarked, and his hand attempted to squeeze my shoulder but grabbed a fistful of the humongous chiffon butterfly instead. He knit his brows and tried to fluff the fabric that he'd crushed.

"Gory sums it up pretty nicely," I replied with a sigh. I felt lucky to be marrying a guy who was such a good listener, especially since I did a lot of talking. Brian reminded me of my dad in that respect. My father was never too busy for me, never too wrapped up in work or my mother to pause and lend me an ear, and I had loved him all the more for it.

When I got inside, I dropped my bag and the borrowed shoes to the floor. Then I turned and reached for Malone. I needed a hug, and how. Only all I caught was air. Malone wasn't right behind me anymore. He'd skedaddled over to the sofa and plunked himself down in front of the TV.

Ah, so much for being a good listener, I thought, although I noticed he was paying very close attention to the hockey announcers.

I walked over and stood in front of him, my hands on my hips. "I thought you wanted to hear the whole gory story," I griped.

He leaned to the right so he could see around me. "Third overtime has started, babe," he said without shifting his gaze from the screen. "Can it wait until the game is over?"

I wanted to shout, *No, it can't!* Only describing my afternoon as my mother's date at Penny Ryan's wacko wedding wasn't urgent, and I knew how much Brian wanted to watch this game. If I'd been bleeding, I'm sure he would have diverted his attention from the TV at least long enough to assess whether or not he needed to call 911.

"Hooking? Are you freaking kidding me?" Malone complained and threw his hands in the air as I went into the bedroom to change.

When I emerged a few minutes later wearing my yoga pants and a Dallas Stars T-shirt, the game was over and Brian was frowning.

As I settled beside him, he glanced at my shirt

with his bespectacled eyes and said, "I think I liked you better in that butt-ugly purple dress."

"The Blues lost?" I asked.

He grunted in response.

I wriggled over and wrapped my arms around him as tightly as I could. He looked like he needed a hug even more than I did.

"Hey, it's four out of seven, right? They'll beat the Stars next time," I remarked.

"If you can't win on home turf—" Brian shook his head and nudged at his specs.

"I know how to make you feel better," I said, and he raised his eyebrows as if expecting something salacious. Instead, I started in on my zany tale of Penny's wedding, from having my cell phone confiscated by Lester Dickens's hired goons, to seeing Olivia La Belle rip Millie apart about the $10,000 cake that was late, to prying the pregnant, hoop-skirted bride from the toilet, and walking down the aisle in the role of bridesmaid number nine.

When I finished, Brian let out a soft, "Whoa." He took off his glasses, rubbed the lenses on his shirt then propped them back on his nose. His blue eyes blinked from behind them. He said nothing, although I heard him slowly exhale.

My pulse thumped. Was he having second thoughts about tying the knot with me? He was such a good guy, funny and sweet, as down-to-earth as his Midwestern roots, and one of the best young defense attorneys in Dallas. I was a wannabe artist who worked as a Web designer (and tried not to touch my trust fund except in emergencies). My mom was a well-meaning lunatic. Maybe

Malone was considering what would happen if he mixed my DNA with his. Our children had a fifty-fifty chance of being whack-a-doodles.

"I know what you're thinking," I said, because he kept looking at me so strangely. "That I'm like a living, breathing episode of *I Love Lucy*, especially when Mother's involved." My mouth went dry when he didn't respond. "You're wondering if you should be marrying someone who's a magnet for lunatics. You're probably afraid our wedding is going to turn into the deb ball I never had, which it very well may if my mother has anything to do with it."

An amused smile slipped over his lips, and he shook his head, reaching out to touch my hair (which I hoped wasn't quite the rat's nest Olivia had implied).

"No," he replied quietly. "I'm thinking how lucky I am to be with someone who cares so much about other people. You did your mom a favor today. You stood up for Millie. You got the bride out of a jam. Hell, several jams. You've got a big heart, Kendricks. It's what I love about you most."

I was so relieved I nearly burst.

"And I thought it was my killer bod," I cracked, because I wasn't good at mush.

He screwed up his face. "Okay, yeah, it's your killer bod first then your big heart. My bad."

I opened my mouth to make another joke but bit down on my lip. Instead of zingers, I wanted to spout vapid Hallmark card thoughts about love. I can't believe I'd ever doubted that there was some-one out there just for me. It wasn't that I'd felt like half a person without Brian; but falling for him had made me feel *more* than whole. Malone had experienced firsthand the insanity that was my life, and instead of running away from me as fast as he could, he wanted to stay with me for better or worse. If he wasn't The One, then there was no such thing on earth.

"It's me who got lucky," I whispered back—the least I could say—and leaned forward to press my lips against his.

I couldn't tell you what came on the TV after the hockey game. I didn't even realize it was dark until we surfaced for air a few hours later. We were both hungry enough to order pizza from Besas (the Meat Lovers Special for him and green pepper and onions for me). By the time I'd eaten enough to fill my belly to the brim, Malone had popped another of his old Star Trek movies into the DVR. This one had to do with saving whales in San Francisco Bay. I snuggled into my fiancé's shoulder and tried hard to watch, but somewhere in the middle I drifted off.

Malone must have put me to bed after the movie ended. When I forced my eyelids open, the yellow haze of early morning filtered in through the shutters. I rolled away from the noisy lump that was my fiancé snoring. Picking up the alarm clock on the night table, I saw the hands pointed at 7:45.

Time to make the doughnuts, I thought and rolled off the mattress. I figured I might as well run down to Olivia's office and drop off the dress and shoes before Malone even woke up. Then I wouldn't have to ruin my *entire* Sunday.

So I tiptoed around the room, pulling on

clothes. I did a quick toothbrushing and an even quicker splash of water on my face. Just in case Malone awoke from his stupor, I left a note in the kitchen saying, *Gone to Olivia's to return Hideous Dress. Back soon. Don't make pancakes without me! Love U, Andy.* I didn't bother to drag a brush through my bird's nest before stepping outside and closing the door.

It was kind of nice being up early on a Sunday. Usually Malone and I slept away half the morning and then made pancakes—blueberry or chocolate chip, whatever we felt like. Sometimes we stayed in our pajamas until noon.

When I stepped outside, I heard birds chirping. The sky looked like a canvas of brilliant blue that some invisible hand had swept with hazy white brushstrokes. I wanted to run back inside to my easel so I could paint it. But that would have to wait. The tiniest breeze ruffled the trees and shrubs, and I drew in a big whiff of honeysuckle. Once I got in my Jeep and headed out, I found traffic was almost nonexistent, something rarer than a natural blonde in Big D.

I'd looked up Olivia's business address and knew right where to go. I'd grown up in Highland Park and my mother's favorite shops were located in Highland Park Village, so it was familiar enough turf.

When I turned off Preston Road and rolled into the shopping center, the parking lot was pretty much empty. I pulled into a space near the Stella McCartney boutique, which was on the same side as Harry Winston, Dior, and Balenciaga. It was hardly surprising that Olivia liked to keep such pricey company. I was sure the snob in Olivia appreciated, too, that the buildings were on the historical register, so Highland Park Village was a landmark as well as *chi-chi*.

I locked the Jeep and headed toward the building that housed the Wedding Belle's office suite. As I approached the glass doors, another vehicle caught my eye, and not just because there were so few cars in the lot at 8:15 A.M. on Sunday.

It was a white Acura SUV with a discreet but readable sign across the rear window: MILLIE'S CAKES, it said in hot pink, LET THEM EAT CAKE! There was a phone number and Web URL as well.

The sight made me uneasy.

Why would Millicent Draper show up at Olivia's office so bright and early the day after Penny Ryan's wedding?

Had she gotten wind of Olivia's trash-talking and driven over first thing to have it out with her? Or had Olivia summoned her here?

Whatever the answer, it didn't bode well for Millie. She was such a nice woman. Olivia would shred her up like taco cheese.

I swallowed hard and kept walking, thinking the grandmotherly baker would surely need backup defending herself against my prep school enemy yet again.

The bad feeling in the pit of my stomach only deepened as I entered the doors to Olivia's building and climbed the stairs to her second floor office. I'd barely gotten halfway up the steps when I heard a gut-wrenching cry. Without a doubt, I knew it came from within Olivia's suite.

That danged bully! She was probably tearing into sweet Millie again.

I ran up the remaining stairs, turned the knob, and pushed my way inside to Olivia's reception area.

"Millie?" I said and glanced right and left, looking for the cotton-haired baker and hoping she was okay. But I saw no one and nothing seemed out of place in the anteroom with its trendy black-and-white patterned wallpaper, upholstered chairs, and shabby chic painted tables topped with stacks of bridal magazines.

Then I heard the mournful wail repeated.

"No, no, no," a voice sobbed in a tone that broke my heart.

I dropped the borrowed dress and shoes, hurrying as fast as I could through the waiting area. Without further preamble, I burst into Olivia's office.

"Millie, are you o—" I started to say, and then my tongue lodged in my throat. "Dear God," I breathed, taking in the frightening tableau before me.

Millie kneeled on the rug not six feet away, looking anything but okay. She turned her wide eyes upon me, her time-worn face stricken.

"Oh, Andy! This is bad," she choked out and shook her head, "very bad."

Very bad?

That had to be the understatement of the year.

For Millie held a silver cake knife in her hand, its blade slick with blood. And lying on the rug before her was Olivia La Belle, her body still and her eyes rolled to the heavens, her throat slick with blood as well.

Chapter 9

The scene was too surreal to believe.

In fact, it was so surreal that I couldn't help but suspect it wasn't real at all. Was this some kind of prank? Was it another despicable attempt to drive up Olivia's TV show ratings? Could Olivia be that desperate for attention?

I looked around for Pete the Cameraman with his rose and thorn tattoos, but I didn't see him or anyone else. It was just me, the knife-wielding Millie, and the lifeless Olivia.

"Is there a hidden camera? Is this some kind of publicity stunt?" I said out loud, because I wouldn't put anything past Olivia La Belle. If there hadn't been so much red goo all over her—was it ketchup?—I would have nudged the prostrate Olivia with the toe of my shoe and told her to get up.

"It's not a stunt," Millie whimpered, "she's dead. I did everything I could but it was too late . . ."

Her voice trailed off, and I noticed the wadded up fabric near Olivia's head that looked like a big ol' bandage drenched in red. Was it a table linen sample? Had Millie used it to try to stop the blood from flowing?

"Olivia's really and truly dead?" I said, and my voice sounded hollow. "She's not playing possum?"

Millie shook her head.

I gulped.

A chill raced up my spine, lifting the hairs on my neck. The red goo wasn't ketchup, and Olivia wasn't going for broke to drive up her TV ratings. She'd gone boots up for real, and they were expensive boots, too. They looked like the Jimmy Choo snakeskin ankle boots that Mother had tried to foist on me at Christmas and I'd made her return.

"I watched her die," Millie said in an eerie half whisper. "I was here when she took her last breath."

Whoa.

"What?" I would have run like a bat out of hell but my legs felt like rubber. "Oh, God, this is crazy," I said, and I grabbed hold of the nearest chair to keep my knees from giving out from beneath me. "This is not real," I told myself. "This can't be real."

"I wish it wasn't"—Millie's voice shook—"but it is. And I have no idea what to do. I should have called 911 instead of trying to save her. But it's too late now."

"What the hell happened?" I asked, staring at her, horrified. "What do you mean you watched her die?"

I wasn't sure how I got out the questions. My mouth had gone bone dry. I had no clue what to do. How did one deal with something like this? Had Millie truly walked in on Olivia in the throes of death with a cake knife sticking out of her throat, or had she stabbed the wedding planner in a fit of rage over the $10,000 cake brouhaha? I suddenly remembered that Millie's departing words yesterday had something to do with Olivia getting what was coming to her.

"You didn't—" I started to ask, but couldn't finish.

But Millie seemed to know where I was headed.

"No," she cried, bursting into tears. "I didn't do anything, Andy."

Though my eyes might have wanted to convince me that Millie was guilty as sin, my gut had a hard time buying it. Fingers shaking, I pulled my phone from the pocket of my cargo pants.

"You can tell me the truth, Millie. Did you and Olivia fight because of Penny's cake? Did she attack you? Was it self-defense?" I asked as I attempted to call 911, but my trembling fingers hit the wrong buttons.

"No, no, it was nothing like that." Millie shook her head as she slowly got up off her knees. "Yes, I came by this morning to have it out with her. She texted me to say the Ryans wouldn't pay the bill for the cake, and I knew she was pulling one over on me the same way she did Jasper. I'd had it up to here with her antics." She raised the cake knife to her chin. "But we didn't fight—it wasn't what you're thinking," she insisted, lowering her arm to her side. "The door was unlocked when I arrived, and she was on the floor. The knife was sticking out of her neck, and she was gasping and twitching and"—Millie gulped—"*gurgling*. I pulled it out but I think that made things worse!" She glanced down at the blood on her shirt and hands. "I grabbed something off her desk to stop the blood but it was too late."

"What if it's not too late?" I said and tried to dial my cell again, pressing the three digits successfully this time. What if Olivia's heart was still beating? What if she needed pressure applied somewhere beneath all that blood? What if we could save her?

Millie shook her head. "She's not breathing. There's no pulse."

I sunk to my heels, knowing Millie was telling the truth. Olivia had lost so much blood. She looked like she'd bathed in it. Whoever had killed her had done the job right.

Oh, boy, oh, boy, oh, boy.

"What is your emergency?" I heard a voice say in my ear, and I swallowed hard, finding my voice to tell the dispatcher to get someone over to Highland Park Village pronto, that Olivia La Belle had lost a lot of blood and needed medical attention. Although by the time I hung up, I knew Millie was right. Olivia was good and dead.

Millie cried as I got up on my wobbly legs and stared down at the sight of my old enemy lying so still, the patterned rug beneath her stained with red. I could smell the blood, too. The sticky sweet scent of it filled my nose and head. Bile rose into

my throat, and I pressed a hand to my mouth,
gagging.

I had so often wished Olivia dead when I was
in school and she was tormenting me. There were
nights I'd even prayed that she'd get hit by a bus or
have a meteorite drop from space smack onto her
head. But seeing her now, like this, wasn't how I'd
hoped it would end. I hadn't *really* wanted her to
die. I had just wanted her to go away.

"Who?" I asked, then again, "Who?" sounding
like an owl. "Because if it wasn't you, it had to be
someone who was here right before you."

"I don't know," Millie said tremulously. "I
didn't see anyone when I arrived." She must have
read the skepticism on my face because she added,
"I swear I didn't kill her, Andy, no matter how it
looks."

Swallowing the horrid taste in my mouth, I
shifted my focus from Olivia to stare at the knife
in Millie's hand. "How it looks is pretty bad," I
said, because it did. "You'll have to tell the police
what you told me. You really didn't stab her?"

"No, I didn't stab her!" But as she said it, Millie
glanced down at the knife as well. I heard the
sharp intake of her breath, like she'd only just
realized what she was holding. "Oh, dear," she
whispered and dropped it. The knife clunked
onto the rug beside Olivia. "Oh, dear," Millie said
again and began to wipe her hands on her tan
pants, leaving brick-red smears. "My fingerprints
will be all over it, won't they?"

"Yes," I said. It was a no-brainer.

"I didn't do anything but try to help," she insisted, her eyes wildly darting about the room and settling on the door. "I have to get out of here, Andy. If anyone sees me like this, they'll get the wrong impression."

Um, hello? *I* was somebody. *I* had seen, and I would never forget.

"You can't just take off," I said, even though I wanted to get the hell out of there, too. I wanted to run home to my condo, jump in the shower, and scrub my brain clean of the past few minutes. But that wasn't possible for many reasons, one of which was the cry of sirens fast approaching. "You have to stay," I said, because it was the right thing to do, "they have to find out who did this."

Millie rushed to the window, parting the blinds. "They're here! There's an ambulance and a police car, oh, God," she whimpered. She glanced down at the blood on her pants and her blouse. "They'll think I'm guilty. They're going to take one look at me and get the wrong impression."

She was probably right but I tried to calm her down. "You just have to tell them the truth, Millie. I believe you," I said, and I meant it.

"Yes, of course, the truth," Millie said and turned away from the window, nodding. "They'll find whoever did it, and they'll know it wasn't me." As she talked to herself, she circled her arms around her middle, further smudging brick-red on her white blouse. "Then everything will be okay."

"Yeah, it'll be okay," I said, but my voice was like a mouse's squeak. I hope she bought it. I wasn't so sure.

As the sirens stopped smack in front of the building, I used my cell again, this time to call Malone. I prayed he wouldn't sleep through the ring tones and let the call go to voice mail.

"Andy?" I heard him say groggily. "Where are you?"

"I'm at Olivia's office at Highland Park Village," I told him as tires screeched down below in the parking lot and car doors slammed shut. "Can you get dressed and come down here *now*?"

"What? Why?"

"Wait, scratch that," I told him, my heart pounding. I had a feeling Millie and I were going to end up in the backseat of a squad car before Malone would even get here. "Better make that the police station." I turned my head toward the door and caught the distant sound of the outer doors opening and closing downstairs.

"Andy," Malone's voice had turned from groggy to panicked, "what the hell's going on?"

I said all I had a chance to say before I heard the footsteps on the stairwell. "Olivia La Belle was murdered, and I'm a bit in the thick of it."

"What is that supposed to mean?" he asked.

"Just hurry," I said and hung up.

I took deep breaths, trying not to freak out. Would the police think I had something to do with Olivia's death, too? Would they arrest me and Millie both? What had I gotten myself into?

I did have enough presence of mind to tell Millie not to say a word until Malone met us at the station.

"I shouldn't have come," Millie murmured,

wringing hands streaked with drying blood. "I should have ignored the text." Tears slipped down the older woman's cheeks beneath her owl-like glasses.

I heard noises at the door to the suite before it flew open and the place was suddenly swarming with people, EMTs coming first followed by a pair of uniformed police.

"I'm the one who called," I said as they took in the scene. "I think Olivia La Belle was attacked," I added in a croak.

The officers—a short middle-aged white male followed by a tall young woman—quickly ushered me and Millie into the anteroom, away from Olivia, so the EMTs had enough room to do their thing.

"Are you injured, ma'am?" the female cop asked Millie, and I saw her name tag said SHANDS.

"No," Millie replied and started shaking hard.

I put a hand on her shoulder. "She's in shock," I told the cops. "She found Olivia with the knife in her neck and tried to help her."

Before either could respond, one of the EMTs emerged from Olivia's office, blood all over the latex gloves on his hands.

"Is she gonna make it?" the male cop asked, and the paramedic shook his head.

Millie loudly wept.

Officer Shands cursed under her breath. Then she nodded at her partner. "Let's secure the scene." She gave me a hard look. "Don't either of you so much as twitch," she instructed, before turning to speak into her shoulder mic. I heard her mention a "DB" and my head began to swim as everything started to fully sink in.

Olivia La Belle would no longer push around Millie or anyone like her. My prep school bully was now a DB, and that didn't mean dumb blonde. It meant dead body.

Ding dong, the Wedding Belle was gone. I just hoped to God there was a guilty butcher or candlestick maker out there and it wasn't the baker who killed her.

Chapter 10

 Malone was waiting at the police station—aka the Highland Park Department of Public Safety—when I arrived in the back of a squad car. He had on blue jeans and sneakers, and his face looked unshaven and grim. Millie had been whisked away from Olivia's office in a separate patrol car. Officer Shands and her partner had separated us as soon as their backup appeared along with officers from the Criminal Investigations Division and a van from the county morgue.

I knew from every cop show I'd ever watched that witnesses at crime scenes were kept apart so they didn't start talking and change their stories or let someone else's perception skew what they'd really seen. I realized, too, that Millie was probably more than a witness in their minds, especially with all that blood smeared on her clothing. And maybe I was a suspect, too. They'd taken my cell phone—the second time in two days I'd had to give it up—and my driver's license along with it.

But I was far more worried for Millie than for myself. She'd looked so lost and afraid when they led her away. Even from afar I had seen her hands shaking. I heard a detective tell her that she had to change out of her bloodied clothes, that they'd be taken for evidence. When I saw Millie again inside the station, she was wearing what looked like hospital scrubs.

As she was shepherded through a nearby hallway, I tried to catch her eye, but she kept her head down. She wasn't handcuffed so I wasn't sure if she was being booked for murder or just being questioned. Even though I believed her story about finding Olivia with the cake knife in her throat, I couldn't deny that she looked guilty on the surface. For one, there was Olivia publicly dissing Millie over Penny Ryan's wedding cake. Two, Millie admitted to being the last person to see Olivia alive. And three, when I walked into Olivia's office she'd been hovering above the dead body holding the bloodied silver cake knife. Okay, that most of all.

"I need a moment with Ms. Kendricks, please."

Malone's voice pulled me out of my reverie. I turned to see him converse briefly with the desk sergeant. Then he walked over to where I sat holding a paper cup with water in my trembling hands.

"Hey," he said by way of greeting.

"Hey," I replied and tried not to burst into tears.

"Can we have a little privacy?" he asked the officer who was babysitting me while I waited to be interviewed.

With a nod, the blue uniform stepped a few feet away.

"Oh, God, what a mess," I murmured as he crouched before me so we were eye-to-eye. "What a freaking mess."

"I should stay with you while you make your statement," he said in a quiet tone. "You were found at a crime scene with a woman holding a knife and wearing bloody clothes. If you're not a person of interest then you're a potential witness."

But I shook my head. "Millie needs you more," I told him. I wasn't scared of the police, and I hoped I wasn't stupid enough to say anything that would get *me* into trouble. I hadn't done anything wrong besides. I was far more worried about Millie. "You have to help her, Brian. She's in big trouble."

He glanced over at my babysitter cop and leaned in closer. "What the hell happened at Olivia's? I thought you were just dropping off that butt-ugly dress?"

"I was," I assured him in a shaky voice, "but when I walked in the door and saw her on the floor and Millie, oh, man—"

I couldn't even describe it, not in a sound bite. I bit my lip, shaking my head. I didn't want to risk blurting out anything with the police officer so near. I didn't want to do Millie more harm than good when she was in such deep doo-doo as it was.

"Would you mind giving us just a little more

space?" Malone asked the officer who stood not three feet away, keeping an eye on us.

The guy didn't look happy but wandered over to talk to the desk sergeant.

"Tell me what you saw, everything you remember," Malone said, sliding into the next seat. He turned so that we leaned into each other. Our foreheads nearly touched.

I tried hard to focus as I recounted what had happened once I arrived at HPV, how I'd heard Millie cry out and what I'd seen when I walked into Olivia's office. I finished in a breathless minute. Then I felt compelled to add, "Millie didn't kill her. I feel it in my bones. Olivia was half her age and twice as strong. It makes no sense."

Malone gave me a funny smile. "I remember you said something like that when I first met you. But it was Molly O'Brien you were so sure about."

"And I was right," I reminded him.

"Yeah, you were right." Malone glanced toward the hallway through which they'd taken Millie. "I've got to go, Andy. Are you sure you're okay? I can call someone else from the firm for Millie if you need me in there with you."

"I'm okay," I lied, but my hands were shaking so badly I dumped the cup of water onto the floor. It splashed my shoes and made a puddle around them. It wasn't the end of the world, but tears spilled onto my eyelashes.

Malone took the cup from my hands and set it aside. "If you feel pressured . . . if you need me there . . . stop talking, all right? Tell them you want an attorney present."

"I will, I promise," I said once I stopped choking up and could get the words out. "I didn't do
anything. There's no blood on my hands. I'll be
fine."

"Just tell them what you told me."

"Okay."

Malone squeezed my shoulder before he left
me. He motioned to the desk sergeant, and the
uniform who'd been my babysitter escorted my
fiancé up the hallway to wherever it was they'd
squirreled away Millie.

I let out a slow breath.

"Come this way, ma'am," a voice said, and I
looked up from my chair to see Officer Shands
standing with her hands on her hips.

So I got up and followed.

She led me toward a door with a plaque that
labeled it as INTERVIEW ROOM 1. I wondered if
Malone and Millie were nearby, perhaps in Interview Room 2, unless Millie rated something more
sinister, like the Third Degree Room or the Spanish Inquisition Room.

Poor Millie! I couldn't help but feel sorry for
her. She'd gone from exclusive cake baker for
Highland Park's glitterati to murder suspect in a
matter of hours.

"Could I get you water or a soda?" Shands
asked, showing me to a chair in the tiny room no
bigger than a closet.

"No, thanks," I said, thinking of the water I'd
spilled on my shoes already. "Can we get started?"
I asked, not that I was any too eager to discuss the
scene I'd stumbled upon at Olivia's. But I figured

the sooner we did, the faster I'd get out of there. "I don't have that much to tell."

"Oh, I'm not the one who'll be interviewing you, Ms. Kendricks," she said, and without another word she ducked out.

Of course, Officer Shands wouldn't be asking the questions. I'd probably be grilled by some hardened detective from the CID, who'd break me faster than Rachel Ray could crack an egg for a meat loaf.

God, help me.

I put my hands in my lap and closed my eyes, wishing I knew how to meditate to slow my racing heart. Instead, my mind began to race as well, wondering what was going on with Millie. Thank God she had Malone with her. Otherwise, I feared she'd completely crumble and confess to killing Olivia, even if she didn't do it.

At least five minutes passed and then ten (I was counting the seconds). I squirmed in my seat and stared at the walls. More time ticked by, and I drummed my fingers on the table. I started humming nothing in particular until it turned into something in particular, namely Clapton's "I Shot the Sheriff." So I cleared my throat and stayed quiet.

Where was everyone? Was this a psychological trick to get me to break down? Did they figure if they left me alone in a dreary cubicle with two plastic chairs and a table bolted to the floor—I shook it just to check—I would quickly go bonkers and confess to a crime that I didn't commit?

Before I had much of a chance to dwell on all

the sordid scenarios my imagination could cook up, the door clicked open and someone walked in.

I quickly realized my interrogator wasn't just any old grizzled veteran of the department but one of the higher-ups: a petite, gray-haired woman with a military bearing and pale eyes that could see right through me.

Chapter 11

"Deputy Chief Dean!" I breathed a sigh of relief.

I wasn't sure how I rated the deputy chief of police but I had a feeling it was because she knew my mother. I'd met Anna Dean at Cissy's when one of Mother's friends had died unexpectedly. The deputy chief knew Cissy well from all the work my mother did to raise money for the Highland Park Police Department's annual Breakfast in Blue.

"Are you taking my statement?" I asked. "I didn't think that was your kind of thing. Not that I'm complaining."

In fact, I was relieved.

"Oh, Ms. Kendricks," she said in that tone my teachers had used at prep school when I was daydreaming or hadn't read the right chapter from my history text the night before. "What on earth have you gotten yourself into? Your mother will be beside herself."

"You didn't call her, did you?" I said, knowing that Cissy would indeed flip out if she heard I'd been taken down to the Highland Park police station to answer questions about the murder of my Hockaday classmate.

"No, I didn't notify her that you'd been brought here," the deputy chief assured me as she settled into the chair catty-corner from mine. "Unless you'd like me to—"

"No, thank you," I quickly said. This definitely rated high on the "break it to her gently" scale. I'd explain everything to Cissy later over tea at the house on Beverly Drive when I was sure she had a couple of Xanax handy.

"Why don't you explain how you ended up at Ms. La Belle's office this morning?" the chief deputy asked.

Gripping the table, I leaned forward. "It was one of those wrong place and wrong time situations, or is that right place, wrong time?" I replied in a rush as Anna Dean glanced at some paperwork she'd brought along with her. "It was my bad luck to even run into Olivia yesterday at the stupid wedding. If only I'd told my mother no and stayed home to watch the playoffs."

"Stupid wedding, the playoffs," Anna Dean repeated, looking puzzled. "How about you just answer the questions without embellishment?"

I swallowed hard. "I'm sorry. I'm babbling, aren't I?"

"It's all right," she assured me, then she tried

again. "How did you know Ms. La Belle would be at her office on a Sunday morning?" she asked, looking me dead in the eye. "It's not typically a workday."

"I know, I know, and I wish I hadn't gone. I should have been back at the condo, making pancakes with Malone. I'm sorry, that's not important," I said and jabbed the heels of my hands into my thighs, realizing I was rambling again. But I was so nervous. "Olivia told me she'd be at her desk at eight. She said she had a wedding later in the day, and Sunday morning was the only time she could work without her assistant hanging around."

"So you went there for a professional consultation?"

"Me? Oh, God, no," I said and went on to explain, "I was returning a bridesmaid's dress and shoes that I'd borrowed from her yesterday at Penny Ryan's wedding. That's Senator Vernon Ryan's daughter," I added, in case Penny Ryan's name alone meant nothing. "I went with Cissy because her fiancé, Stephen, was out of town."

"So you're a friend of the senator's daughter?"

"Not exactly, she's quite a bit younger," I said, trying hard not to get too off-track, "but Cissy's tight with Shelby Ryan, the senator's wife. The wedding was supposed to be late summer but they pushed it up because Penny's prego." I paused as Deputy Dean cocked her head. "Oh, wow, was that TMI again?"

"Just keep talking," Anna Dean said, "and I'll try to keep up."

"I know, it's confusing," I admitted. "You see, I didn't have the right thing to wear, at least according to Cissy, so she brought me something from Saks that was too tight," I rattled on. "The stupid dress ripped up the back when I was getting the bride and her hoopskirt out of the toilet. Olivia had the spare bridesmaid's dress because Penny's cousin got pink eye and didn't show up. I didn't want to put on the butt-ugly thing, but I didn't have a choice, and Olivia didn't want the wedding party to be asymmetrical so she asked me to fill in."

I stopped to draw a breath.

"I see," Deputy Dean said, although she didn't appear to see at all.

She gave me a funny, squint-eyed look and ruffled the paperwork. I tried to read upside-down but I couldn't make out what was written. Were they notes from the crime scene? My FICA scores? Her career horoscope for the month of April?

"So you went to Ms. La Belle's office around eight o'clock to return a bridesmaid's dress, is that correct?" she summed up, editing out the rest.

"I got there at eight-fifteen on the nose," I said.

"Did you call ahead?"

"No," I replied, "I didn't need to. Olivia specifically told me she'd be there, and she'd threatened to show up at my place if I didn't drop off the dress and shoes first thing. I figured I'd go ahead and get it over with so I didn't ruin my entire Sunday."

For all the good that had done.

Deputy Dean leaned back in her chair. "And what did you see when you arrived? Be as specific as you can."

I wet my lips, approaching this one more carefully. "There weren't many other cars in the parking lot but I did notice Millie's SUV. It has a bright pink sign on the window so it's hard to miss."

She nodded and said, "Go on."

"I entered the building and went upstairs to Olivia's suite. I heard someone cry out, like they were hurt. My first thought was it was Millie because Olivia had been pretty harsh with her when she'd delivered Penny's cake to the wedding," I said, the memory fresh in my mind. "The door was unlocked so I walked right in."

"You saw no one else on the way?"

"No, not a soul," I confirmed, very sure of my answer. "No one was in the stairwell or hallway or waiting in Olivia's reception area. At least, no one I could see, though it's not like I peered behind doors or checked in the closets or anything." I paused, collecting my thoughts. "It wasn't until I entered Olivia's office that I saw Millie. She was— she was standing there, and Olivia was—" I was about to explain what I'd seen but couldn't get it out. Everything I said seemed to implicate Millie. So I clammed up.

"Olivia was what?" the deputy chief asked, cautious not to lead me. "It's okay, Andy, take your time."

I was pretty sure that calling me by my first name was a deliberate attempt to make me trust her. I guess it worked well enough because I took a nice deep breath and made myself continue.

"Millie was kneeling beside Olivia with the cake knife in her hand. Olivia was on the floor, covered in blood," I said, and I imagined I could smell the raw metallic scent all over again. My stomach pitched but I kept it together. "Millie looked petrified. She told me she'd found Olivia with the knife in her throat. Millie had pulled the knife out trying to help her. There were balled-up fabric samples on the floor that she'd tried to use to stop the blood flow. Why would she have done that if she'd meant to kill her? Why wouldn't she have just run?"

I had to pause and swallow.

"Was Olivia La Belle alive when you arrived?"

"No," I said and shook my head. "At least, I don't think so. Millie said she'd checked for a pulse and that Olivia was dead. She *looked* dead to me."

"But you didn't see what happened, any of it?"

"No." I raised my chin. "But I don't believe Millie Draper committed murder. She doesn't have it in her. The woman baked my first birthday cake and every cake after until I was sixteen. She's about as nonviolent as anyone I've ever met."

"Hmm," Deputy Dean said and wrote something down on the paperwork. "How well did you know Olivia La Belle?"

I'd had a feeling this was coming. How best to put it?

"We were at Hockaday together a lifetime ago," I explained without going into detail. "I hadn't seen her in a dozen years before yesterday, but she hadn't changed a bit. She wasn't the nicest person, if that's what you're asking."

"So you weren't friends?"

"We were classmates," I said. That was as diplomatic as I could get. "She was captain of the tennis team, and she was strong, way stronger than Millie. If there'd been a fight, Olivia would have been the winner. There's no way Millie could have taken her down—"

"Did you happen to see Ms. La Belle's laptop or her cell phone?" the deputy chief asked, trampling over my opinion. "We didn't find either in her possession."

"Maybe she left them at home," I said, but I figured that was a stretch. Olivia probably had both soldered to her hip. "Or else the killer took them," I suggested, "which would tell you right there that it wasn't Millie who did it—"

"Thank you, Miss Kendricks," Anna Dean cut me off. "I think we're done here." She gave a crisp nod. "I'll have your statement transcribed and be right back."

"Millie Draper is innocent," I said pointedly, but the deputy chief didn't appear moved. "Okay, yes, Olivia treated Millie really badly yesterday, but that doesn't mean Millie would stab her with a cake knife. I mean, that'd be pretty stupid. Olivia had a lot of enemies."

"Thank you, Ms. Kendricks, but we're done," Deputy Dean said for the second time, and it was as infuriating as the first.

I wasn't getting anywhere. All my protests weren't doing Millie a damned bit of good.

The police wanted cold hard facts not my personal observations and insight, however well-intentioned. Sighing, I leaned back and glanced up at the camera slanted down from the wall. It reminded me of Pete, skulking around Penny's wedding.

A light went on in my brain.

"Wait!" I said as Anna Dean went toward the door.

She paused and turned.

"Olivia had been filming for the second season of her reality show. She had a cameraman named Pete following her around Penny Ryan's wedding. I can't believe she didn't have a camera stashed in her office somewhere."

"We're going over her office quite thoroughly, Ms. Kendricks, believe me," Anna Dean replied. "If there's a camera or anything else there, we'll find it."

There was something else that niggled at me, too.

"The shopping center parking lot must have surveillance," I said, thinking of the high-end retailers and restaurants there. They'd want to make sure their wealthy customers were well protected. "You can see for yourselves who came and went before Millie even got there."

"Of course, we'll be looking over surveillance camera footage. We're already working on it," Anna Dean said, and she gave me a *Do you think I'm stupid?* look.

"Yes, of course you are," I murmured. I was the one who felt stupid.

"Is that it?" the deputy chief asked. "Otherwise, I'll have your statement ready for you to sign in a few minutes."

Was that it? I asked myself. I was tempted to tell her a few facts about Olivia La Belle I was sure she didn't know. Like, Olivia had been one of the cruelest people I'd met in my life; how she could act charming enough when the occasion warranted and humiliate a person in the next breath; that I thought she was a sociopath and, as a child, I'd wished her dead more times than I could count on my fingers and toes?

No, I hardly figured any of that was worth bringing up unless I wanted to be considered the prime suspect right alongside Millie.

Call me a coward, but I swallowed hard and said, "Yes, that's it."

"Be right back," Deputy Dean said.

She picked up her paperwork and stood. She disappeared for maybe ten minutes, just long enough for me to mull over what I'd divulged and hope I hadn't done anything to hurt Millie's case. When the deputy chief reappeared, she was all business. She asked me to read over the brief transcript to see if everything was as stated. Then once I had, she gave me a pen to sign the papers. After eyeballing my signature, she opened up a manila envelope she'd brought with her, dumped out my cell phone, keys, and driver's license and pushed them across the table. Then she collected the signed paperwork, stood, and nodded.

"We'll be in touch, Ms. Kendricks. We may need to interview you again so, please, don't leave town. Oh, and tell your mother hello for me." She paused before adding, "I'm sorry for your loss."

"My loss?"

"Ms. La Belle," she said with an arch of her eyebrows, "your school mate."

"Oh, yeah, of course," I replied vaguely and squirmed.

I wasn't sure how I felt about Olivia's death. I knew she had parents in Monte Carlo, maybe even other relatives who presumably loved her. She might even have a friend or two, probably living in foreign countries, like her folks, so they didn't have to see her often. Yes, I was sorry that a human being had been killed violently. I was sorry that I had to see the bloody aftermath. I was sorry, too, that a kind woman like Millie Draper was going through hell at the moment. But sorry for *my* loss? If I'd lost anything because of Olivia, it was the part of my childhood that she'd tarnished. Even all these years after, I still kept in my heart that insecure girl whom Olivia had tormented. Now that Olivia was gone, maybe it was time I let that girl go for good.

"You're done with me?" I asked, because it all felt too fast, like what I'd done—what I'd said—wasn't enough.

"Would you like to stay?"

"No," I replied honestly, yet I was reluctant to leave. I didn't want to abandon Millie.

"Then you may go." She opened the door with a click and held it wide, but I still couldn't get my legs to move. "Ms. Kendricks," Anna Dean said firmly. "Do I need to call your mother and ask her to come get you? You'll need a ride to your car."

"No," I told her as I got up from the chair and walked toward the open doorway. "I'll wait for Brian . . . Brian Malone. He's my fiancé, and he's with Millie," I started to babble. "He's a lawyer

with Abramawitz, Reynolds, Goldberg, and
Hunt—"

"Good for him," the deputy chief cut me off.
"Do give your mother my best, Ms. Kendricks,"
she added, then turned on a heel and walked off.

I let out a slow breath and headed in the opposite direction toward the station lobby, where
I planned to sit and wait until Malone was done
holding Millie's hand during her interview with
the police. Or was it an interrogation? Would she
be released? Would she have to stay in jail overnight until she had a bond hearing? If she needed
me to pay her bail, I would do it in a heartbeat. I
couldn't bear to imagine Millie in prison orange,
locked behind bars with violent offenders. It
wouldn't be like Martha Stewart's stint at Camp
Cupcake.

I was about to text Malone, wondering how long
he'd be, when I heard a voice say my name—my
full name—in a horrified North Texas drawl.

"Andrea Blevins Kendricks!"

I glanced up from the screen of my cell phone
to see Cissy striding into the station. Once she
spotted me, she bypassed the desk sergeant with
an impatient flick of her hand. Her steps didn't
even stutter as he called out after her, "Ma'am!"

"Good Lord, sweet pea!" Cissy drawled dra-
matically as she approached with arms extended.
"You couldn't call your own mother to say that
you'd tripped over a dead body? I had to hear it
secondhand?"

Chapter 12

 "I was just figuring out what kind of pastries to pick up for our girl-talk this morning when your Mr. Malone phoned," Cissy explained before I'd even asked how she knew. "And thank heavens he did, or I could have been waiting and waiting for you to show up after you dropped that dress off at Olivia's, and I wouldn't have known where you were. You certainly didn't see the need to inform your own mother that you'd been arrested."

"Because I wasn't arrested," I told her, sure that her fondness for exaggeration had confused the issue, not anything Brian had said. "I just had to answer some questions."

Her fingers clutched at my upper arms. Her pale blue eyes were wide with fright as they wildly darted around the police station. The rest of her was impeccable as usual. Her hair was styled, her makeup subtle and done to perfection. She had on tan linen slacks, a pale pink shirt, and an alligator belt that made her waist look tinier than Scarlett O'Hara's eighteen inches. One of these days I wanted to see my mother race to my side with bed head and pajama pants.

"Oh, Andrea, why didn't you phone me yourself?" she asked, her drawl turned mournful. "I could have used my connections to spring you sooner. You know the mayor and I went to school together."

I was about to remind her that I hadn't needed springing because I was never behind bars but I figured that to argue would be fruitless.

"There wasn't time," I said simply, which was only partly the truth. "Brian shouldn't have dragged you into this," I told her, and I so wanted to be ticked at him for pulling my mother into this black hole. But then again, she had dragged me into plenty of disasters, like the wedding yesterday. Maybe this would put us even.

"Your Mr. Malone did the right thing!" She bristled. "What if I'd had to hear about your bein' hauled down here in the back of a police car from someone else? Or, heaven forbid, what if I'd seen your mug shot in your friend Janet's column in the *Park Cities Press*?"

My best buddy Janet Graham was a society columnist for the *PCP* and usually wrote about socialites and their fund-raising luncheons, debutante balls, and various art gallery openings. Although lately she'd been dabbling in more serious news stories, like a rather contentious debate over required reading for freshmen at the high school. ("*Romeo and Juliet*? They're teenagers who have unprotected sex, right? How dare that Shakespeare pen such filth," Janet had mocked one parent's protest at the latest PTA meeting and rolled her eyes.)

"Janet doesn't write the police blotter column, Mother," I said as she reached up to push bangs from my eyes. "Besides, I don't have a mug shot. I didn't commit a crime. I just happened to see Olivia's—" I bit off the end of the sentence. I couldn't seem to get out the words "dead body."

"Oh, sweet pea," Mother moaned. "Brian told me that you found her. I hope it doesn't haunt you, seeing Olivia like that."

"I didn't actually *find* her," I clarified, "because Millie was already there. But I'm sure Millie had nothing to do with it."

"Of course she didn't! Millicent Draper is a saint. I can't tell you how many times she's rescued me when I've needed pastry in a pinch. She's a treasure, that's what she is," Cissy replied and leaned forward to whisper in my ear, "although I couldn't blame her for being upset after what Olivia did yesterday at the wedding."

"Millie didn't kill her, Mother," I insisted, but I got the feeling that wasn't Cissy's primary concern.

"My dear, sweet Andrea," she let out in a rush of breath. "What if something had happened to you? I couldn't have survived that," she added and looked me over from head to toe as mothers were wont to do. I half expected her to put a bit of spit on her thumb and wipe my chin. But instead she hugged me hard against her slight bosom. She was thin enough that I could feel bones.

"You need a sandwich," I grumbled, fighting

the sudden rush of tears. But I hugged her back and briefly closed my eyes, letting the gentle cloud of Joy wash over me along with the ever-present scent of Aqua Net.

"I need a sandwich? But it's not even noon," she countered, missing the point entirely.

I laughed into her shoulder, feeling strangely glad that if Brian was going to be delayed with Millie, he'd phoned my mom. She was good for the comic relief alone. It had been a long, difficult morning, and I was ready to go home. Maybe I'd even crawl back in bed and hide under the covers for the rest of the weekend.

"Andrea, are you truly all right? You're shaking like a leaf," Cissy said.

I wasn't sure how I was exactly, but it was far from all right. Part of me still felt like I was caught in the midst of a bad dream. With a sniffle, I drew apart. "Can we get out of here?" I asked, looking into her concerned face, and she didn't argue.

Although I hadn't been inside the DPS for more than an hour, it felt like days. I blinked at the brightness of the sun as we exited the Spanish Colonial building with its stucco walls and red-tile roof. I glanced at the neighboring Town Hall, which housed the library, admiring the convenience of being able to get an occupancy permit or vote and check out a book all in one fell swoop.

Cissy had parked her Lexus in the slot reserved for the chief of police. I almost called her on it but reconsidered. I happily slipped into the sedan when she unlocked the doors and I sunk into the leather seat, clicking my belt into place.

"Thanks for coming to get me," I said, and I meant it. Maybe my relationship with Cissy didn't involve lots of warm and fuzzy moments, but this surely counted as one of them. "Can you take me to my car? It's still in the parking lot at HPV."

Mother frowned as she started the engine and the Lexus began to purr. "How about we go back to the house for breakfast first? Sandy's not there to whip up waffles, but I can still scramble an egg when I have to."

"Can you really?" Did my mother even know how to turn on the stovetop in her kitchen? "I would pay to see that."

"Andrea, for goodness' sake," she said, shaking her head.

"How about this?" I searched for an alternative, otherwise I had a feeling my mother was going to chauffeur me straight to the house on Beverly Drive no matter what. "How about you take me to get the Jeep first? I promise to follow you home and stay there until I hear from Brian."

Mother had slipped on her Jackie O sunglasses and was about to shift gear. But she hesitated, leaving the car in park. Her face tightened in a way that had nothing to do with the nips and tucks she discreetly had done during periods when she claimed to be on vacation. "You promise you'll go directly to the house?"

"Cross my heart," I said. I was about to add *and hope to die*, but decided that wasn't wise, not after what had happened that morning.

"All right," she agreed, but sounded reluctant. "It's a deal."

"Great." I tried to sit calmly in the car seat and look out the window. I sought out the same beauty in the clouds and sky that I'd seen upon first walking out my front door nearly two hours before. But instead all I saw was Olivia on the rug bathed in red as though the image had been carved on the back of my eyeballs. "It's just so weird," I said, speaking my thoughts aloud.

"What, sweet pea?" Cissy asked.

"I just can't believe Olivia's dead." My brain still hadn't quite digested the fact. "I saw her yesterday afternoon for the first time since graduation. Now she's in the morgue."

I never even found out what she'd been trying to tell me. Had she wanted to apologize? I'd like to believe that was the case. Or maybe I was just being a Pollyanna to hope so.

"I got the impression that you didn't like her," my mother replied as she drove toward Mockingbird Lane.

"I didn't," I admitted as I gazed out the window. "That's why it's weird. I should feel all torn up inside, shouldn't I? Someone I know was just killed. But I mostly feel bad for Millie getting caught up in a murder investigation, and I'm a little freaked out that I could have been there when the killer showed up to stick Olivia with the cake knife—"

"Don't say that!" my mother cut me off. She diverted her attention from the road and stared at me from behind those big sunglasses. "Thank God you didn't get to Olivia's office any earlier. There are plenty of crazy folks out there, Andrea. It was hard enough for me to fall asleep at night knowing you were living alone in that condo in North Dallas before Mr. Malone moved in. If he wasn't staying there now I'd insist you come home until this blows over."

She had said "North Dallas" as though it were the projects when it was anything but. Still, I knew what she meant because I worried about her, too, living by herself in such a big house in Highland Park (which was *so* not the projects). Okay, she wasn't even really by herself, because Sandy Beck was there most of the time and Mother had other help that came part-time. And once she and Stephen, her golf-playing, former IRS agent fiancé, tied the knot—whenever that might be—he'd be moving in permanently.

"So even though you know I don't approve of Mr. Malone stayin' over at your place until he's your husband . . ."

"Yes, I know," I said during her very pregnant pause. I'd heard her entire *cow giving the milk away for free* lecture a dozen times already.

". . . these days I think it's safer for a woman to have a man around because the world has gone berserk. Everyone's angry about something and no one takes responsibility for anything. It's not like it was before I met your daddy," she said, finishing her thought. "People used to talk to one another, face-to-face. Now everyone just Tweets and takes those selfish pictures."

Selfish pictures? Did she mean *selfies*?

"It's definitely a different world than before you met Daddy," I agreed. My mother had lived at home with my grandparents until she married my father when she was twenty-two and fresh out of SMU. I wanted to remind her that it was the twenty-first century and lots of women lived alone despite the world being bat-shit crazy. Though I didn't think it would do any good.

"I like your Mr. Malone, I truly do," Cissy went on, "but it'll be so much better when you two are married and find a place to raise a family, perhaps somewhere closer to me. Highland Park has a fine school district, Andrea. If you didn't want to go private with your children, I wouldn't raise a stink . . ."

Here we go again.

As she rambled on about how to rear the gang of imaginary children Malone and I would have, I sighed and gazed past her, out the windshield to the left.

The Lexus sailed past the Dallas Country Club, and I was a bit surprised the car didn't automatically steer itself onto the grounds.

Soon enough we were turning off Mockingbird into the lot at Highland Park Village. As we approached where my Jeep was parked, I noticed the police still working the scene. Millie's SUV had been loaded on top of a tow truck. Would they put it in a police impound lot and scour it for evidence? What would they find, I wondered, except perhaps a trail of flour or fondant fingerprints?

Yellow tape that declared POLICE LINE DO NOT CROSS boxed off the front doors of Olivia's building. Early shoppers and restaurant patrons out for Sunday brunch collected on the sidewalk and in the lot, watching the goings-on. Through the plate glass of the nearest boutique, I saw several officers in their blue uniforms talking to shop owners. Had anyone else seen anything?

"Oh, my," Cissy said and removed her sunglasses as she took a gander. "This is just like one of those *Law & Order* shows, isn't it?"

"You watch *Law & Order*?"

I thought of my mother as more of the *Downton Abbey* type, not police drama. Maybe she was merely mortal after all.

"I used to watch the new episodes but not anymore." Cissy made a face. "It hasn't been the same since Jerry Orbach died. Did you know your father and I saw him on Broadway in *42nd Street*?"

I shook my head.

"He was brilliant. What a versatile man. He could make you believe anything."

"He sounds like your buddy Senator Ryan," I cracked.

"Oh, Andrea, stop." Mother gave me a look.

At least I could count on her to distract me, if only for a moment.

"I'm getting out now," I said.

"Are you okay to drive?"

I inhaled deeply before I answered, "I am."

"Meet you back at Chez Kendricks?"

"I'll be right behind you," I said and opened the door. My mother's house was practically around the block. "I won't even drive-through Starbucks for a latte."

"Oh, Andrea." Mother breathed my name and glanced over at the building with the crime scene tape fluttering near its doors before replacing her sunglasses on her slim nose. "It's just so unsettling. Things like this shouldn't happen here."

Things like murder shouldn't happen anywhere, I thought. But they did and would continue to as long as Homo sapiens roamed the earth.

I ducked out of my mother's car and headed over to my Jeep. I kept my head down as though that made me invisible, and maybe it worked. No one seemed to pay me the least bit of attention. Within a minute or so I had my car unlocked and climbed inside. Thankfully, the late morning sun hadn't made things too steamy, so the interior felt more like a tepid bath than an oven.

As I backed out of the space, I turned to look at Olivia's building and saw her assistant, Terra Smith, standing in front of the police tape. She was talking to a reporter who had a microphone stuck in her face. Her blond-on-black hair blew in the slight breeze, and she kept pushing it back behind her ears. She wasn't smiling but she hardly looked distraught. Then again, Olivia had called her a Hoosier and implied she wanted to can her, so maybe she wasn't that shaken up. I remembered, too, that Olivia had said firing Terra could get "messy," so was this the kind of mess she'd meant?

I started to wonder about the people around Olivia.

What would happen to her business now? Would Terra inherit her clients? Would the business be sold? Who would benefit the most by wiping her off the face of the earth? Was she in a relationship that had soured? Did she have a vengeful ex? How many people were out there who had a motive to kill her?

I simply didn't believe Olivia's death was a random act of violence. It was hard to imagine someone entering the upstairs suite on a whim and icing her with a cake knife. Her office hadn't appeared ransacked by a thief, though her phone and her laptop were apparently missing. Why steal from a wedding planner anyway? Wouldn't any of the posh stores that surrounded Olivia's office make better targets for robbery? Or even the Starbucks around the corner?

No, I firmly believed Olivia had been attacked by someone she knew. The key was in figuring out which of her enemies hated her enough to want her dead. There was only one big problem with my theory: Olivia La Belle probably had more enemies than most.

I knew so little about Olivia's life beyond Hockaday. If I wanted to learn anything about why she died, I was going to have to find out more about how my prep school enemy had lived. Luckily, I had someone in mind who could help me catch up on anything and everything to do with Olivia La Belle . . . someone who knew the deepest dirt on everyone who was anyone in the Park Cities.

Honk, honk.

A horn tooted loudly, and I glanced in the review to see the tow truck with Millie's SUV idling behind me.

I pulled back into the parking space and let the truck pass. While I did, I got my cell phone out and I called my pal from the *Park Cities Press*, Janet Graham.

Chapter 13

When I turned into the half circle in front of Cissy's house on Beverly Drive, I saw her peering out from the doorway, waiting for me.

As I exited the Jeep, the smell of roses filled the air, and I eyed the lush pink blooms as I ascended the stone steps. No matter the season, the grounds always looked so pretty, kind of like my mother. I'd always felt so rumpled in comparison.

"Good, you're here." She put an arm around my shoulders. "Let's get you fed," she said, and she ushered me inside, her Cole Haan loafers clicking softly on the marble tiles. "I found a dozen eggs in the refrigerator," she remarked brightly, as if that was a huge accomplishment, though I guess it was for her since she so rarely set foot in the kitchen. "I located a small mixing bowl and a whisk but I'm not quite sure if I should use a skil-

let or the griddle for the actual cooking part, and
I'm concerned about turning on the gas burner. I
don't have to light it with a match, do I? Heaven
knows, I don't want to set something on fire while
Sandy's away," she remarked, guiding me toward
the kitchen. "If you'd do me a favor, sweet pea,
and pick out the right pan and get a burner going,
I'll start crackin' the eggs."

Um, maybe I should just make the eggs myself.

Martha Stewart she wasn't. But it was sweet
that Cissy was clucking over me like a mother
hen. When I was growing up, it was more often
than not Sandy Beck who'd assumed that role,
bandaging my scraped knees and making me Toll
House cookies when I'd had a bad day at school.

I was about to tell my mother that cereal
would be fine—I wasn't really that hungry—
and I opened my mouth to do just that. But as we
neared the stairwell my mind suddenly shifted in
a different direction entirely. I stopped at the base
of the steps and reached for the carved wooden
finial. What ended up coming out of my mouth
instead was, "If you don't mind, I think I need to
go up to my old room for a while."

"What?" Cissy swiveled on a loafer. She looked
equal parts relieved and concerned. "Andrea
darlin', do you feel ill? Would you like some tea?
And, yes, I do know how to make that. Or how
about a Xanax?" she asked, and she wasn't kidding. "I would have fallen apart without them
after your father died."

Like a tiny pill could rid me of all my worries.

"No, thanks," I said, because I wasn't big on

medicating myself when I didn't truly need it. Plus, I was counting on my adrenaline to fire up my brain and help me figure out what to do next. "I just need to go upstairs for a few minutes if it's all right."

"Do you want company?"

I shook my head.

"I understand." Mother closed the gap between us and touched my cheek. "Take all the time you need. If you feel like napping, you should do it. I don't have anything important on my schedule today so I'll be around."

"Great." I gave her a halfhearted smile.

Then I wandered up the staircase, which creaked and groaned despite the thick Oriental runner. When I reached the first room at the top of the steps, I paused as I always did. It had been my father's study, and Cissy had left it untouched through the years. If I sat in the worn leather chair behind the desk, I could still smell the Cuban cigars Daddy had given up after his first heart attack. My artwork hung on the walls between actual masterpieces. Old books with richly colored leather covers filled built-in shelves.

Would Stephen change things once he and Cissy got married? I guessed he could if he wanted to (or rather if Mother would let him). I wouldn't want to be in his shoes, moving into a house that held decades of memories; taking over another man's closet; trying to feel at ease while walking in another man's indelible footprints.

Much as I liked my mom's fiancé—and I did, I really did—the idea of him turning my father's study into his den made my heart hurt. But I couldn't expect it to remain untouched forever. The house wasn't a museum. It was for living, and my mother had done a bang-up job continuing to live after my father had passed, despite how that loss had shaken her. It had shaken us both to the core.

My heart heavy, I continued down the hallway to my old bedroom. With a flick of the switch, I lit up my childhood. Bypassing the canopy beds and rows of Madame Alexander dolls, I walked straight toward the built-in shelves above my desk. First, I pulled out an old Hockaday yearbook, and I thumbed through the senior pictures, finding my own—dear God, what was with the frizzy perm?—and then homing in on Olivia La Belle's.

She wore pearls and had her blunt-cut blond hair flipped up at the bottom. She smiled with perfect white teeth, and her pale eyes appeared so at ease with the camera. My picture looked like a *Glamour* magazine fashion don't, while Olivia's looked like an ad for Pantene. During our senior year, *Seventeen* magazine had come to Dallas searching for students for a special back-to-school issue. Of course, Olivia had been picked for the feature because she was tall and pretty in the way of Texas pageant girls who seemed to emerge from the womb leggy and slim and perfectly groomed. Janet Graham had been hanging out with me when the issue showed up in my mailbox. Surprise, surprise, Olivia's face was on the cover. Janet had torn it off and set it on fire in my bathtub.

Frowning, I stowed away the prep school annual and glanced up at the next shelf, which held my collection of Nancy Drew mysteries. I felt drawn to the row of yellow spines, and I ran my fingers across the titles: *The Secret of the Old Clock, The Hidden Staircase, The Bungalow Mystery,* and on down the line. My father had given me a complete set of the hardcover Nancy Drew books when I turned eight, and I had treasured them all. Someday when Malone and I had a daughter—and I thought of it as *when* not *if*—I would pass them down to her. I only hoped she would love them as much.

How I wished I could channel Nancy Drew now and figure out *The Secret of the Dead Wedding Belle.* I had my own Ned Nickerson, didn't I? And I had a widowed mother who stuck her nose into everyone's business, which trumped Nancy's father the lawyer who was always out of town, leaving Nancy alone with the housekeeper. I was just missing one thing—

I heard the distant ring of the doorbell, the *tap-tap* of my mother's shoes on marble, and then the front door coming open.

Shortly after, Cissy called up the stairs, "Andrea! Janet Graham is here to see you," as she had so many times when I was a kid and Janet came over to play.

Ah, there was my Bess! Or was she George?

It didn't matter, I thought as I turned off the light in my old room and headed down. Janet Graham had it going on over either of Nancy Drew's best friends. Neither Bess nor George had been a reporter. Having a buddy whose profession involved asking questions was a big bonus when there was a mystery to be solved.

"Hey, Jan," I said as I descended the stairs and caught sight of Janet in her long magenta skirt with clunky boots poking out beneath. Her blouse was a deep shade of purple and her hair was pretty much burnt orange, maybe in deference to her alma mater, the Texas Longhorns. She was a feast for the eyes, to be sure, and she'd brought along a feast for my belly, if the bag from La Madeleine in her hand was any indication.

"Chocolate croissants," she said. "They're still warm."

"Nice," I replied, and I would have hugged her if either of us had been the hugging type.

"Oh, Janet darlin', how lovely of you," my mother said and clasped her slender hands together. "Looks like I won't have to fix breakfast, will I, sweetie?" She gave me a quick pat on the back. "Why don't you take Janet to the kitchen, and I'll head upstairs to call Stephen and catch him up on the goings-on." Mother clicked tongue against teeth. "He'll probably feel compelled to cut his golfing weekend short and race home," she said with a look on her face that had me wondering if that wasn't exactly the result she was hoping for.

The stairs creaked gently as Mother headed up. I motioned Janet to follow me into the kitchen. Once I'd poured us each an orange juice and we settled at the old pedestal table that predated my birth, the conversation instantly turned to Olivia La Belle's demise.

"Can you believe the bitch is really gone?" Janet said without an ounce of sympathy in her voice, "and, I mean, *gone* as in dead as a doornail."

Still slightly numb from the morning's turn of events, I stared at Janet, not sure how to react. I was glad that Cissy wasn't around to hear her remarks. My mother frowned on cursing in her house, and I'm sure she would have taken Janet to task for speaking ill of the newly dead as well.

But I had to agree with her.

"Brutal but honest," I said with a sigh and pulled a croissant from the bag. It smelled heavenly so I took a big bite. My stomach growled like it was hungry, but the anxious lump in my throat was making it tough to swallow.

"I thought only the good died young," Janet went on. "I guess this proves that theory wrong, huh? It's just so bizarre knowing someone's dead that you hated so much. Do you realize how many birthday wishes I wasted hoping some kind of doom would befall Olivia? I prayed she would move to China or fall off the planet."

"Me, too," I said. Similar thoughts had passed through my head upon seeing Olivia lying on the blood-smeared rug in her office.

"Well, there goes one more bully in a world full of bullies," Janet said, sounding so bitter I could taste it on my own tongue. Her eyes flashed fire behind her smart girl glasses. "She may have been all that on the outside but she was ugly as hell on the inside." When I didn't speak up, she loudly sniffed. "C'mon, Andy, you didn't like her any better than I did."

"You're right," I said. "I didn't. She picked on us both."

"Picked on?" Janet's voice rose. "She humiliated us at every turn. I can't tell you how many times I found pictures of clowns taped to my locker. She called me Bozo."

Ever since I'd known her, Janet had always been loud in personality and voice and her bold color choices, both for her clothing and her hair. Because she'd never been a cookie-cutter prep school drone, she'd been on the receiving end of Olivia's taunting, too. I couldn't blame her for sounding so cold about Olivia dying. She wouldn't miss Olivia's presence on this planet any more than I.

"I'm not sure how people like that can sleep at night or look in the mirror every morning without hating themselves," she grumbled between bites of a croissant. Clearly, Olivia's death hadn't spoiled her appetite.

"She won't have to look in the mirror anymore," I said, and I wondered who else would not be grieving over the untimely passing of Olivia La Belle. How many other girls from Hockaday alone—now grown women—would breathe a sigh of relief knowing they'd never have to risk running into her from this day forth?

"What a nasty piece of work," Janet said and brushed crumbs from her blouse. "Olivia was hateful from her fake blond roots to her toes. I couldn't believe when she became a wedding planner. That woman wouldn't have known what love was if it had walked up to her and punched her in the nose."

"She did get to boss people around," I commented, having seen it for myself.

Janet snorted. "She would have been a better prison guard than a wedding planner. How did you even bump into her again, Andy? I thought you stayed as far away from Olivia and her ilk as possible. You didn't exactly run in the same circles."

While I'd mentioned on the phone that I'd dropped by Olivia's office and found her dead, I hadn't taken the time to explain the events leading up to my morbid discovery. So I drew in a deep breath and told Janet the whole sordid tale of Cissy dragging me to Penny Ryan's wedding, including how I'd caught Olivia screaming at Millie, ended up in the borrowed bridesmaid's dress, and found myself seated with the former president and Lester Dickens at the reception dinner.

By the time I was done, Janet's eyes had gone wide. "Oh, my God, that's like being Alice and falling into the rabbit hole and having tea with the Mad Hatter and the March Hare."

Yep, add in the Dormouse who kept falling asleep, and that pretty well described my experience in a nutshell.

"I wish I'd known you were going to Penny Ryan's wedding," my friend said wistfully. "I only got wind of it being moved up about an hour beforehand. I tried like hell to get an invite but they weren't letting any of us media types in. Did you snag any photos the *PCP* could pilfer? My boss would love me if I could get something for the Society pages."

I shook my head. "They confiscated cell phones at the door."

"So no pics at all?"

"There was a hired gun taking photographs," I told her. If I'd overheard the wedding photographer's name, I couldn't recall it. But I did remember another name. "Olivia had a cameraman following her around for her reality show. She called him Pete. All I know is he had a beard and tattoo sleeves."

"Sounds like every camera guy I've ever worked with," Janet murmured. "I'll have to call Salvo Productions and see if they'd give me a still. Sometimes reality shows like to leak photos, you know, to pump up the publicity. I still can't believe Olivia has her own show. When I first heard about it, I had to wonder who she was blowing—"

"Janet," I said sharply, thinking of my mother's bat ears and hoping she hadn't heard that one.

My friend shrugged. "Well, I figure it was either that or blackmail. Why else would anyone want to give that bitch a show? She wasn't that interesting." Janet pulled out her phone and started thumb-typing on the keyboard. "Samantha Garber," she said, nodding. "That's who I dealt with in *The Wedding Belle*'s production office for a piece I wrote for the paper. I should follow-up and see what they're going to do now that Olivia's out of the picture. That would make a great Page One feature. I'll bet Sammi's more than happy to give me whatever I need to write it."

I was hardly surprised that Janet was speaking so dispassionately about Olivia's murder and penning a story for the *Park Cities Press*. That was how her mind worked. Everyone was a potential lead. And it wasn't like either of us had lost someone worth grieving over.

"Hey, would you talk to me, Andy, on the record, I mean?" She put her cell down and looked over at me eagerly. "You were first on the scene when Olivia's body was found, right? I could use the angle that Penny's wedding was the last one Olivia would ever plan. It's just so dramatic what with your showing up to return that borrowed dress and seeing her lying there—"

"Janet, stop," I said, cutting her off. Maybe I wasn't mourning Olivia either but I wasn't quite ready to dance on her grave yet. Heck, she wasn't even *in* her grave yet. And if Millie was arrested for her murder, it would be partially my fault.

"Stop, what?" She blinked bespectacled eyes. "You don't like the idea?"

I almost blurted out, "Like it? I hate it." No matter how I felt about Olivia, I didn't want to be part of a story about her violent end. And I wasn't sure Malone would embrace the idea of me blabbing about what I'd witnessed to a newspaper. He had his work cut out for him already.

"You can interview every guest at the wedding and write whatever you want about Olivia and her last wedding, but leave me out of it, okay?" I told her and felt the bits of croissant I'd eaten curdle in my belly. "I don't want anything I say at this table used in your exposé."

Janet didn't look any too happy about that. But after a moment's pause she said, "What happens at Cissy's house stays at Cissy's house. Got it."

That was something we used to tell ourselves as kids when we got into my mother's walk-in closet while she was gone and Sandy was babysitting or even when we found the keys to the liquor cabinet and got our first taste of fifty-year-old Scotch (*blech*).

"Thanks," I told her.

Truly, I understood why my friend wanted to write such a piece. It could be a career maker, or a solid notch on her J-School belt at the very least. Maybe once everything was sorted out and the police had the actual killer in custody, I'd feel more comfortable going on the record about what I'd walked into this morning. But I didn't think that would happen before the story was old news.

"I'll see if I can chat with Penny Ryan about her wedding being Olivia's final affair," Janet said. Then she sighed. "With my luck, she's honeymooning on some Pacific island without cell towers."

"I'm sorry I can't help you, Jan, but I have to watch myself. I don't want to say something to make Millie Draper look worse," I tried to explain. "I'm so worried about what's going to happen to her. What if she's arrested and tossed in jail with hardened criminals? She's a sweet old lady who bakes cakes."

"Oh, God, you're right. I forgot about Millie." Janet paled.

But Millie was all I could think about. "I feel like I'm the reason she's in so much trouble," I confessed, and a rush of tears filled my eyes. "I'm the one who walked in on her at Olivia's office. She was so scared. She wanted to get out of there but I made her stay until the police arrived. I should have gotten her out of there . . ."

"Andy, for God's sake, it's not your fault!" Janet pushed her plate aside and half stood to reach across the table for my hand. She patted it gently. "What were you supposed to do? Aid and abet? Then you would have been an accomplice."

"But she didn't *do* it," I repeated.

"Even still, the police were going to catch up with her," my friend said as she released my hand and sat back down. "Millie admitted that she pulled the knife out of Olivia's neck. There was blood everywhere. They would have found her bloody fingerprints on the knife and a bunch of other places. Someone would have seen her or they'd find her on the footage of some traffic cam at just the right time, and it would have looked even worse for her then, if she'd run." With a nod, she added, "Worse for you, too."

She was right. I couldn't have done anything other than what I did.

"I know, I know." I wiped at my eyes and sniffled. I felt guilty nonetheless. "I have a bad feeling Millie's going to be booked for Olivia's murder. Malone's still at the DPS with her. I don't know what's going on but it's taking forever."

"They can't book her this fast, can they? Unless she confesses, I mean, or they have footage showing Millie in the act."

I shrugged. I might have been engaged to a defense lawyer, but that didn't mean I was as well-versed in criminal law as Brian.

"Millie's such a lamb." Janet put her elbows on the table and dropped her chin into her hands. "We used to call her the Cake Lady when we were kids, remember? You think she's really the prime suspect?"

I recalled the look on Officer Shands's face when she realized the blood on Millie's clothes and hands hadn't come from Millie. "Yeah, I think they do."

"That stinks." Janet loudly exhaled.

"Yeah, it stinks," I repeated. "I know she didn't kill Olivia, and I'm hoping you can help me prove it."

Chapter 14

"Me?" Janet wrinkled her brow. "How am I supposed to do that? I'm not a private investigator, Andy. I'm sure Brian's law firm has somebody who can poke around even if the police are piling up evidence against Millie."

"But you know Highland Park," I said, wanting to remind her that Bess and George hadn't been PIs either, but they'd always helped Nancy. "People trust you, Jan. They tell you things."

Janet had been writing exclusively about the Dallas social scene for years. If anyone could dig up dirt on Olivia's life—private or public—it was Janet.

"I appreciate the flattery." She blushed. "But I'm not a priest. I don't sit in a confessional while socialites spill their deepest, darkest secrets. If the police charge Millie, Brian's going to do a bang-up job defending her," Janet said, as if I needed reminding. "I don't know how anything I could do would trump that."

"But the police won't *need* to charge Millie if we can turn over a few rocks before it comes to that."

Janet shook her head.

"Come on, Jan, what if the cops don't look anywhere else besides Millie?" I asked the question that kept running through my mind because I had seen it happen before. "Why wouldn't they figure they had their prime suspect when she'd been caught—literally—red-handed at the crime scene?"

"This is a bad idea," my friend warned me, and not for the first time. I'd asked for her help before.

"We have to do something," I insisted. "I can't just sit around and twiddle my thumbs while Millie spends her sunset years in jail. I'm not saying I want to hunt down her killer. I just want to prove there are plenty of other viable suspects out there."

"And if that doesn't work, maybe Millie will give us a recipe for baking a cake with a file in it," Janet joked, but I didn't laugh.

"I'm serious. Will you help me or not?"

"All right, all right, I can see you're going to be OCD about this." She tugged a strand of dark orange hair and began to twist it around her finger. "What can I do that isn't immoral or illegal? Okay, never mind immoral. But the illegal part stands."

I could have kissed her.

"For now, just fill in some blanks for me, will you?"

Jan stopped playing with her hair. "Shoot."

"Was Olivia in a serious relationship?" I asked, because her murder sure looked like a crime of passion to me.

"Was she in a serious relationship," Janet repeated. "Hmm," she intoned, delaying her response while she snagged a second croissant. Her brows arched above the rims of her black glasses as she chewed. Then she swallowed, took a sip of juice, and wiped a smudge of chocolate from the corner of her mouth. "Yes and no," she finally replied.

"Which is it?"

"Both," Janet answered. "On the surface, Olivia was involved with a man formerly known as Melvin Mellon." She paused as if waiting for some kind of reaction.

"Formerly known as? Is he a con artist or a rock star?" I was stumped.

"Hmm, maybe a little of both," Janet said with a grin. "You *are* hopelessly out of the loop, Kendricks. Melvin Mellon is a fashion designer from the Midwest who lost in the finals on last season's *Operation: Runway*, another Salvo Productions show. The producers had the brilliant idea of plunking him down in Dallas so he could open up shop seeing how much we love rhinestones and glitter. He goes by the name Draco, he's about all of twenty-five, and he was reportedly living with Olivia."

Draco. I wrinkled my nose. Why did that ring a bell?

"Oh, my God, he's the one responsible for Penny

Ryan's horrific bridesmaids' dresses," I said, wondering if he'd named himself after the evil wizard
kid in Harry Potter. "So he was Olivia's boyfriend?
But if he's a fashion designer, isn't he . . . ?"

"Gay?" Janet laughed. "Not all male fashion designers are," she said and gave me a look. "Come
on, Andy, I thought you were more enlightened
than that."

"Me, enlightened about fashion? That's a good
one," I remarked, although I had been raised in a
house with a mother who saw fashion almost as
a religion, so I could tell a Pucci from a Gucci, but
only if my life depended on it.

"There's Ralph Lauren and Tommy Hilfiger,"
Janet rattled off, cocking her head and squinting
at the ceiling as though more examples were written up there. Or perhaps she was just channeling
Cissy, who could likely recite the names of every
fashion designer in the world, gay or straight,
male or female, dead or alive. "Um, Yves Saint
Laurent, Elie Saab—"

"Okay, you can stop now. I'm enlightened already." I waved a hand to cut her off. "Tell me
more about the gossip around Olivia's boy toy."

Janet scooted forward in her chair. "Well, not
everybody bought the story they were selling.
Plenty of folks figured Draco and Olivia were a
match made in TV heaven. Some said they were
each other's beards, and that he was using her
for the publicity on her TV show, and she was
using him to hide what was really going on in her
boudoir."

I took a stab. "Was *she* gay?"

Janet shrugged. "That's part of her mystery," she said noncommittally. "If she was, she kept it on the down low, and I can't blame her. She ran a very traditional business in a *very* conservative town. You know how folks are around here. Mamas don't dream of their little girls becoming cowboys or engineers or astronauts. They want them to debut, pledge a sorority, get pinned, marry money, join the Junior League, and have babies, all in that order."

"Tell me about it," I said, because that was precisely what Cissy had wanted for me, although that hadn't exactly panned out, had it? "So what do you think? Did Olivia have a secret girlfriend?"

"Maybe she did, and maybe she didn't."

I groaned. "Come on, Jan, give me a crumb here. Which is it? You know everything about everyone in this burg."

"Speaking of crumbs, I'm hungry," Janet murmured and took another bite of a croissant before brushing the crumbles off her hands. "A few of the Highland Park ladies who lunch swore that Olivia's Achilles' heel was playing house with married men, but I think they were just guessing like everyone else."

"Ah," I murmured, because that one made more sense, considering the Olivia I had known back in prep school always wanted what she couldn't have and thought rules, respect, and common decency were for sissies. "So she did the nasty with married guys."

Janet put up a hand. "Don't get too excited, Andy. Like all the rumors about Olivia, it's just talk. She was extremely good at keeping the spotlight on her business, not on her love life. So nobody seems to really know anything except what she put out there."

"But sleeping with other women's husbands would have been very bad for business, wouldn't it? Was she shagging the grooms or fathers-of-the-brides?"

"Why not throw in the mothers-of-the-bride, too?" Janet tossed out, just to make my brain even dizzier. "Your guess is as good as mine."

"You must know *something.*"

"Cut me some slack, would you?" Janet frowned. "Olivia's private life was not Watergate, and I'm not exactly Woodward or Bernstein."

"No, you're the Socialite Whisperer," I told her, and she sighed.

"All right, all right, I did try to find out more about Olivia when I interviewed her last year for the *PCP*. It was the Wedding Belle's tenth anniversary. She had chatted up my boss about running a big promotion in the paper. So Gary thought we should do a nice sidebar about Olivia. You know, the whole 'local girl makes it big' angle."

"You met with her?" I said, wondering how Janet had remained civil with Olivia when she'd despised La Belle from Hell as much as I. "You didn't tell your boss you and Olivia had a history?"

"Not exactly," Janet said. "I did mention we were at Hockaday together, but I left out the part about her tormenting me and my friends. I was dying to see the Turtle Creek penthouse she and Draco moved into a few months back. She must have been raking in some serious bucks, because I know Draco's not bringing home enough bacon for Turtle Creek, not yet."

"Maybe the reality show pays better than the wedding planning," I suggested.

"I'm told they pay peanuts, relatively speaking," Janet remarked, "and that it's more like free advertising than real income."

"So what happened? Did you get to the penthouse?"

Janet made a face. "Unfortunately, Olivia declined to meet my photographer and me at her Turtle Creek digs. We had to go to her office instead." An angry blush began to bloom on Janet's cheeks. "And when we got there, she totally acted like she didn't know who I was. If my name rang a bell, she didn't let on. She probably didn't even remember all the times she harassed me. If I hadn't been doing the story, I would have called her out. But I didn't want to lose my job."

By the time Janet finished, her face was a hot shade of red.

"What a jerk," I said, quickly adding, "If it makes you feel any better, Olivia didn't recognize me either. Not for a few minutes anyway. We were standing face-to-face, and I haven't changed *that* much."

"Troll," Janet muttered.

If I wasn't such good friends with Janet, I might have wondered if she didn't stab Olivia in the neck herself.

"So did you get any scoop from the interview?" I pressed. "Did Olivia divulge anything earth-shattering?"

"I asked her about being in love since love is her job," Janet said. "I kind of hoped she'd jump on the couch like Tom Cruise and make a big deal about Draco, trying to convince everyone they were really a unit." Janet tightly crossed her arms. "But you know what she said?"

"That she was an alien from the planet Be-otch and didn't have a heart?" I suggested to Janet's snicker.

"Oh, it's even better science fiction than that," my friend replied. "She said that planning events to celebrate milestones in other people's lives was her one true love and that anyone in her life had to understand that." Janet let out a snort. "Is that the lamest thing you've ever heard or what?"

"It sounds like a nonanswer."

"Exactly"—Janet bobbed her head—"she was completely avoiding the question." She squinted thoughtfully. "I didn't see a single photo of Draco in her office, not a romantic one, anyway. The only pictures of Draco showed him with Olivia's brides in the gowns he'd designed for them."

"Interesting," I murmured.

So was Olivia's relationship with Draco a farce? Was she hiding behind it because she either had a lesbian lover or a married one? Even if that was the case, was it any reason for someone to want Olivia dead? Unless Olivia was tired of faking it and Draco wasn't ready for his ride on the gravy train to end.

"I would love to meet him," I murmured, "just to size him up."

"What if you're barking up the wrong tree?"

Janet asked. "Maybe her death has zero to do with her love life. Olivia had plenty of enemies on the job. For example"—she began to tick off on her fingers—"every assistant she'd ever hired and fired, other event planners whose clients she stole, vendors who didn't like to have their arms twisted."

"Like that florist, Jasper Pippin," I blurted out, recalling a tidbit my mother had shared. "Although Olivia didn't just twist his arm, she drove him out of business."

"Ah, Jasper Pippin." Janet tapped her chin. "I remember last fall when he sold his shop piece by piece. I think he started dismantling the place even before Olivia's infamous show aired, because he was supposed to do the flowers for the White Glove Society's annual deb ball and he bailed on them. They were in a tizzy, trying to find someone else at the last minute. The fact that Olivia tarnished his rep on TV was just the final nail in the casket. The whole mess got Jasper unseated as chair of the state floral association. The poor guy practically went into hiding."

"He was selling his store *before* the show even aired?" Geez, I thought, he must have been terrified, knowing what was to come. "Can you find him?" I asked. "He's a prime suspect as far as I'm concerned."

Janet pursed her lips then sighed. "Well, if he hasn't picked up stakes and moved to Key West, I'll hunt him down and see what he's been up to."

I sat up straighter, finally feeling as if I was getting somewhere. "And I'll talk to Terra Smith,"

I told her. "Olivia sounded like she was getting ready to can her. Maybe she gave Terra the axe after Penny Ryan's wedding, and Terra popped a gasket. Olivia did tell me that if she canned Terra, things could get messy."

"Well, they got messy all right," Janet said with a loud *hmph*. "What do you plan to do? Phone the girl and ask if she killed her boss? My God, that's brilliant!" She smacked her forehead with the heel of her hand. "Why didn't I think of that?"

"Oh, ye of little faith," I said with a sniff, having just come up with the most perfect idea. "I thought I'd ring her up and see if she wanted to plan a wedding."

"Whose?" Jan asked, and her brow wrinkled.

"Mine," I said. When Janet gave me a *Whatchu talkin' about, Willis?* look, I explained, "What can it hurt to pretend I'm plotting the course for my pending nuptials while asking a few subtle questions to see what I can find out?"

"You? Subtle?" Janet guffawed. "You're the proverbial bull in a china shop."

I ignored that. "It's the least I can do for Millie."

I didn't add that going upstairs to visit my Nancy Drew books had inspired me to sniff around, although Janet would probably have found that equally amusing.

My friend opened her mouth to say more but my cell phone interrupted, playing a quick burst of Def Leppard's "Animal," my personal ring tone for Malone. I had it tucked in my back pocket and grabbed for it, answering breathlessly, "Hello?"

"Are you at your mother's house?" asked my very tired-sounding fiancé.

"Yeah, I'm still at Cissy's," I said, "but if you need me to go home—"

"No," he cut me off. "Stay put."

"Did they arrest Millie?" I asked, and my pulse zinged like I'd had too much caffeine when all I'd drunk was orange juice.

"Not yet," he said, "but they're working on it."

"What's going on?"

"They're executing a warrant right now to search Millie's house and the shop. They're building a neat little case for the prosecution. They've already got Olivia's blood on Millie's clothes and shoes, and they have the knife with Millie's prints on it, although she's admitted to handling it. They're looking for Olivia's missing computer and cell."

"Which means what? Are they holding Millie while they gather more evidence? Can they do that?" I felt sick to my stomach, thinking of Millie behind bars for as much as a minute.

"No, babe," Malone said, "they can't hold her unless they charge her. They have to follow due process. But they're working on it as we speak."

"So where is she?"

"I just put her in my car, and she doesn't want to go back to her house. She can't stomach watching the police rip the place apart, so I'll head over and wait for them to arrive with the warrant." His voice lowered even further. "She's exhausted and scared, and I don't want to leave her alone."

I glanced across the table at Janet, who mouthed, *What's going on?* I shrugged and asked Brian, "So where are you taking Millie?"

"I thought that maybe"—he cleared his throat—"well, I hope your mom doesn't mind if I drop her off there. I'm just getting behind the wheel so we'll be there in five. See you soon."

He hung up, and it was probably just as well.

I wouldn't have been able to come up with a coherent reply. My gray cells were still processing the fact that Malone was bringing Millie Draper over to Cissy's.

Chapter 15

 When I told Janet that Malone was on his way with Millie, she got up to leave, and I didn't stop her.

"I know she wouldn't want to find me here, Andy. She's probably already got the media stalking her," my friend said as she carried her crumb-filled plate from the table to the sink. "It would freak her out, thinking I was ready to pounce on her for the sake of a story."

I nodded, because I knew she was right.

As I walked Janet to the door, I saw my mother standing just inside the butler's pantry. I'd been too wrapped up in talking with Janet to catch the creak of her footsteps coming down the stairs. I wondered how much of our conversation she'd overheard. By the tense look on her face, I imagined she'd overheard plenty.

She didn't say anything until I'd shown Janet

out, my friend promising to do her best to track down Jasper Pippin and unearth further details on Olivia's life.

Before I could get into it with Mother that Malone was en route with Millicent Draper in tow, she dug into me about something else entirely.

"I know what you're up to," she said, her pale blue eyes homing in on mine. "You're not calling Olivia's assistant for an appointment because you want her to plan your wedding. You want to pump her for information about Olivia and see if she rats out the perp," she said point-blank.

Dear Lord, she did watch *Law & Order* reruns.

"Geez, Mother," I said, squirming beneath her very direct gaze, "what if I just changed my mind and figured you were right about having a professional involved in Brian's and my wedding?"

"Oh, please, do you think I just fell off the turnip truck?" She sniffed. "Listen here, sweet pea," she went, her voice deadly serious, "if you're gonna play undercover agent with Olivia's assistant in order to find out who killed her, I'm going with you, and that's that." She jabbed her chin in the air and crossed her arms rigidly over her pretty pink blouse. That was definitely Mother's *don't mess with me* stance.

How to delicately tell her to mind her own business?

"Oh, you are so wrong," I lied.

"Am I?" She arched her perfectly drawn eyebrows. "Well, then, if there's nothing more to it and you really do want to start plannin' your nuptials, what's the harm in letting your dear old mother join you?"

I nearly choked. "Well, um, for one thing," I muttered, trying to come up with a fast excuse, "I'm a grown woman. You don't have to hold my hand. For another, we don't want the same things."

I did *not* want Cissy getting involved in my wedding planning, even if it was all a ruse. It was one thing sticking my neck out, but I didn't want to risk my mother's pearl-draped throat if anything should go awry.

"You're a bad liar. You always were," she informed me, unfolding her arms so she could reach for mine. She held me in a death grip. "Why don't you just accept my help? There's a lunatic running around out there, and I don't want anything to happen to you. How can it hurt to have backup?"

"This is America. There are *always* lunatics running around," I said, "just turn on the news or read the paper." Or look in the mirror, I mused, only half kidding.

Mother frowned. "I'm not jokin'," she warned. "You've been doing this since grade school, and one of these days it could catch up with you."

"What have I been doing?"

"Getting involved in other people's problems," she said and clicked tongue against teeth, finally letting me go. "It's like a compulsion. You can't leave well enough alone."

I stared at her and rubbed my arms where she'd dug in her talons. "*I* can't leave well enough alone," I repeated. This coming from a woman who had worn a wig and dressed in velour warm-ups with rhinestones in order to infiltrate a retirement home and figure out who was poisoning her bridge partners?

"Don't make me have you followed," Mother added, and I sighed, knowing that she had the contacts and the deep pockets to do just that. "Whatever it takes, Andrea. If you're going to stick your finger in this pie, I'm going to keep tabs on you one way or another. It might be easier if you just let me play undercover agent with you. No one's going to mess with the two of us, not while I've got Anna Dean on speed-dial."

"Okay, okay," I said reluctantly, giving in to her verbal arm-twisting. She did present a good case. Maybe she should be on Malone's defense team. And it would make the whole scenario more believable if I went to talk wedding deets with my pushy mother in tow. "I'll call you as soon I've got an appointment with Terra, and you can tag along if it makes you feel better."

Cissy smiled, and her face softened. "Oh, it does," she remarked and gently patted my cheek, "immeasurably."

The doorbell rang, and we both swung around toward the noise.

"That must be Malone," I said nervously. "I'll get it."

I dashed away, hurrying toward the foyer in order to let Brian in, knowing who'd be with him as I pulled the door wide.

There stood my knight in shining armor with his arm wrapped around the slumped shoulders of a very weary-looking Millicent Draper.

"Hey, babe," my fiancé said before he patted Millie's arm. "Hang out here for a while, okay? No one from the media will find you," he assured her in his warm masculine voice, which even had me convinced. "Stay put until I get back to you," he told her. When Millie nodded numbly, he leaned over to kiss my cheek. "I've got to run but I'll see you back at the condo in a bit."

Without further ado, Brian took off, loping down the steps toward the driveway. Millie stood unmoving on the doormat in her police-issued scrubs, and I quickly took her hand, attempting to draw her inside.

"Oh, Andy, I hate to impose," Millie said in a scared little whisper. "Are you sure it's all right with your mother?"

I looked into her lined face and tired eyes magnified by her giant round glasses, and I had a sudden flashback to all the times Millie Draper had driven up to the kitchen door on the morning of my birthday. I used to peer out the window, eagerly awaiting the white VW van with pale pink printing on the sides—because that was what she'd driven back then, not a fancy SUV—and it was like opening a present on Christmas morning to see what marvelous fantasy Millie had brought to life with my cake.

"Andy?" she said, squinting at me. "Are you feeling all right?"

"Sorry, yes, I'm good," I told her and quickly ushered her in. "I'm even better now that you're here. Brian's right, you'll be safe with Cissy. My mother might look like a delicate Texas bluebonnet, but she's a pit bull in pearls," I remarked. "If any reporters sniff around, she'll send them packing."

Before I closed the door, I glanced out toward Beverly Drive. I was thankful it was Sunday and traffic was at a bare minimum. Hopefully, no one had seen Millie standing at Mother's door in her jail scrubs.

As we stepped into the foyer, Cissy appeared. She strode toward the center of the entry and planted her hands on her hips. There was no welcome on her face. Instead, she watched us with a pinched face and tight lips.

"Look who's here," I said, cutting through the silence. "It's Millie Draper."

Since it was clear that Mother had heard about my intentions to meet with Terra Smith, I darned well knew she'd heard about Brian stashing Millie here for a while. But that didn't mean Cissy wouldn't veto the plan. It was her house, after all, and Sandy Beck wasn't around to act as a buffer. I just prayed she'd be open-minded.

"What a nice surprise, eh, Mother?" I said and let go of Millie. "Brian had to go, um"—I chose my words carefully—"take care of a few things for Millie. He thought she might be better off with you for a while. Is that okay?"

My heart pounded as I awaited a reply. I guess if Mother said no, I'd take Millie to the condo with me. No harm, no foul.

But Cissy's tough expression crumbled, and her brow tried its hardest to wrinkle as she took a step toward us and said, "Oh, Millie darlin', you've had quite the morning, haven't you?" She reached a nervous hand up to tug at her starched collar.

Millie bit her lip, nodding. "I've had lots better," she replied, and her eyes filled with tears.

"Of course you can stay while Mr. Malone is helping you out. In fact, you can stay as long as you need to," Mother added, giving me a sideways glance. "I wish I could convince Andrea to stay, too, until this whole thing's been solved and the madman who killed Olivia is caught. I just hope they find him soon."

"Amen to that," Millie whispered.

If my mother had any fears about Millie—if she thought for an instant that the Cake Lady had really committed murder—she certainly didn't show it. Heck, if *I* felt Millie was a homicidal maniac, I wouldn't leave her alone with Cissy, not even for a minute. No, I knew in my heart that Millie couldn't hurt a fly, and I could tell my mother felt the same.

"My dear Millicent, whatever I can do for you, consider it done," my mother offered, her voice as warm as honey.

"Thank you, Mrs. Kendricks," Millie replied and swayed on her feet. "I wasn't sure where to go. Mr. Malone wanted me to lie low. He said the press had caught wind of the story and would be swarming my house and the store, what with how fast social media spreads information."

"And misinformation," I murmured.

"So true, so true," my mother said and stepped toward us, giving the older woman a soft smile as she took her elbow and led her away. "Perhaps we can pick up some things from your place later on. But, for now, how about we get you some clothes to wear . . . I'm sure Sandy's got somethin' you could borrow, and she's just about your size . . . then I'll make you some tea and you can put up your feet. Does that sound all right? And do call me Cissy. We've known each other for too long to be formal."

"Thank you, Cissy," Millie replied meekly, "and, yes, a change of clothes and tea sounds lovely. I don't exactly feel human wearing these." She tugged at her scrubs.

I wondered if Mother would crush a Xanax or two into the teapot, and I figured that might not be such a bad thing.

Whatever happened, I had a feeling Millie would be in good hands, even without Sandy Beck around to do the fussing.

I shook my head, listening as my mother's voice trailed off and thinking that maybe Stephen was good for her. Maybe he was responsible for her turning into a kinder, gentler Cissy. Or was it just that she was getting older and the tough shell she'd lived in for so long had developed cracks?

At least Millie's presence had distracted Cissy enough that I could escape. I took the opportunity to slip out of my mother's manse and get into my Jeep without her standing on the doorstep and watching me every step of the way.

Chapter 16

I took Preston Road north, hardly seeing anything I passed. Even though I played my favorite oldie but goodie, Def Leppard's "Rock of Ages," hoping to take my mind off things, hearing *Pyromania* didn't loosen me up the way it usually did. Instead, I kept picturing Olivia covered in blood, lying on her office floor.

As soon as I got home, I shed my clothes and showered. For a long while I simply stood there motionless, letting the hot water rain down on my head and my body. Then I scrubbed shampoo fiercely into my hair and soaped up my limbs before rinsing off thoroughly, desperate to wash the memory of Olivia's death from my pores and my brain.

When I turned off the shower, my fingers were as wrinkled as raisins. While I watched the suds disappear, gurgling down the pipes, I found

myself wishing it was as easy to send the whole
ugly morning down the drain like dirty water.
Unfortunately, I figured it would be a long, long
time before what I'd seen was forgotten.

While I toweled myself dry, I heard the faint
strains of "Animal" and realized my phone was
ringing. Holding the towel on, I raced into the
living room to answer.

"Andy?"

"What's going on?"

"I should be back soon," Malone said. "The cops
didn't take much from Millie's house or her shop. It
seems they were mostly interested in her computers."

"All right," I replied, not sure if that was a good
or bad thing.

After I hung up, I got dressed. Then I started
looking around the room for Terra's business
card. I had tucked it into my bra at the wedding
yesterday after the rescue of Penny from the toilet.
But I'd forgotten about it. There was no sign of it in
the bedroom so I wandered into the living room.
If it wasn't there, I'd probably lost it, since that
was about the only other usable space besides the
galley kitchen and the bathroom in my tiny place.

Ah, there it was! I struck gold on the floor near
the sofa where I'd removed my bra the night before
when Malone and I had— Well, anyway, I hadn't
lost it. I smoothed it out, reading her handwritten
number on the back.

Then I located my cell and dialed, once I'd figured out what to say. I was going to stick with
simple. I didn't even want to mention Olivia at all.

Luckily, Terra's voice mail picked up, and I

managed not to ramble too much in the message
I left her: "Hey, Terra, it's Andy Kendricks. I'm the
one who helped you get Penny unstuck yesterday.
Maybe this isn't the best time to call . . . things are
probably crazy for you right now . . . but I need to
start thinking about my own wedding plans, and
I was hoping we could talk."

If I didn't hear back from Terra, I wasn't sure
how else I'd learn more about Olivia's business
from the inside. Terra was my best bet at finding
out who might have had it in for her boss, though
I figured that list might include Terra herself.

After I'd grabbed a glass of water and my
laptop, I settled down on the couch. It struck me
that there *was* a way I could find out about Olivia
that didn't involve anyone else. I went to iTunes
and proceeded to download Season One of *The
Wedding Belle* for $9.99. Luckily, that was as long
as the show had been airing. Thank God there
weren't nine seasons. I don't know if I would have
survived watching that much of Olivia La Belle.

I sat cross-legged with my laptop on a pillow
and leaned back as I played the first episode. I had
to fight not to roll my eyes through the zippy mu-
sical prelude that included plenty of church bells
ringing and a slow shot of Olivia's long legs as she
exited the back of a chauffeur-driven Escalade
with her phone at her ear and a big white Hermès
bag in hand while her voice-over drawled, "I'm
Olivia La Belle, the premier event planner in
Texas, where everything's bigger: the hair, the ball
gowns, the jewels, the egos, and especially the
bank accounts of my brides' dear old daddies."

Good God, I found myself groaning as the images flashed by: a bride with her blond hair bumped-up to high heaven, a glittery white gown with a train at least twenty feet long, an engagement ring with a brilliant-cut diamond as big as a quarter, a face-lifted mother-of-the-bride in a sparkly dress, and a good ol' boy in a Stetson hat with a bolo 'round his neck flashing a fat money clip.

Way to reinforce tired old stereotypes, Olivia, I thought.

Then again, what had I expected? Particularly since Olivia had been a stereotype herself: the pretty, leggy blond trust fund baby who acted like she owned the world and everyone in it.

Sometime deep into Episode Three, Malone came in, and I put Olivia on pause.

He looked like he'd been through the wringer. After a lingering hug where he pressed his face into my hair, he whispered, "I'm so glad you're all right. We need to talk, okay? But first, I need a long hot shower." Then he disappeared into the bathroom, leaving the door half open so I could hear the fan go on and the water start falling.

I pushed play again and sat there like a zombie, eating up every melodramatic moment of the reality show like it was a never-ending bowl full of Cookie Dough Häagen-Dazs. It was tacky and show-offy, and, in parts, mean-spirited, but I couldn't get enough.

I was starting the fourth installment of *The Wedding Belle* when Malone emerged from the bedroom in clean clothes, wet hair, and slightly foggy glasses. He sat down beside me and didn't say a word, just leaned in to watch as Olivia turned from sweet drawling Southern girl into a raging bull, verbally attacking various vendors, claiming late delivery, wrinkled linen, or in the case of Jasper Pippin, wilted flowers. She routinely snipped at her then-assistant, Debbie, for all sorts of minute blunders. It was no wonder the girl looked terrified every moment she was on camera. By the end of the show Olivia pulled a Donald Trump and told Debbie she was fired. Debbie cried but I was guessing those were tears of relief and not sorrow.

"Andy, what the hell are you doing?" Malone asked when the show ended, and I queued up the next episode.

"I'm catching up with Olivia," I said. I wasn't sure if I was ready to tell him about my plans to do a bit of digging into the life of my old nemesis, but maybe I didn't have to.

"Why? You didn't even like her," he reminded me.

"That was when she was living and breathing," I said, "but now she isn't."

"Let me get this straight." He cleared his throat. "You were just not that into her when she was alive but now that she's dead, you're suddenly a fan?"

"I wouldn't call myself a fan exactly," I tried to explain and looked into his skeptical blue eyes. "I'm more like a rubbernecker watching a train wreck while it's still smoldering. I want to find out how it all came to pass."

He pushed at the bridge of his glasses and shook his head. "Andy, c'mon, you can't get involved in this any more than you already are. You'll likely be a key witness for the prosecution, albeit a bit of a hostile one."

"That's why I can't sit still," I informed him because, well, I was responsible. Not for Olivia's murder. But I was the one placing Millie squarely at the scene of the crime. "I can't just stay on the sidelines while Millie takes the heat for something she didn't do. I have to do *something*."

"So what does that make me? Chopped liver?" Malone made an unhappy noise and got up off the sofa. "I'll do my damnedest to get Millie out of this."

"Of course, you're not chopped liver! If anyone can get her off, you can," I called after him, because he was taking this the wrong way. He was an amazing lawyer. There was no doubt about that. He wouldn't be working at Abramawitz, Reynolds, Goldberg, and Hunt if he wasn't. "It's not *you*," I said, setting the laptop aside and dumping the pillow to the floor as I followed. "It's me. I feel guilty about Millie. I can't help it."

He had his briefcase open and shoved some paperwork inside it. "You have no reason to feel guilty."

"Really?" I said and came around the kitchen table. "*I'm* the one who puts Millie at the scene with the cake knife in her hand. *I'm* the one who made her stay put and wait for the police."

Brian's wide eyes blinked behind his glasses. "No," he said pointedly. "Millie puts Millie at the scene. She knows now that should have called 911 when she saw Olivia on the floor with the knife in her neck. But she did what she thought was right at the time, and she's too nice a woman to lie."

"So the police are pinning this case on her because she tried to help a dying woman?" I said, because that was how it felt.

"No, Andy," Brian said in an exasperated tone. "They're making a case against her because that's where the evidence is pointing." He paused before adding, "At least so far. But Millie's got the best team in town on her side so that's going to change. We'll get our own investigator on it and review whatever evidence the prosecution drums up. We'll catch their mistakes, find the holes. You have to trust me."

"I *do*," I said. I trusted Brian more than anyone on the planet. "I'm just scared for her," I admitted. "It's like someone's trying to toss my own grandma in jail."

"They're doing the autopsy now," he said, "so we'll have some preliminary findings by tomorrow. That could help Millie's case."

"Or hurt it," I remarked, being realistic.

"The more information we have, the better for Millie," he replied. "Then we'll know better how to attack the prosecution's case."

That sounded logical. But what if the evidence had already been manipulated to make Millie look guilty? What if she'd been set up? I didn't often believe in conspiracy theories, but I'd begun to wonder if one might actually apply here.

"So if they're not arresting Millie yet, are you off the hook until tomorrow? I mean, it is still Sunday," I said. "I'll make chocolate chip pancakes, and we can save part of the day."

I didn't mean to sound cold or uncaring. I just desperately wanted to—needed to—salvage some normalcy after a horrible morning.

"Sorry, Andy," he said, as I knew he would. He ran a hand over his hair, which had been damp a minute ago but had air-dried in record speed. "I wish I could hang around," he added, closing the buckles on his briefcase, "but I've got to head into the office."

"You can't go in, say, an hour?" I asked, hating that I sounded whiny.

"I'm meeting Allie so we can get started preparing motions to file on Millie's behalf. We need to be ready for anything, particularly now that the cops have possession of Millie's hard drives. Who knows what they'll dig up that looks incriminating," he was saying, "emails, something from Instagram, or a Facebook post—"

"Wait, what?" I cut him off. "You're working with Allie Price?" I said, because she was Brian's old girlfriend. The last serious girlfriend he'd had before he started dating me. I didn't hate her anymore—though I didn't really like her either—but that couldn't stop a spark of jealousy from igniting.

"Yes, Allie," Brian replied matter-of-factly and came around the table to kiss me. "If I'm lucky, I'll be home in time for dinner."

He'd be spending all afternoon with Allie working on Millie's case? This whole mess was getting worse by the moment.

"You're okay with it, right?" he asked, as if my saying, *No, you can't work with her, I won't allow it*, would make any difference.

"Huh? Oh, sure, I'm fine," I murmured as my vivid imagination pictured him sitting side by side with pretty blond Allie, their heads bent together, an undercurrent of electricity crackling between them as Allie said something like, *Remember when we used to team up on cases and then go home and have wild monkey sex?*

"Love you," Brian called over his shoulder and gave me a wave as he headed out the front door.

"I love you, too," I replied feebly as the door shut with a *thunk* behind him.

I knew then and there that Olivia was screwing with my life even in death. And somewhere—from the depths of hell, I figured—she was smirking.

Chapter 17

It was pathetic how quickly I got hooked on Olivia's show. Though I had pangs of guilt for enjoying it so much, I told myself I was viewing it all in the name of research. My butt didn't shift so much as a hair for a solid hour after Brian left, not until my stomach growled in protest.

Reluctantly, between the fifth and sixth episodes of *The Wedding Belle,* I put the thing on pause and grabbed a banana and tub of yogurt for sustenance. Olivia had already fired five assistants— one per episode—and I'd lost count of how many other folks she'd dressed down behind the scenes. It was a wonder anyone kept working with her at all . . . except out of fear. It confirmed my suspicions that she hadn't changed an iota from the girl she'd been at Hockaday. Even as an adult, she'd still bullied her way through life. I can't imagine how such behavior could have ended anything but badly.

When my phone rang, playing a burst of AC/DC's *Highway to Hell*, I knew it wasn't Brian. So I let out an annoyed sigh and put the show on pause. My mouth full of banana, I picked up.

"Hello?" I said, though it sounded like, "Uh-oh."

"Andy Kendricks? It's Terra Smith."

My heart skipped a beat. "Oh, hey," I replied, swallowing down the mush in my mouth. "Thanks for calling me back so fast."

"I was pretty surprised to hear from you," she admitted. "You must know about Olivia by now."

I guess she hadn't heard that I'd been at Olivia's office that morning and was the one who'd called 911. Maybe it was better not to bring it up.

"Yeah, I know. It's all over the news," I told her, because it was. A local celebrity being murdered in Highland Park was a big flipping deal. Heck, a missing dog in Highland Park made headlines. It was one of the richest zip codes in the country. Not exactly a cesspool of crime. I tried to choose my words carefully. "What happened to Olivia was awful."

"It's so bizarre. I mean, I'd just talked to her late last night, going over the to-do list for today." Terra sighed. "We're deep into spring weddings and June's coming up fast. We have so much going on that things are kind of chaotic right now, as you can imagine," she went on, and I was afraid she was going to tell me she couldn't meet. "I've got the onerous task of contacting all of Olivia's current clients to see if they want to continue with me, but a lot of them are running scared."

"I'm sorry," I said, wondering not for the first time what would happen to Olivia's business. And I wondered, too, if there was more to Terra Smith than met the eye. Who used the phrase "onerous task" these days? There was definitely a brain behind the two-toned hair and bad makeup.

"I just never figured things would end up like this, not in a million years," Terra told me, sounding frustrated. "Without Olivia steering the ship, well, there's no Wedding Belle. I guess I'll keep whichever clients want to stick with me if there are any."

"There's no one else with a stake in Olivia's company? She didn't have a partner?" I dared to ask.

"No," Terra insisted. "Olivia would never have gone for that. She liked to run things herself. She did a lot of contract hiring rather than keep a big staff. She was kind of a control freak."

Kind of?

"I want to work with you, Terra," I said, feeling sorry for her. "I haven't even begun to think about my wedding, and the clock is ticking. I don't even know where to start, and it's making me sick to my stomach," I added, and it wasn't a total lie.

"What date have you set?"

"Um"—the fact was, Brian and I hadn't gotten around to that yet, so I did a bit of spur-of-the-moment fudging—"we're thinking this fall, October maybe?"

"Ah, six months is pretty tight, but I think I can pull it off," Terra told me, and I had a sense she was taking notes. "Anything less than six months would basically be a mad dash to the altar. Do you have ideas for a reception venue, caterer, music, flowers . . . ?"

"No," I said, and laughed nervously. "I'm horrible, aren't I?"

"You're hardly horrible. Some brides are just more into this stuff than others," Terra remarked, and I found myself warming up to her, skunk hair and all.

"So I guess we should meet soon, huh?" My heart thudded in my chest. "I feel so far behind already."

"Are you busy right now?" Terra asked, taking me by surprise. "I've got a couple hours to kill before a wedding and reception later today at the Adolphus. The bride's totally pissed that Olivia won't be there, like she up and died on purpose." Terra's voice caught but she quickly regained her composure. "The police are still at the office. They can't seem to find her computer or her iPhone, so they've taken a bunch of paper files, and they asked me to surrender my laptop, too, since it's networked to Olivia's. It's a pain, but don't worry. I have everything important backed up on a spare that I use for personal stuff. It's my insurance policy," she said. "You can't be too careful these days."

"That's smart," I told her.

"I would ask you to come to my place," she went on, "but I've been staying with a relative since I moved to town. Maybe we could do a coffee shop? I work out of those a lot."

I wasn't sure the public atmosphere of a coffee

shop would be the best place to discuss wedding plans—even fake ones—or elicit any kind of information from Terra about her dead boss. So I decided to go for broke.

"Could you come here?" I asked, my palms sweating. "My mother wants to join us so it'd probably be better if we had some privacy. Besides, I'd prefer if we kept Cissy away from hot beverages while I'm disagreeing with her about the dress and the venue and linens . . . well, everything."

Terra chuckled. "Oh, yeah, it's much safer to keep the mother of the bride away from burning liquids and sharp objects."

"Give me half an hour to alert my mom and tidy up," I said and gave her the address of my condo.

"That'll work," she told me and said good-bye.

I hung up and immediately dialed Mother.

"The Eagle has landed," I said, only to hear her pregnant pause.

"What eagle?" she sputtered. "What on earth are you talking about, Andrea? You haven't been drinking, have you?"

For Pete's sake.

"No, I haven't been drinking!" I told her, and I took a deep breath. "I talked to Terra Smith, Olivia's assistant," I said. "You know, mission accomplished."

"Ah," she murmured, "I see. You were being cryptic, like a spy."

My eyes rolled involuntarily.

"Look, she's coming over to my place in thirty minutes. If you want to play the part of the obsessive mother of the bride"—which would hardly be a stretch—"you're welcome to join us. If not, no worries. I can handle this myself. It's not like I'm meeting her in a dark alley."

"Is Mr. Malone there, or are you alone?"

"Brian had to go into the office," I said stiffly, trying to stop further images of him and perky Allie cozying up over paperwork. "He's got to prepare all sorts of motions and stuff on Millie's behalf so they're ready when the police file charges." Speaking of, I wondered if it was a good idea for Cissy to leave Millie alone so soon after being grilled by the Highland Park police. "Maybe you should stay home for Millie's sake," I told her, biting my tongue before I tacked on *and for mine.*

"Oh, the poor dear's fast asleep," she told me. "She'll be out for at least an hour, maybe two."

My voice went up right along with my pulse rate. "Mother, what did you do to her? Did you spike her tea?"

"Well, I might have given her a little something. She needed to rest, Andrea, and she wasn't going to get it unless I helped."

"You gave her a little of what exactly?" I asked, hoping she hadn't ground up an Ambien, or Millie might end up sleepwalking around Highland Park in her underwear.

"She's fine," Cissy assured me without doling out further details. "As we speak, I'm writing her a note with my cell number in case she wakes up before I'm back."

"I can do this alone," I told her, but she brushed me off.

"No need," Mother replied, "when I'm already on my way out the door. See you in a few," she cooed before ending the call.

Oh, Lord. I hung my head and groaned. What had I done? I'd invited my mother to come talk wedding plans at my condo. I hadn't debuted. I hadn't pledged a sorority. But I was getting married, and she would have her say, even if this meeting was nothing but subterfuge. Terra would probably not make it out of here alive, and I had doubts I would survive the meeting either. It was akin to unleashing Frankenstein's monster on a bunch of villagers who'd given up pitchforks for Lent.

Well, fake as the appointment might be, I didn't want my condo looking like a mess when Mother arrived.

For the next fifteen minutes, I ran around the space, picking up random socks, shoes, books, and whatever else I found littering the kitchen and living area. Before I'd met Malone, I'd been obsessively neat. Funny how his presence made me worry less about how often I picked up and more about how often we laughed together. Once I'd tossed the detritus into the bedroom and shut the door, the place looked pretty good, definitely presentable enough for both my mother and Terra.

I even ran a brush through my still-damp hair so Terra wouldn't have cause to tell me it looked like a rat's nest; though something told me that Terra didn't care as much about appearances as her dead boss.

The hum of an engine propelled me to the

window, and I peered through the blinds to see Mother's Lexus pulling into the spot belonging to my nosy neighbor, Mrs. George, a fact I reminded her of when she walked in the door.

"Oh, pooh, I'm sure she won't mind," Cissy said as she dropped her keys and kelly-green Birkin bag on the kitchen counter.

I guess she figured if she could take the Highland Park police chief's spot, using my neighbor's was no biggie. Besides, Mother and Mrs. George were practically buddies. They used to do Bible study together at Highland Park Presbyterian, and I knew Cissy had enlisted the snoop upstairs to spy on me in the past. Although it seemed that since Malone and I had gotten engaged, Mrs. George had lost interest. I guess the ring on my finger made all the difference in the world.

"So what's the plan?" she asked and faced me with hands on hips. "Should I be the good cop or the bad cop?"

Good cop, bad cop? Did she think we were Starsky and Hutch?

"Just be yourself," I said and heard a knock on the door. "Pretend we're doing this for real, okay? Follow my lead, and you'll be fine."

"Pretend it's for real, yes"—Cissy nodded—"I can do that." Then she drew in a deep breath, scooping her hands up in front of her as though gathering air for her lungs before an opera debut.

Talk about a drama queen.

Oh, boy.

I went to the door and opened it to find Terra standing on the welcome mat. She had a big hobo bag slung over a shoulder and a hesitant smile on her glossy red lips.

"Sorry I'm a little slow," she said, "but my old Honda crapped out and I had to borrow a ride."

"It's okay," I told her. I hadn't even realized she was late.

"So are you ready for me?"

I nodded. "As I'll ever be," I told her, and I smiled nervously. "Come on in."

Chapter 18

Before I had a chance to introduce Terra to my mother, Cissy stepped forward, clasping her hands between her breasts. "What a pleasure it is to meet you, my dear," she drawled with cheerleader enthusiasm. "I saw you at Penny Ryan's wedding yesterday but we never had the chance to chat. I'm Andy's mom, Cissy Kendricks."

"Very nice to meet you, Mrs. Kendricks," Terra said, looking pleased as punch. "I've heard your name mentioned so often that I feel like I know you already. You do so much for area charities."

"How kind of you to say." My mother smiled, her ego stroked. Then as quickly, Cissy turned sober, touching Terra's arm and telling her, "I'm sorry to hear about Olivia. It's such a shame to see a young life cut short."

I cringed though I realized Mother bringing up

Olivia's death couldn't be avoided. That particular pink elephant couldn't have hidden in my tiny
condo if he'd wanted to.

"Yes, it's a shame that she had to go like that.
The world is a harsh place. Sometimes I wonder
how anyone survives without a lot of scars," Terra
said quietly. "Life can be so twisted."

Wow. I didn't know what to say to that.

"It can be twisted, indeed," Cissy said and
looked right at me, as if proving a point. "But we
must march forward as best we can."

"I just wish things would get back to normal,"
Terra remarked with a sigh. "My life hasn't been
the same since I met Olivia, and now . . ." She let
the thought trail off with a shrug, and she began
biting her lip.

Oh, God, this was turning rather maudlin.

Mother's pale eyes met mine.

"Hey, let's talk about happy stuff," I said, "like
getting married."

Terra stopped gnawing her lip. She perked up
and reached for my left hand. "Where's your ring?
I have to see!" She held my hand up, turning it
in the light. "Eyeing the bling is an occupational
hazard."

"I'm not sure this qualifies as bling," I joked as
she studied my engagement ring, which was at
best a carat. "Brian, my fiancé . . . he got it from
an antiques dealer in town," I told her. "He was
told it's from the twenties. He knows how I love
old things, and the setting's so cool. It's very Deco.
But it's hardly the kind of rock you're probably
used to seeing on your clients' fingers."

"It could have been a wee bit bigger," my mother murmured, and I was about to jump on her when Terra stepped in.

"No, it's perfect, very understated and cool," she said, bravely contradicting Highland Park's resident Queen Bee. "Not many fiancés think to get something so meaningful." She let go of my hand and smiled. "Good for Brian for not going overboard. I'm used to seeing sparklers so large I wonder how long it'll take the poor groom to pay it off. You don't know how many couples start off their marriage in serious debt."

"It *is* the American way," Cissy said with a lift of her penciled-in eyebrows.

"Thank God, it's not my way," I stated, because I hadn't wanted Brian to feel financially bogged down by a piece of jewelry. Like Baby Bear's porridge, my ring was just right. I loved that it was true to my taste—and to me—and it showed that Brian knew exactly what I wanted. I would never have felt comfortable wearing a huge stone from Tiffany that cost more than my Jeep. I would have been too scared to leave the house with it on my finger.

"Terra darlin', you should hear the story of how I interrupted Mr. Malone proposing. Why, he was down on one knee when I burst in with news of my own—" my mother began, and I cut her off with a loud cough.

"Save it, Mumsy," I said under my breath.

Terra glanced around my little condo, and her gaze stopped on the easel perched in the corner by the picture window. "Andrea, do you paint?" she asked, artfully changing the subject.

"I dabble," I admitted, liking that she'd noticed. "I do abstracts mostly. I've tried still lifes and landscapes, but I'm better when I don't go for any kind of realism."

She walked nearer, inspecting my work in progress, which pretty much looked like a crazy quilt of brushstrokes.

"So you use acrylics not oils?"

"Yeah," I said, intrigued that she knew something about the process. "I like acrylics better for creating texture and depth. They dry faster, too."

"I love art," Terra told me. "I started out wanting to be an interior designer. I even went to the Art Institute of Indianapolis for a while. Then I came here with a friend who knew Olivia and heard she was hiring. Not sure we were the best match but I ended up really loving the business. So despite everything, I guess I should thank her for that."

That was hardly a ringing endorsement.

"I went to Columbia College in Chicago," I told her. "I studied Web design but I love art in all its forms."

"I've dabbled in Web design," Terra said, seeming more interested in me suddenly. "I'm working on something new, as a matter of fact."

We ended up chatting for a bit about my Web design business. While we talked, I noticed my mother doing a little surveillance of her own, checking out Terra's two-tone hair, squinting at the overdone makeup and the mix-and-match attire complete with teetering heels. I prayed Cissy wouldn't say something rude, like, "Hello!

The eighties called and they want your whole look back."

Fortunately, Mother kept her lips zipped.

I caught the faint tightening of her mouth, a sure sign of disapproval, but I figured Terra hadn't seen it. Besides, what did Cissy expect? That Olivia's assistant would sashay in looking like a page out of *Vogue*? Maybe Olivia could afford to dress like the socialites she worked for, but I doubted Terra could. From what I'd learned by watching those episodes of *The Wedding Belle*, Olivia had practically made her assistants work for free.

Personally, I appreciated the fact that Terra had her own sense of style and hadn't tried to copy Olivia. It seemed that most of Terra's predecessors on *The Wedding Belle* had desperately attempted to dress like their boss, act like her, and try to *be* her, down to her dyed-blond roots. It made me respect Terra Smith in a way I hadn't upon first meeting her yesterday when I'd thought she was clueless.

"I can tell you're artistic just by looking around," Terra said, taking note of the rest of my space, just as Mother had taken note of her. "The place is so cozy and homey. I like shabby-chic."

"Thanks," I said, tempted to remark that my decorating style was more shabby than chic, but I wasn't sure if Terra needed to hear about my penchant for hunting down finds at local flea markets and estate sales. Maybe she'd already figured that out.

Mother cleared her throat and gave me a pointed glance. "Could we get started? I have a guest staying with me, and I'll need to get back to her shortly."

"Yes, let's sit down," I suggested, gesturing toward the kitchen table with the four chairs I'd bought at the Junior League rummage sale in Richardson and painted black. "You need anything to drink?" I asked, looking at Terra. "I have water, juice, and green tea."

"I'd love a Perrier," Mother replied, though I wasn't talking to her.

"I've got tap water and ice," I said.

She winced. "Thanks, sweet pea, but I'm fine."

"I'm fine, too," Terra replied. "I've already sucked down too much coffee this morning. I can feel my stomach sloshing. I had to talk to the police before I came here. I think they need to invest in a Keurig."

I was tempted to say something more about Olivia. But I couldn't just barrel ahead and ask, *So, who hated her enough to stick her with a cake knife?* I doubted that would go over very well. I was going to have to ease into things.

"If no one needs their whistle wet"—I rubbed my hands together—"then let's do this."

I let my mother and Terra settle down at the table before I pulled up a chair. I ended up across from Terra and next to Cissy.

"On the phone, you said the date is October, right?" Terra remarked as she propped her laptop on the table and opened it. I admired the hot pink smiley face sticker she'd slapped over the Dell logo. "We'll need to move quickly," she said and started clicking away at the keys. "We have to get your venues booked, lock in a caterer, and find the perfect dress ASAP."

"The wedding is *this* October?" Cissy repeated and looked at me. To call her expression delighted was an understatement. "That's a mere six months away!"

"So it is," I replied, hoping my eyes conveyed the message that this was just for show because Brian and I hadn't set any firm date yet. But even if I'd actually uttered the words, I wasn't sure she'd believe them. She was going to enjoy this mission far too much, I could tell that already.

"Here we go. The new site I've been playing with," Terra said, she and swiveled the laptop screen so Mother and I could see it.

A hot pink logo floated boldly across the screen. PLANET WEDDING, it read, in a circle like a ring. Beneath that, *Make All Your Bridal Dreams Come True with One Click.* I noticed there were buttons labeled Dresses, Floral, Venue, Music, and so on.

"Planet Wedding, huh," I said, because it definitely wasn't the Wedding Belle. "It's catchy."

Terra blushed. "It's just a beta test," she replied. "I'm sure Olivia's lawyers won't let me use her brand much longer, and it's time I struck out on my own anyway. So"—she gave me a look, like a puppy begging for approval—"what do you think?"

"It's very inventive," I told her, wanting to sound enthusiastic.

But I had to wonder if Terra hadn't been making other plans even before Olivia's murder. Or else she was fast on the draw and had whipped up the graphics for her Web site since this morning.

"Thanks," Terra said, smiling. "I'm trying to move forward, like you said." She nodded at my mother.

"You're a wise young woman," Cissy remarked,

and Terra blushed. "But, by chance, do you have a book I can hold in my hands? I'm not as fond of computers as Andrea."

"Of course," Terra said. Grabbing up her bulky purse from the floor, she reached a hand in and pulled out a big pink binder. With a push, she slid it across the table.

"Great." I reached for it first and opened it wide as Mother craned her neck, peering at the pages as I flipped through them.

"It's got a bunch of ideas for pinning down your wedding style," Terra said, "and images of every gown you can imagine, plus floral arrangements, venues for the wedding and reception, photographers, caterers, musicians, everything you'll want. I'll leave the book with you if you'd like."

"Yes, please," I said. As I skimmed the pages, my brain felt overloaded by all the pictures. It was like looking at the Cheesecake Factory menu. There were so many options it was overwhelming, especially since I'd barely begun to consider what I wanted. I must have looked particularly bug-eyed as Terra cocked her head in my direction.

"I know, I know," she said. "There's a lot to think about. It's an important day."

"*The* most important," Cissy drawled and batted her lashes at the young woman. "It's right up there with having a baby," she added. "That's why it's so helpful to have a true professional on our side."

"Thank you, Mrs. Kendricks," Terra said and blushed again.

I nudged Mother with a toe under the table. Overkill, I was thinking, but she merely grinned.

Chapter 19

 "So how about you all just give me an overview of what you're thinking right now," Terra suggested, and she tapped another key on her laptop so the wallpaper morphed into a slide show with photographs of beautiful brides, shoes, gowns, rings, churches decorated with endless flowers, string quartets poised to play, ad infinitum.

"What I'd like for my wedding," I began, my mouth strangely dry for someone who was merely role-playing, "is something simple . . ."

"Simple but lush," Cissy said, butting in, "with no expense spared." When I looked at her sideways, she added, "I didn't wait over thirty years for my baby to get married to skimp on this."

"*Mother*," I said, hating the whine I heard in my voice. It seemed to appear out of nowhere when Cissy and I crossed swords. "To be perfectly honest," I told her, keeping my cool, "I don't see myself getting married in front of hundreds of your closest friends. Don't get too pushy or Malone and I might decide to elope."

Mother's eyes went so wide, I thought they might pop out.

"Well, we can always keep things small but elegant," Terra said in an effort to intercede, but Cissy wasn't done yet.

"*Elope?*" she squawked like a parrot. "Dear Lord," she muttered, fanning her face with a hand. "Do *not* say that word again." Her hand settled on her heart. She looked fit to burst. "You think being married by an Elvis impersonator in Vegas is preferable to being married by the pastor at Highland Park Presbyterian in front of pews filled with friends and family?"

"Yes," I said, because I did, hands down, no contest. I couldn't even think of more than a hand-ful of friends and family who I wanted around to share such a special moment, much less four or five hundred of them.

"Oh, Andrea, I love you, but you're out of your mind," Mother remarked, shaking her head. "You've already deprived me of seeing your debut. Now you're going to deprive me of the kind of wedding for you I've always dreamed about?"

"But it's my wedding, not yours," I said.

"It's a little bit mine if I'm paying for it." Cissy's gaze met mine, and her pale eyes flashed fire.

My back stiffened. "Who says you have to pay for it?"

"Whoa, ladies, let's take a step back, okay?"

Terra said and clapped crisply, trying to get our attention from across the table. It didn't work.

"We're not turning my wedding into a three-ring circus, Mother," I said as civilly as I knew how. "If you try, I will skip out."

"You wouldn't dare!" Cissy turned such a bloodless shade of white that her subtle makeup looked suddenly clownlike in contrast. "Eloping is for drunken fools and girls who find themselves in a pickle," she announced in that sharp tone she'd always used when I did something to embarrass her. "Oh, no," she murmured and stared at me, unblinking. "Oh, sweet pea, please, tell me Mr. Malone hasn't gotten you—" She hesitated and tried again. "That you aren't—"

"Knocked up like Penny Ryan?" I replied, nearly choking on the words. "For Pete's sake," I said and started laughing. I couldn't help it. Did she think I was a horny college sophomore?

"Goodness, Andrea"—my mother frowned, clearly miffed—"it's not the least bit funny."

She was right. It wasn't funny. It was hysterical.

I finally caught hold of myself enough to tell her, "Don't worry. I'm not having your grandchild any time soon. So you can untwist your Spanx and breathe easy."

"I would much prefer that you wait until after the wedding, thank you," Cissy replied in a stern drawl, and she began fiddling with her double strand of pearls. "I could only imagine the looks I'd get if you walked down the aisle in one of those horrid maternity gowns." She wrinkled her nose.

I raised my eyebrows. "So you think I'd look better in a giant marshmallow dress?"

"If you mean a gown that covers your chest and has proper crinolines and train," my mother said, "then, yes, I would."

God, give me strength.

I opened my mouth to fire back, but Terra leapt up from her seat.

"Ladies, please, you're not the first bride and MOB who've disagreed," she said, snatching her laptop from the tabletop.

"Mob?" Cissy echoed. "As in Al Capone?"

"As in mother of the bride," I clarified, although my mom was certainly acting like a mafia don.

"What if we find a happy medium," Terra offered, dragging her chair around the table, and plunked down between Mother and me, as though trying to prevent a catfight. She pulled her computer up closer so she could tap the keyboard. "It's all doable," she said, reminding me of the encouragement I'd given her before we'd had to free Penny Ryan and her hoop skirt from Lester Dickens's toilet. "We just have to find things that will satisfy you both. No worries. I do this all the time." She looked eagerly at me and then at Mother. "What do you say? Can we compromise?"

Cissy sighed. "I guess you're right." She leaned back so she could see around Terra. "After all, this is your wedding, Andrea, not mine."

"Although Mother is engaged, too," I threw out in retaliation.

Terra perked up. "Is that true?" she asked.

"It is," Cissy said, and stopped fingering her

pearls so Terra could admire her emerald spar-
kler; which was, of course, from Cartier and far
bigger than my modest diamond.

"Have you two thought about a double wedding?" Terra asked, and I had to grab the table to
steady myself.

"What?" I gulped.

"Why, no, the idea hadn't occurred to me before
now," Mother said and gave me a look, as though
seriously entertaining the idea.

I hoped to God she was saying that for the
sake of our undercover sting and not because she
meant it.

"You know, that might be fun," she remarked
with an overzealous twinkle in her eyes, and I felt
a frisson of fear race up my spine.

"No," I said firmly, "we are absolutely, positively not doing a double wedding." It would be
a disaster of epic proportions. And, besides, we
weren't here to actually plan *any* wedding. We
were supposed to be finding out about Terra's
relationship with Olivia. "Let's just stick to one
wedding for now," I suggested, *"mine."*

"You are a spoilsport," my mother drawled,
acting disappointed. "But I'll do whatever you
want, pumpkin."

If there was sweat on my upper lip, it was for
good reason. If this whole thing wasn't a charade,
my mother would have gone ahead and planned
a double wedding, if that was what she really
wanted. She would have ordered me a marshmallow dress and had us both marching down the
aisle in tandem. Because no matter how much I

fought her, in the end she would grab the wheel and steer the ship. She was Cissy Blevins Kendricks, the Doyenne of Dallas Society, a blue-blooded Texas filly to the core. I could insist on a simple, small wedding until I turned blue in the face, but she would never listen. Mother never did anything small and never would.

Terra must have heard me hyperventilating, as she said, "I agree, let's focus on Andy for now and talk about dresses."

She clicked a few keys on the laptop and brought up photos of wedding gowns. They were very simple with clean lines, many of them ivory and some knee-length. I leaned forward to better see them.

"They're pretty," I said, "but maybe a bit too traditional."

"There's nothing wrong with being traditional," I heard my mother say with a sniff, but I ignored her.

I was about to point to a cute cocktail-style dress that had an overlay of antique-looking lace when I remembered why Terra had come to my condo. I was supposed to be finding out more about Olivia, not picking out my wedding attire.

So I made a noise of disappointment. "You know, I was thinking maybe I'd have someone design my dress. I've heard Draco does really cutting edge bridal fashions. Is he available?"

"Draco?" Terra repeated. "Are you sure? You sound like you want something different but quiet, and Draco's designs can be very loud."

Hmm. Shouldn't she have encouraged me to

order a dress from Olivia's supposed favorite designer cum boyfriend? When it sounded like she didn't want me going near the man, it prompted me to dig in my heels.

"I'm not sure what I want yet," I told her honestly. "Is it possible just to talk to him? I'd like to see more of his work. Oh, wait—" I made myself pause. "—he was involved with Olivia, wasn't he? No wonder you're so reluctant. It's probably not a good time to meet him. He's undoubtedly devastated."

Terra pursed her lips tightly before she haltingly spoke. "Yes, he's as devastated as I am that she's gone."

I thought at first she was being facetious but maybe I was wrong. Her expression turned stoic and unreadable. She sat there quietly for a long moment, and her lack of response made me nervous.

I hoped I hadn't jumped the gun, asking for an appointment with Draco. At least I hadn't asked if Jasper Pippin could do my flowers, too. If Terra got suspicious of my motives and backed off, I'd have to find another way to figure out who hated Olivia enough to kill her.

"Yoo hoo, can I ask a question?" my mother said, breaking the uncomfortable silence. "Who's this Dracula fellow? I know vampires are big these days, but I don't want you in a black dress on your big day, sweetheart, unless"—her expression turned mortified—"you're planning to do some kind of Halloween theme."

What?

"No," I said, and I raised my foot to nudge Cissy but ended up toeing Terra's shin instead. "Oops, sorry, I thought you were a table leg," I said lamely, though Terra didn't even flinch. I looked past her at my mom. "No, we're not doing a Halloween-themed wedding, and Draco is not a vampire. He's a hot young designer from the show *Operation: Runway* who set up shop in Dallas."

Her eyebrows lifted. "Oh, yes, of course, how did I not know that?" she remarked, though I could tell she'd never heard of him. "Well, if Dracula's too busy, there's always Vera Wang, pumpkin, even though she's been done to death," she went on, improvising so beautifully that I had to wonder if she was being earnest. "I have her private number. I'll phone her this afternoon if you'd like."

"Hmm, I guess I'd consider talking to Vera," I said, playing along, and apparently it was enough to get Terra's attention.

Terra swiveled toward me. "No, it's all right." Her darkly outlined eyes looked worried. "If you want to meet with Draco, I can arrange it."

"If you're sure, well, okay," I said, trying to project nonchalance.

"Let me give him a call." She pushed away from the table and left her laptop sitting between me and Mother while she retrieved her hobo bag, pulling out her cell. "I'll just be a few minutes," she declared before heading out the front door.

"I guess she doesn't want us to eavesdrop," I said and, with a glance toward the door, grabbed Terra's laptop keyboard and minimized the window she'd opened with all the wedding gowns. I wanted like crazy to get into her emails but that was password-protected.

Damn.

I clicked on the desktop icon with photos, opening up a folder within labeled *Big Money Shot*, which turned out to be a photo of a man's very white bare butt with a big brown mole and some kind of frog tattoo.

Cissy let out a sharp breath. "What is that?"

"The big money shot," I said and grinned. "Terra must have a boyfriend with a tat on his ass."

"Andrea!" my mother scolded and wiggled her fingers. "Make it go away."

So I shut the windows and maximized the one with Terra's Web site. She wasn't lying about it being in testing stages. I hit the link button for Dresses to see if Draco's designs would be available on Planet Wedding, but the link went nowhere. Ditto the link for Flowers.

"Andrea, what are you doing?" Cissy asked.

"Snooping," I said under my breath. Did she forget that was why Terra was here?

"I meant, why are you being so obstinate about your wedding dress?" Cissy clarified. "A marshmallow dress?" She shook her head. "Is that what you think I'd pick out for you? Truly, Andrea, if you believe that, you don't know me at all."

I sighed. Why wouldn't I believe she wanted me in something big and poofy? That was exactly the type of gown she'd picked out for my debutante ball. It was still hanging in my childhood closet on Beverly Drive, as a matter of fact. Perhaps she'd just want it altered so I could finally wear it for something and she'd get her money's worth.

"I'm not going to fight over a dress," I told her.

"Oh, sweet pea, you don't get it," she said and let out a laborious sigh. "In all honesty, I don't care what you don on your Big Day so long as you don't wear something strapless with your bosoms falling out. The things I have seen." She wrinkled her nose. "Whatever happened to modesty?"

"My bosoms won't fall out, I promise," I said and tried not to smile. Like I had enough boobs to fall out of anything, as Olivia had so often reminded me from the time I got my first training bra.

"Now don't take this as carte blanche to get pregnant before your wedding, but, for your information"—she squared her jaw and finished with a straight face—"if you marched down the aisle in a maternity gown, I would neither have a heart attack nor would I disinherit you."

I smothered laughter. Was she serious?

"It *is* a different world than when I married your father, and I accept that," she went on, still not giving any indication that this was a joke, and we were a few weeks past April Fools' Day so it couldn't be that. "Just promise me that my grand-baby won't be illegitimate. The ceremony must come before the birth. That's not too much to ask, now is it?"

Um, what?

I stared at her, barely able to choke out, "Sure."

"See," she said and clapped her hands, "we *can* agree on something!"

It was a good thing Terra came back inside at that moment, or I might have dialed 1-800-Loony-Bin and had them pick up my mother. What was happening to the uptight, überconservative Cissy I had known and feared? I couldn't imagine such a thing coming out of her mouth a year ago. Did she want a grandbaby so much that she'd eschew propriety to bounce one on her lap?

Perhaps Olivia's death had really gotten to her, and she'd rather have me around breaking rules than lose me. It was enough to make me teary-eyed.

"It's all set. You can meet with Draco tomorrow," Terra announced, although she wasn't smiling about it. She looked tense and her cheeks were flushed, as though she and Draco had argued.

"Is everything all right?" I asked.

"Everything's fine," she murmured, and I thought she was going to settle back into the chair between Mother and me. But she merely leaned in and snatched her laptop off the table. "He's doing a bridal show at the World Trade Center at eleven o'clock tomorrow so he wants us to come, and he can give you a few minutes after. I figure you'll want to watch the show anyway as it's his latest bridal couture. It might give you a better idea of what you want. He has his showroom there, too, so we can see more of his samples."

"Sounds good," I replied, a little surprised that Draco was still conducting business as usual despite Olivia's untimely demise. Perhaps he wasn't any more torn up about her passing than Terra seemed to be. Or maybe I was just cynical. "Are we all going together?"

"How about I meet you there?" Terra said as she scribbled something on the back of a card she pulled from her bag. "Here's the address for the building and suite. All the bridal showrooms are on the fourteenth floor." She pushed the card into my hand. "If I don't make it on time, I'll reserve you some seats."

"Why wouldn't you make it?"

Her face pinched. "I got a voice mail from the Highland Park police. They want to talk again in the morning, and I'm not sure how long that'll take."

No wonder she looked tense.

"It's no problem at all, Terra. Andrea and I will meet you at Market Center," my mother said before I had the chance.

"If you have any questions or thoughts about your wedding at any point in time, you can always email, text, or call. I've got your file started," Terra said as she tucked her laptop into her giant hobo bag. "I'll probably be working on the fly for a while. I don't know when the police will be done with Olivia's office, or if her lawyers will ever let me go back in, for that matter."

"Whatever works," I told her, getting up to walk her to the door. "Thanks for coming by. We'll see you tomorrow at the show."

"Yeah, see you tomorrow." She nodded, glancing over my shoulder to say, "It was very nice meeting you, Mrs. Kendricks."

Then she took off, and I closed the door behind her, though I quickly raced to the window to peer through the blinds. I saw her get into a dusty old

Mercedes wagon with a sticker that read TSFA on the rear window and another sticker on the bumper that declared: HONK IF YOU STOP AND SMELL THE ROSES.

I hadn't even heard my mother come up behind me until she quietly said, "You're right, Andrea. That girl is definitely hiding something."

"Is that so?" I turned around with a sigh. "What makes you so sure? The fact that you don't like her hair or the way she dresses? So what if she's not Junior League material? She seems okay to me."

I hated thinking that Terra might have something to do with Olivia's murder. She seemed to be a nice person. I'd even begun to like her a little.

Cissy clicked tongue against teeth. "Oh, sweet pea, that's not it," she said. "I'm not talking about her awful clothes or her bad hair. Didn't you notice anything strange about this?" She very deliberately tapped her third left finger, the one that used to wear the platinum and diamond wedding band my father had given her and now sported the radiant-cut emerald engagement ring from Stephen.

I shook my head. Nothing came to mind. As far as I could recall, Terra had all four fingers and an opposable thumb on that hand.

"What strange thing should I have noticed?" I asked.

"She had the tattoo of a wedding band on her finger," Mother said, her mouth pinched. "Is she married? Is that some newfangled thing kids are doing these days to save money on rings?" she asked.

But I could only stare back at her dumbly because I didn't have a clue.

"Do you know what TSFA stands for?" I asked, suddenly wondering if Mother wasn't right about Terra's secrets.

Mother shrugged. "I haven't the foggiest."

So I got my laptop from the sofa, opened it up, and did a Google search to see what came up while Cissy sat down beside me.

"Tax-free Savings Account, Tri-State Fast-Pitch Association . . . ," I murmured the names as I went down the list of results, although nothing seemed just right. ". . . Toronto Society of Financial Analysts, Toasted Sub Franchise Association, Tobago Sheep Farmers Association, Texas State Floral Association . . ."

Ah-ha!

I stopped on that last one as something Janet had said earlier came to mind.

. . . he was supposed to do the flowers for the White Glove Society's annual deb ball and he bailed on them. They were in a tizzy, trying to find someone else at the last minute. The fact that Olivia tarnished his rep on TV was just the final nail in the casket. The whole mess got Jasper unseated as chair of the state floral association. The poor guy practically went into hiding.

It made sense that the "state floral association" was the TSFA, particularly with the "Honk if you stop and smell the roses" companion sticker.

Now a bigger question: was there a connection between Terra and Jasper Pippin besides having worked with Olivia? And was that connection close enough that Jasper would loan Terra his car?

"What's wrong, sugar?" my mother asked.

"I'm not sure," I told her, knowing exactly what Nancy Drew would do in such a situation. She'd keep sticking her freckled nose where it didn't belong until she found some answers.

Chapter 20

Five minutes after Terra took off, my mother left, too.

But before Cissy made her grand departure, she'd invited me to bring Malone to dinner at her house so we could distract Millie for an hour or two. Millie was staying overnight, which I thought was great. That way, she wouldn't be alone if she woke up with nightmares about Olivia, and it gave Mother someone else to fuss over besides me. I told her I wasn't sure if my fiancé would even be back in time to eat. When I'd mentioned he was working Millie's case with Allie, she raised an eyebrow and said, "Allie Price, the blonde who helped us find Brian when he went missing? My, oh, my."

Yes, even Cissy knew about Brian and Allie's history, and since she'd met the woman, it made her "my, oh, my" even worse.

"Well, if Mr. Malone can't make it, come alone, and we'll have a girls' night in," she'd suggested before kissing my cheek and disappearing in a wispy cloud of Joy perfume.

Normally, that type of invitation would have made me run screaming in the opposite direction. But then I realized it wasn't a half bad idea. I could use some distracting, too. Knowing Brian was spending time with his ex was killing me, though I was trying hard not to let on.

I kept reminding myself that it was a small price to pay to keep Millie out of the penitentiary. So, much as I resented Malone working alongside his former flame on this one, I knew the pair would leave no stone unturned. Allie might be too pretty for a lawyer—much less for her own good—but she wasn't stupid. That combination of looks and brains had made her a killer in the courtroom. And Malone was no slouch either. He was Atticus Finch in the flesh, a real-life Eagle Scout who earnestly believed in truth and justice.

Millie was lucky to have them both on her side.

As for me, I'd just have to bite the bullet and tough it out until this whole thing blew over, which was why I needed to work fast and gather as much information as I could these next few days. I didn't want Brian spending any more time with Allie than he had to. The sooner the police had the real culprit in hand, the better it was for everyone.

I called Janet Graham to check in. "So, what have you got for me?" I asked only to hear her dry laughter.

"Geez, Andy, it's been maybe three hours since I left your mom's house. You do realize this isn't *CSI* where a homicide investigation gets wrapped up in sixty minutes give or take twenty for commercials?"

After I'd grumbled for her to "get cracking," I hung up and got back to my homework: watching the rest of Season One of *The Wedding Belle*.

This time, I settled down on the couch armed with a bottle of Honest Tea and a bag of veggie chips. And it was sustenance I would need to get through endless scenes where Olivia and her minions prepared for some of the most garish weddings I'd ever seen, or heard of, for that matter. Cakes coated with twenty-four-karat gold dust, four hundred guests dressed up like characters from *Game of Thrones,* even a bride arriving by helicopter and messing up everyone else's hair in the process.

Oh, yes, and there was plenty of drama involving Olivia and anyone else who dared stand in a frame with her. She argued with bossy mothers-of-the-brides, cajoled fathers-of-the-brides into expanding their wedding budget ad infinitum, and she fired and hired more assistants, all but one running off in tears. The sole standout was a blonde named Candy. Instead of crying, she called Olivia a bitch, claimed she'd ruined her life, and slapped her hard enough to leave a handprint on La Belle from Hell's cheek.

For a few minutes anyway, I had Candy on my suspect list, until I Googled her name and saw that she'd ended up on another Salvo Productions reality show called *The Devil's Apprentice*. In that one, contestants vied for a position in the firm of a pompous real estate mogul. I figured that after her experience working for Olivia, Candy had a good shot at winning the whole shebang.

I found myself wondering if the slap had been written into the script. The further I got into the season, the more everything about the show seemed very deliberate, if not downright staged. Surely not every day was jam-packed with drama in the average event planner's life.

But on *The Wedding Belle,* the soap opera quotient ramped up and up and up until the final episode of Season One when things really exploded. That was the show where Jasper Pippin stood up to Olivia and got his ass kicked to the curb. It also featured the hiring of Terra Smith—seemingly Olivia's opposite—and showcased the relationship between Olivia and Draco with Olivia inadvertently (ha, right!) catching a bride's bouquet and later walking into her bedroom with the ribbon-tied blue succulents and white spray roses in one hand—and Draco in the other—before shutting the door.

The moment I saw them together, I let out a snort.

I knew in my gut that they weren't a real couple, and it wasn't because of anything either of them did or didn't do. The designer formerly known as Melvin Mellon was nearly a decade younger than Olivia and he was *way* prettier. She might have had the face of a homegrown Texas pageant girl, but he had an air of mystery and the looks of an Eastern European hunk with silky dark hair, brown eyes, slim nose, and full lips. If he were on the cover of a romance novel, it would sell a million copies. Plus, he openly flirted with other women—especially Terra—right under Olivia's nose.

But the real kicker was something only a school mate of La Belle from Hell would know: Olivia had always dated older guys, all with nice cars and rich fathers, but never more than average looks. Everyone at Hockaday could recognize her M.O. Nope, she never would have hooked up with anyone who outshined her in youth and beauty, but Draco did both in spades. Maybe he wasn't gay, but I didn't buy that he was sleeping with Olivia. I had to wonder how much of the show—and her life—was real and how much was fake.

I shut down my laptop and pressed my fingers to my aching temples.

Something told me that Terra knew the truth. As Mother had pointed out, there was more to Terra than met the eye. I just had to hope she didn't see through my faux wedding planning before I had a chance to learn what deep, dark secrets Olivia had been hiding.

When my phone rang, playing the ring tone for Def Leppard's "Animal," I jumped and dumped my laptop to the couch.

I knew it was Malone before I picked up.

"What's wrong?" I said, ever the optimist.

"Sorry, babe"—he sighed—"but I'm not going to make it home for dinner. Allie just talked to her friend in the DA's office. It sounds like they're working hard and fast to build a case against Millie. They're setting up interviews with anyone who knew Olivia La Belle and subpoenaing footage for Olivia's show that hasn't aired yet. Sounds like an arrest warrant could come down anytime, so we've got to get our ducks in a row ASAP."

"Oh, my God, they *are* going after Millie. They're not looking for anyone else," I breathed the words, my heart pounding. How could this be happening? There were plenty of other suspects, people who despised Olivia more than the Cake Lady.

"We're gearing up for the worst," Brian said, "but we believe in Millie. So don't give up, Andy."

"I'm not," I assured him. I just had to work faster to find some answers.

"We're ordering pizza so we can keep working," Brian said. "You okay?"

No, I wasn't okay. My faith in the justice system was being shaken yet again. I wanted to believe that innocent people never went to jail, but I knew otherwise. Still, I drew in a deep breath, exhaled, and managed to sound halfway calm as I answered, "I'm all right. I'm getting ready to head to Mother's for dinner. Should I say something to Millie? Have you talked to her? Does she already know?"

"Look, I'm bringing her downtown to the office tomorrow so she can talk to the whole team. We have to go over every minute detail of her relationship with Olivia and set up interviews of our own, like with you," Malone replied. "Maybe you can come down in the afternoon?"

"Yeah, sure," I said. I would be more than happy to talk their ears off about Olivia La Belle and what I knew.

"We should get some autopsy results by then, too. So chin up, Kendricks, and don't make tonight any rougher for Millie, okay? Let her enjoy a nice meal and get some sleep tonight if she can. She's going to have a rough road ahead."

"This sucks," I said, and not for the first time. "Give me a call when you're heading home. I love you," I said.

"Ditto."

Then he was gone.

I gathered up my things to head to Mother's house, hoping I could act something other than morose at dinner knowing the cops had set their sights on Millie.

Chapter 21

I heard the voices coming from the kitchen as soon as I let myself in. There was music, too, and it sounded very much like Frank Sinatra singing, "I've Got You Under My Skin." As I pulled my key from the lock and shut the door, I realized I was bopping to the beat, my shoulders swaying.

It had been a long time since I'd heard these walls filled with song. The house felt alive again, like it had a real beating heart. My dad used to play music all the time when I was growing up. I still remember the old LPs he reverently placed on the turntable of his RCA stereo with the big-ass speakers. He loved the Rat Pack, Elvis, and Nat King Cole, and he'd introduced me to Maria Callas, Luciano Pavarotti, and Beverly Sills before I even understood what opera was. "It's as though the words alone aren't enough. There's so much raw emotion," he had told me, "that they have to be sung."

He was every bit a man's man. He liked skeet shooting—but not hunting anything with a beating heart, thank God—and he loved sports, especially golf and Malone's passion, hockey. But my father wasn't afraid to admit he loved the arts, too. I think he was the reason I'd fallen in love with drawing and painting and sculpture back in school. And books—how he adored books! It was no wonder I'd been such a daddy's girl. I had always found him to be the more sensitive of my parents, and I went to him more often than to my mother when I had a problem.

How I wished he were here now, I thought, and I felt myself choke up.

If only I could run to him and have him enfold me in his arms. It didn't matter how much time had passed. I still missed him like crazy.

I wondered how I was going to get married without him walking me down the aisle. There was no one who could fill my dad's shoes, not even my soon-to-be stepfather, Stephen, as nice as he was. That was another reason I was dragging my heels over actual wedding plans. I was no more certain of what to do about my Big Day than I was about how to find Olivia's killer and clear Millie's name.

What would Daddy have advised me to do? Would he tell me it was best if I stayed out of the mess entirely? Would he suggest that I sit back and let the police—and Malone—do their jobs? Would he have insisted I twiddle my thumbs while I waited to be called as the prosecution's star witness?

No, I thought, letting out a slow breath. I was sure that my father wouldn't choose any of the above. He would tell me what he always had: to follow my heart. Maybe it got me into trouble sometimes. Maybe it even made me act like a brainless fool. But I didn't care. I had to do what I felt was right.

I cleared the lump from my throat and called out, "Hello, hello!"

Not surprisingly, no one answered.

Clearly, more was going on in the kitchen than just the music. There was the warm, inviting scent of something baking in the oven, and I knew my mother couldn't possibly be responsible. Was Millie playing chef?

As the final notes of "Under My Skin" trailed off and Frank began to croon "Strangers in the Night," I followed his voice and the tantalizing smell. Halfway there, I heard a throaty burst of laughter.

Was that my mother?

Was she *drunk*?

As soon as I'd passed the butler's pantry and entered the kitchen, I hesitated, my eyes doing a double take. For an instant I thought Sandy Beck had returned early from her visit with her sister and was dancing around the room in oven mitts while Cissy sat on a stool at the granite island, singing out loud and tapping the toe of her pump against the foot rail. She waved a glass of wine in the air, and I saw the bottle nearby. It looked like she'd broken out her favorite Château Margaux Bordeaux.

I very nearly blurted out, *Sandy, you're home!* Then I blinked and realized it was Millie dressed in a pair of jeans and one of Sandy's classic sweater sets. She had her white hair brushed away from her face and held back by a plaid headband. Her eyes looked bright behind her owlish glasses. And she was singing as loudly—and as off-key—as my mother while she opened the double oven doors to check on whatever scrumptious-smelling recipe she was cooking.

After closing the oven doors, Millie did a quick spin as if twirled by some imaginary partner, and my mother chortled merrily.

My hand went to my mouth, and I stifled my own laughter.

What a pair! You would have thought the two of them were long lost friends. And maybe in a way they were. They had known each other as long as I'd been alive, yet they'd never really mixed or mingled. I couldn't help but think it was a good thing they'd been brought together like this. My mother could use more down-to-earth friends like Millie and Sandy. She had enough superficial society pals to field several ball clubs.

For a moment I just hung back and watched them, loving the sight of Millie and my mother so relaxed. It was wonderful that Millie had taken up Cissy's offer to stay over, since apparently Stephen wouldn't return until the next afternoon. That Millie didn't want to be alone was understandable. I'm not sure I'd want to go home to an empty house that had been rifled through by the cops, especially after having spent the morning at the police station being treated like a criminal. That kind of thing tended to shake a person up.

I waited until Sinatra's voice trailed off again before I made a point of stomping through the doorway into the kitchen and saying, "Hey! It looks like a party's going on. What have I missed?"

"Andrea!" Mother drawled, swiveling on the stool and nearly missing the granite when she set down her wineglass. "I didn't hear you come in!"

"Oh, Andy, you're here! Wonderful!" Millie chimed in. She plucked off an oven mitt and reached for the CD player that Sandy had installed beneath the cabinetry. Poor Frankie got cut off in the midst of crooning about the summer wind that came blowin' in off the sea. "I'm making beef Wellington," she told me, her face aglow, "and I've got glazed carrots and green beans almondine in the oven as well. There's plenty for four." She glanced around me. "Where's Mr. Malone?"

"He couldn't make it," I said. Millie looked crestfallen. "But don't stop dancing on his account. I'll take him home some leftovers," I promised, setting my bag on the floor and slipping onto the empty stool beside Mother. "Wow, beef Wellington. And I thought pastry chefs only knew how to make pastry."

Millie's smile returned, although it seemed to stutter. "My granny was a fabulous cook," she explained, "a disciple of Julia Child more or less. She taught me everything she knew about cooking and baking, and I fell in love with both."

"What a coincidence," I said, leaning over to nudge Cissy with an elbow, "my mother taught me everything she knows about cooking and baking."

"And Andrea's grandmother taught *me* everything she knew, which is a whole lot of nothing," Mother said and guffawed, waving her arms in front of her like a referee after a bad field goal. She narrowly missed knocking over her wineglass. "I can't even boil water to save my life."

"I used to cook for Henry every night until I got too busy with the cake shop," Millie went on, and the hesitant smile vanished. "I actually thought of opening a restaurant back then, one that had its own bakery. Then when Henry passed away, I had no one to cook for. We never had children. It used to eat at me a little but now I'm glad. I wouldn't want them to see what's happening now because of that damned Olivia . . ."

Her voice trailed off, her chin quivering. It made me want to cry.

"Oh, Millie, I'm sorry for you . . . for Henry . . . I'm sorry for everything," I said, and I would have jumped down from my stool to go hug her if my mother hadn't slid off hers and headed Millie's way.

"Now, now," Cissy cooed and draped an arm around Millie's shoulders. "Don't let's get maudlin," she said. "Things are always darkest before dawn, *n'est-ce pas*? It will work out, you'll see. The police will find the bad guy, just like they always do on *Law & Order*, and you'll be free to come over and teach Andy a thing or two about how to use an oven so Mr. Malone won't die of starvation."

"You're very sweet," Millie said, and her smile reappeared. But this time it was melancholic.

"Seriously, Millie, that would rock," I chimed in, trying to keep the mood upbeat. "It'd be a chance to see you more often besides. You were part of my growing-up, you know. Some of my best memories are of your cakes."

"Oh, Andy, that's so dear of you to say." Millie sighed, and I saw a tiny spark ignited in her eyes.

"Please, feel free to come by and take over my kitchen now and then, Millicent. It would be one way to get my darling daughter here more often. I hardly see her as it is," Cissy opined and pouted at me.

I felt a sudden stab of guilt, because it was true that I didn't get to Mother's house much these days. I was always so busy with my work and with painting and hanging out with Malone. I needed to make more of an effort, I told myself. Cissy wasn't getting any younger, and neither was I. Soon Stephen would be my stepfather and, one of these years, I'd have rug rats crawling around my ankles. Life was changing so quickly, and I wasn't doing a very good job at keeping up. I didn't want to get to a place in my life where I was looking back, like Millie, and counting my regrets.

"If you give me cooking lessons," I said, "I could offer my Web design services. Anytime you want a site update, just call."

"I may very well take you up on that, Andy," Millie said, "maybe once we're caught up at the shop. The crew's doing the best they can without me, but I need to get back to work without this noose hanging over my head."

"Malone will have you back to work in no time," I said, avoiding her eyes. I slipped off my seat to wander over to the ovens. Turning on the light inside, I took a peek at the bubbling carrots with glaze and the green beans almondine. They were a nice distraction. "Everything looks amazing," I told her, and that was no lie.

Millie blew out a breath. "Truly, I appreciate what you're trying to do, the both of you, but I'm so afraid that I'll be—" She hesitated. "—that Mr. Malone won't be able to—" She couldn't go on. She put her head in her hands and gently shook it.

"There, there, sweetheart, it's okay," Cissy said. "I'd be frightened, too, but you have to believe in your own innocence, or no one else will believe you."

I watched the pair of them hugging each other, and that darned lump in my throat returned with a vengeance. My mother was surprising me a lot these days.

Millie took a deep breath and lifted her chin. "I want to believe in myself and in Mr. Malone, but it's scary," she admitted and shivered. "I have a bad feeling this might be the last beef Wellington I'll ever make." She stopped talking, and Mother squeezed her shoulders.

"Mother's right," I said. "You can't think like that. You will make beef Wellington again, and you will bake more cakes. Don't let Olivia take that away from you." If I sounded angry, I was. I was furious at Olivia, not only for the misery she'd inflicted on my younger life, but for making Millie's life miserable even after death. "What's going on is totally crappy, yes, but it's not the end."

"On the contrary," my mother jumped in, "it's the beginning, Millicent, of an even stronger you. It's a lot like losing the love of your life and feeling a piece of yourself die as well, or being diagnosed with an illness that seems like a death sentence until you realize that it's not. It's just a dreadful curveball that fate has thrown at you. You're being forced to trudge through the muck, and it's painful. But you will survive. You survived losing Henry, didn't you? And I'll bet at the time you thought you never would."

"Yes," Millie whispered. "I did."

"There, you see," my mother said, "all things are possible."

"Oh, Cissy, you're right." Millie lifted up her glasses to brush tears from her cheeks. "I have to trudge through the muck," she repeated, nodding to herself. "I will get through this. I have no choice."

"Of course, you will," Mother told her. "I have faith in you, Millicent."

I stood there, looking at my mother and blinking, utterly dumbfounded.

The force of her comments—the compassion she'd shown Millie—surprised me far more than Millie's beef Wellington. What the heck was happening to her? She was turning into a fully empathetic being, sensitive to the plight of others and downright huggable.

The timers began to ping on the double ovens, and Millie suddenly forgot her woes. She sprang into action, pulling on oven mitts and withdrawing meat and vegetables from the racks.

The steamy goodness of the food pervaded the kitchen, and I almost forgot that there was anything going on worth worrying about. My stomach growled. I hadn't done enough eating today, and I was suffering the consequences.

"Andrea, could you set the table?" my mother was saying, but I couldn't move for a minute or two as I watched Millie begin to carve the beef, the knife slicing through it like butter. Juice from the pink center of the meat dripped as she filled a silver serving dish with plump pieces. The sight unsettled me, and I pressed my eyes shut, hoping that would ward off the thought of finding Millie standing over Olivia with the bloody cake knife.

"Andrea." Cissy pinched my arm.

"Ouch," I said and opened my eyes wide. I rubbed my skin where she'd left a mark.

"Sorry, pumpkin, but it looked like you were sleepin' on your feet. Can you grab some silverware," she said, unapologetic. "I'll get the napkins from the linen closet."

"Yes, ma'am," I told her, "right away."

Thankfully, no one said anything more about Olivia or the mess she'd left behind. Instead, we all sat down at the kitchen table and Millie led us in a very simple grace, something I hadn't done in longer than I'd cared to admit.

After the "Amen," Mother began nattering on about some upcoming charity ball or another, and I found my appetite again. I dug into the beef Wellington even though I didn't usually eat red meat, particularly when it was pink. But it was calling to me like a Siren's song, and I didn't fight it. As I listened to Cissy and Millie chat about non-earth-shattering events like Penny Ryan Trippelhorn's real due date and a braless Jennifer Aniston appearing at the NorthPark Neiman Marcus to plug perfume, I did nothing but chew, savor, and swallow until I'd cleared my plate of carrots and green beans and beef and, à la Oliver Twist, politely asked, "Please, may I have more?"

Millie seemed thrilled to see me demolish the meal she'd prepared, although I noticed she barely touched hers. Ditto my too-thin mother who ate, like, three carrots, two beans, and two forkfuls of beef before she pushed away her plate, groaning and insisting that she couldn't eat a bite more without popping the button on her size zero pants. Maybe it was the wine—I abstained, but Cissy and Millie managed to empty the bottle— because suddenly Millie began to talk about Olivia.

"It seems wrong, doesn't it, when someone with the face of an angel can be so cruel. She wasn't so bad at first, just arrogant." Millie waved a hand dismissively. "But so many young people are these days, like the world belongs to them. Once she got that silly show, she went from bad to worse, treating us all like we were her minions, there to serve her. She had no respect for anyone's talent or hard work. She only cared about what we could do for her."

Mother and I both made sympathetic noises but neither of us spoke.

Millie paused and wet her lips. "I worked my fingers to the bone on Penny Ryan's cake, and to hear that Olivia had bad-mouthed me at the reception, pretending she didn't know the first layer of the cake was foam? I was horrified. Of course, she knew every detail about that cake. She had what amounted to an architectural drawing of the danged thing on her tablet the day we met to discuss it months ago. She made me study it and sketch it out on paper for my own file."

Very clever of Olivia, I mused, not giving Millie the electronic file or a hard copy so Millie wouldn't have proof to back up her words that the fake first layer had been Olivia's idea.

Hearing that reinforced my theory that Olivia's take-down of Millie was scripted. Was it Olivia's doing? Did she figure that would spice up the drama? Or had someone else written that particular script? What about Janet's contact, Sammi Garber, the producer?

"Did you get the feeling Olivia meant to embarrass you from the start?" I said, because I couldn't help myself. "Like she set you up?"

Millie looked confused. "Set me up? I don't know, Andy. All I do know is that she was trying to get me to write the cake off, and I wasn't going to let her win. I wasn't going to let her drive me out of business like she did Jasper." Her voice turned into an angry whisper. "I could have killed her for double-dealing like that—"

I glanced at Mother.

"—but I didn't," she finished and slugged down what wine was left in her glass. "Instead I was planning to sue her and that show of hers. Someone had to make her stop behaving so recklessly.

Though I guess someone did, didn't they?" She turned her owl eyes upon us. "Only it wasn't me."

"Had you told anyone yet," I asked, "about wanting to sue?"

"I told Olivia." Millie nodded. "I sent her an email telling her I was going to take her down, no matter what it cost."

I groaned inwardly. I could only imagine what the police thought of that email when they'd read it. It sounded like a death threat, not a warning that a lawsuit was forthcoming.

"Is there anything else you can think of that might help your case?" I said. "Maybe there's some small detail you didn't figure was important at the time."

Millie set her mouth in a grim line. "You know, I've been wracking my brains, trying to think of something important that I missed, something that would help the police find her killer, but it's all such a blur. Although"—she bunched up her forehead—"something odd did come to me as I lay down to rest on your guest bed this afternoon, Cissy, but it's so foggy that I'm not sure if it's real or a dream." My mother leaned forward, like she was going to interrupt but didn't. "When I went into Olivia's building and found her office door unlocked, I heard strange sounds above me. A thumping . . . or maybe it was more like a drumming that got dimmer and dimmer."

A thumping or drumming sound?

"Like footsteps?" I suggested. "Could it have been someone running away?"

Millie cocked her head. "I wondered that same

thing. Only the building is just two stories tall. If someone ran, they were going across the roof." She sighed. "I must have been imagining things."

My mother glanced at me across the table, as though she was waiting for me to decipher what Millie meant.

I wasn't sure what she wanted me to do or say. I hadn't seen anyone else in the building. Millie was right: if she'd heard footsteps drumming overhead that meant someone was on the rooftop. So how did they get down? Had they used a fire escape and left a getaway vehicle parked somewhere near the lot at Highland Park Village? That certainly implied lots of malice aforethought.

Unless the noises Millie thought she heard overhead at Olivia's office were something else, or weren't real at all, as she'd suggested, and whatever drug my mother had slipped into her naptime tea had caused her mind to play tricks.

"You need to tell Brian," I said firmly. "He'll know what to do."

"I'm seeing him tomorrow," Millie replied. "He's coming for me early so we can get to work. I hope I can sleep so I'm clear-headed enough to be of help."

"Watch some mindless TV or have Mother bore you with her tale of running into Bill Gates outside the President Wilson Hotel in Geneva and shoving her bags in his hands, thinking he was a dorky-looking bellman," I suggested. "That'll knock you unconscious."

"Oh, Andrea," my mother pooh-poohed me.

"I do need to rest," Millie said and took off her

glasses to rub her eyes. She looked utterly wrung out. "But I'm afraid I might stare at the ceiling all night."

"You will sleep," my mother said, "I'll make sure of it."

I had to wonder if she'd laced Millie's glass of wine or had plans to give her more spiked tea.

"First, let me take care of these." Millie started to stand and pick up her plate, but I made a noise of protest.

"No, no, I'll clear," I told her. "You two should head into the den and put your feet up." I pushed my chair back from the table to start gathering the dirty dishes.

As I took a load over to the sink, I heard my phone playing "Highway to Hell." I scrambled for my bag and dug it up, hoping like heck it was Malone calling from an office phone rather than his cell, telling me he was heading home.

"Hey!" I said without checking the number. "I missed you."

"Aw, shucks, Andy, that's so sweet. I missed you, too," replied a voice that wasn't Brian's, or any man's for that matter. It belonged to Janet Graham.

"Sorry, I thought you were Brian," I said, trying not to sound disappointed. "So what's up?"

"I found him," she said, fairly bubbling with excitement.

But my brain was so addled I couldn't recall exactly who she'd been looking for. "Found who?"

"The florist whose career Olivia turned to toast," she said in a rush, and I heard music and chatter in the background, like she was calling from a party. "I had to ask around . . . and around . . . and around, but I found Jasper Pippin. He didn't retire to the Keys. He's been lying low practically right under our nose, and I've made a date for us to meet with him tomorrow."

Chapter 22

 Malone called not long after Janet, saying he'd left the office and was on his way home. So I kissed my mother on the cheek and squeezed Millie's hand, telling them both "Good night." I had to hope that tomorrow would bring some good news. Malone and his defense team at ARGH were on the offense, and maybe whatever preliminary autopsy results they got would be in Millie's favor. He'd told me to have faith, and I was trying.

Regardless, my chest constricted as I drove away from Beverly Drive. This wasn't how Millie should be spending her golden years. She should be doing what she loved most: working in her shop, baking cakes that made people happy, even opening up that restaurant she'd always dreamed of.

I couldn't turn on the radio as I headed back to

the condo. My head felt so crowded with thoughts that there was no room for music or chatter. I realized I suddenly had a very full Monday and none of it was work-related. In reverse chronology, I had the interview at Brian's office in the afternoon, time to be determined. At eleven o'clock I had Draco's bridal show at the merchandise mart. Before that, at nine o'clock, Janet was picking me up so we could visit a swanky retirement village called Belle Meade.

And, no, I wasn't looking to commit my mother.

I knew the place well because an old bunkmate of mine from Camp Longhorn used to run it before she ran into some trouble. According to Janet, Jasper Pippin had been quietly working at Belle Meade as their in-house floral technician. He was responsible for visiting the downtown wholesale flower market weekly to put together their fresh arrangements, and he taught classes on flower-arranging for the residents.

"Kind of a come-down from owning his own shop and doing galas and weddings for the biggest names in Big D," Janet had remarked, and I couldn't disagree.

But was it enough of a motive for murder?

Janet had talked to the current manager of Belle Meade, who'd given us a pass to attend Jasper's Monday morning flower arranging class. Jan had claimed she was doing a piece on extracurricular activities for the young at heart for the *PCP*.

"It'll make a nice sidebar to my feature on Olivia's life and untimely death," my friend had informed me. "One of those 'where are they now' bits."

"As in, here's what one of Olivia's victims—and possibly her killer—has been up to since La Belle from Hell ruined his career?"

"That's perfect, Kendricks. Mind if I use that for my opening line?" Janet had dryly remarked before hanging up.

I didn't care so much about Janet's cover story as the fact that I'd have a chance to size up Jasper Pippin in person and see if my first impression was, "Oh, yes, I can see him stabbing Olivia in the neck with a cake knife."

When I reached my parking lot and pulled into my slot, I saw Brian's Acura neatly tucked into my guest space. He'd turned on the porch light but I didn't see any lights beaming through the windows. It wasn't that late. Had he already gone to bed?

I went in quietly, setting down my keys and bag on the kitchen counter. The only sound I detected was the air conditioner whirring.

"Bri?" I said as I tiptoed into the bedroom. "Are you awake?"

His reply was a softly grunted, "No."

I toed off my shoes and pulled off my yoga pants, dropping them onto the carpet. Then I struggled out of my bra without removing my T-shirt. I tossed the bra to the floor and crawled into bed.

I snuggled up beside him, setting my hand on his chest and my head on his shoulder. I felt his heart's steady thump beneath my palm. At first I thought he had dozed off in the few seconds it had taken me to undress. Then I heard his voice, quiet in the dark.

"How was Millie?" he said.

"She's trying to be brave," I told him, "but she's scared out of her mind." I felt his arm wrap around my back. "Mother's trying equally hard to distract her." And possibly slipping mickeys in her tea, I left unsaid.

"Cissy's a good egg."

"If not a little scrambled," I replied, and he chuckled, drawing me nearer. For a while I lay there beside him, tucked against his warmth. I listened to him breathe and tried to clear my head. I wanted to close my eyes and drift off. I wished I could. But I imagined I smelled Allie's perfume, and I found myself picturing the two of them working late, Allie sitting much too close to him.

Stop it, I chastised myself and swallowed down my jealousy. Brian and Allie hadn't been downtown at ARGH making out. They were working toward the same goal I was: to keep Millie out of jail. So instead of making some idiotic comment, like, *Can you tell Allie to nix the patchouli?* I asked him, "You're going to get Millie off, right? She's not going to prison for something she didn't do, is she?"

"Not if I can help it," he whispered into my hair. "Let's get some sleep, okay? It's been a long day, and I'm beat. And you've been through the wringer, too."

He was right. It had been one of the longest days of my life.

"I love you, Brian Malone," I said and tightened my hold on him.

He nuzzled my neck and murmured, "I love you, too."

So this time when I closed my eyes, I envisioned Malone and me on our honeymoon, far away from Allie Price and from my mother, on some tropical island in the middle of the Pacific Ocean. Somehow I dozed off.

When I woke up, blurry daylight edged the window shades, and I heard Brian's razor humming in the bathroom. It was almost like yesterday had never happened, I thought as I yawned and stretched before turning on my laptop. Only yesterday's horrors were real as a glance at the local news headlines on my laptop would attest: THE WEDDING BELLE SLAIN, ARREST PENDING SAY COPS.

Oh, boy.

My stomach fluttered.

It was strange, the way nothing had changed and everything had changed in twenty-four hours. My life would go on, maybe better than before. Olivia's death had closed a rough chapter, and the unwritten chapters that lay ahead promised to be the best part of the whole book. There was just one hitch: Millie. Until she was off the hook, my story was bookmarked.

Luckily, I had plenty of nosing around to do, enough to keep me very busy. But first I had to brush my teeth.

Brian waited until I'd rinsed to kiss me. Then he asked what I was doing all day and whether I could come down to the office at two o'clock. I told him I was seeing Janet to help her with a story and then to a fashion show with Mother—he raised his eyebrows at the latter but not the former—

and I should be done by lunchtime. Satisfied, he kissed me again before grabbing his briefcase and leaving to pick up Millie at Mother's house.

Fifteen minutes later I had my face washed, hair brushed, and clothes on. I was eating a banana and trying to get some work done—adding pages to a local breast cancer recovery group's support site—when Janet showed up in her silver VW sedan, tooting her horn out front.

I could see her vintage yellow cloche hat through the glass even before I jumped into the passenger's seat and was able to take in her entire ensemble: orange hair, black glasses, black shirt, black belt, black and yellow striped skirt, and black combat boots with laces up the shins.

"Great outfit. Let me guess. You're the boogie-woogie bumblebee from Company C," I said, smiling as I buckled up and she put the car in gear.

"Good one." She grinned. "Well, Jasper Pippin's into flowers, right? I figured I'd go with the theme."

"So you're going to pump him for pollen?"

"Until it stings," she said with a hearty *yuk-yuk*, and I groaned.

Hey, at least she was in a good mood, I thought as she pushed the car into Preston Road traffic and hightailed it south to Forest Lane. Maybe she'd awakened this morning, too, and realized she could forever close the book on the bad times with Olivia. It was rather liberating.

We'd barely gone a mile before Janet started to rattle on about calling the Salvo Productions office and talking to her friend Sammi about getting stills from Penny Ryan's wedding, but I was only half listening until I heard her say, "I asked about that guy, Pete, but she said they didn't have a cameraman on staff named Pete anything."

"What?" I turned away from the window. "Of course there's a cameraman named Pete. I saw him with Olivia. I heard her call him that. Maybe it's a nickname?"

"I described him to Sammi—the tattoo sleeves, the beard, just like you said—and she seemed really adamant that he doesn't exist. In fact," Janet glanced away from the road as she told me, "Sammi insists they didn't send anyone from *The Wedding Belle* to shoot at Penny Ryan's wedding. She said they couldn't get permission from Lester Dickens. He threatened to have any of the crew arrested for trespassing if they showed up on his property."

"Wait, what?" I stopped her because it made no sense. "Of course Pete was shooting for *The Wedding Belle*. Why else would he have been there?"

"He could have been part of the wedding photographer's party," Jan suggested.

"No," I said, because I knew that wasn't right. Pete didn't seem to have had anything to do with the official photographer. Another guy had shot all the formal wedding pics, and he had his own crew, all women, who'd taken the sanctioned shots of the wedding party and the families. Pete hadn't been anywhere around for that. "Olivia sure acted like he was with her show. When I interrupted her yelling at Millie for showing up an hour late with the cake, she had Pete take five. Then she ranted about ratings and how she had to ramp up the drama to hold onto her show. And when Olivia pulled a hissy fit about the cake, Pete was there, catching it all on his camera. If he wasn't with Salvo Productions, Olivia sure acted like he was."

"That's weird," Janet said, precisely what I was thinking. "You told me they confiscated the guests' cell phones, right?"

"Yep, and security was tight."

"But somehow Olivia snuck this Pete guy in to record for her show? Wouldn't Lester Dickens have had him tossed once he saw him working the wedding?"

"You'd think so," I agreed.

"And if Dickens didn't throw him out, surely the Ryans would have," Jan said, and I nodded. "But no one did?"

"No."

"Something's fishy, indeed," she said.

That was exactly what I'd told my mother after Olivia's wedding cake drama. Who was Pete? And why was he at Penny Ryan's wedding? It was almost as though he'd been present just to record Olivia's dressing down of Millie when she was late with the cake and Olivia's histrionics over the cake-cutting. Was it the Wedding Belle's idea to have a rogue cameraman on-hand so that she could pressure Millie to drop the $10,000 bill? Or was there more to the story that I didn't see?

"Can you ask your buddy Sammi if the routine with Millie's cake was scripted," I said, "because Millie insists Olivia knew the bottom layer was

Styrofoam, that it was her idea in the first place. I got the impression Olivia pulled her pissy diva routine for the camera."

"Sure, I'll ask," Janet said. "Anything else?"

"We have to keep digging," I told her, more convinced than ever that something very twisted was going on with Olivia toward the end, something that had worked its way up to her murder. And either Millie had been unfortunate enough to get caught in the crosshairs or she'd been the perfect patsy.

Chapter 23

Janet and I were both quiet as she pulled the VW onto the grounds of Belle Meade. Once we'd turned off Forest Lane, the car rolled past tall privacy fencing anchored by two stone pillars topped by huge carriage lanterns. Janet slowed down as we thumped over speed bumps toward a security guard's booth.

"Hey, there, I'm Janet Graham from the *Park Cities Press*. I should be on the visitor's list. I spoke with Madge yesterday," she said after rolling down her window to check in with the white-haired guard.

I thought I recognized him from when I'd visited Belle Meade with Cissy about a year ago. Wasn't his name Bob or Sam? I couldn't recall which, and he didn't give me a second glance as he looked into the car and waved us past.

"It's gorgeous, isn't it?" Janet remarked, steering the car beneath the overhang of tall, gnarled oaks toward a plantation-style house with pillars straight out of *Gone with the Wind.* "I hope I stick around to tack on at least fifty more years of mileage. If I do, I want to move into this place. They have every amenity you can think of," she said. "It's like Disneyland for real grown-ups."

"You should probably make your reservation now," I told her. "I think the waiting list is something like ten years."

"I'll check it out while we're here, see if they have a spot I can reserve in another half a century," she said and smiled.

I didn't know if Janet really wanted to book a villa at Belle Meade when she reached Golden Girlhood, but if she did, good for her.

Personally, I hoped that Malone and I could live out our old age in a house we bought together, somewhere quiet on a bit of acreage so we didn't have neighbors too close. I think being in a condo for so long had burned me out on living in what amounted to a human ant colony.

"When I go," Janet said out of the blue, "I hope they have to pry my knotty old hands off my keyboard."

"I want to fade out with my bony claws clutching a paintbrush," I told her, adding, "and if I'm really lucky, with Brian stiff as a board in front of the TV, watching hockey across the room."

"Yep," Jan replied, "that sounds perfect for you two lovebirds. None of that mushy holding hands stuff when you croak in tandem."

"Okay, so I'll clutch my paintbrush one-handed

and hold Malone's hand with the other while he stares at hockey on the forty-two-inch screen across the room," I said, laughing, before I realized what we were talking about. "Listen to us! We're positively morbid. It's Olivia's fault, for making us think about life and death."

Janet shrugged. "If you can't joke about what scares you most, what's the point?"

"Yeah, what's the point," I repeated as Janet pulled the VW into a visitor's spot in front of Belle Meade's pillared façade. She shut off the engine and twisted around to grab her big bag from the backseat.

"We're supposed to stop by the management office and then head to Activity Room 3 where Jasper's holding his class."

So I dutifully followed on Janet's combat boot heels, entering the main building of Belle Meade with its oiled wood and crystal chandeliers. I trailed her into the management office, where she introduced me to Madge Malloy, the woman who'd taken over after my friend Annabelle's departure. I didn't speak except to smile and say, "Nice to meet you."

Janet seemed to have the patter down perfectly, telling Madge she'd send her courtesy copies once the piece on Jasper's floral-arranging class appeared in the *PCP*. Then Madge dropped us off at Activity Room 3. Although we were ten minutes early for class, the chairs were filled with chattering women who gave us the once-over as we walked in. And I didn't think it was just because we were the only ones who appeared to be under sixty. The crowd of bespectacled eyes homed in on Janet and her bee-inspired ensemble.

"Nice topper," one of them said, admiring Janet's cloche hat. She was an elegant-looking woman with her gray hair pulled back into a ponytail and a paisley scarf around her neck. "My mother left me a few Caroline Reboux originals that I should dust off. They're still in their boxes."

"Wow, Caroline Reboux in boxes," Janet said breathlessly, and I half expected her to jump in the woman's lap and wriggle like an excited puppy. "That's vintage gold."

"Real treasures never age," the woman replied with a smile.

Janet smiled back.

"Okay, now that you've made a new friend, can we sit down?" I whispered, nudging her toward the only pair of unoccupied chairs in the back. "Guess you'll have to grill Jasper after class, huh?"

"Yeah, Madge said he'd give me a few minutes," Janet responded and tugged open her bag. She withdrew a point-and-shoot camera, which she passed over to me. "Hold this, would you?" Then she got out a tiny notebook and pen. "Yes, I still take notes longhand," she said when I gave her a look.

Jasper hadn't shown yet, though there was a rectangular table set in the front of the room. Its surface was covered with buckets containing greenery and an assortment of peonies. There were as many vases as women present so I figured that, once Jasper gave some instruction, he let his students have at it.

Soon enough the sound of footsteps could be heard tapping on the tiled hallway and the women seemed to sit up straighter. Their chatter stopped.

And into the room swept the same thin, smartly dressed man I'd glimpsed in a few of *The Wedding Belle* episodes. He had on pin-striped black trousers, a mustard-colored jacket, and a patterned black-and-gold cravat.

I nudged Janet and whispered, "I see he got the memo that it was Dress Like a Bee Day."

"Shh," she hushed me with a finger to her lips.

"It's another beautiful morning at Belle Meade, isn't it, girls?" he said to the room at large, and the group replied in unison, "Hello, Jasper."

"Hello, hello," he replied, winking, and he smoothed a hand over his shiny pate.

He may have been a card-carrying member of AARP himself, but he looked fit and agile, moving behind the table to gesture at all the goodies gathered atop it.

"We're doing peonies today, as I'm sure you can see, because nothing says 'spring' like a peony! We'll just stick to three blooms each and do very simple arrangements that'll look perfect on your dresser or vanity. First, let's pick out some hardy greenery," he said, and all the ladies leaned forward to watch him select his foliage.

Then he plucked a small sharp knife from the table and began to pare off unwanted leaves, describing what he was doing every step. He used the knife again to trim the stems of his peonies before he selected a small silver-footed vase.

While he talked and worked, the ladies would

occasionally pepper him with questions like, "Oh, Jasper, tell us that story again about how you did flowers for Richard Burton to give to Elizabeth Taylor when she was filming nearby," or, "We want to hear the one about Audrey Hepburn . . . Sophia Loren . . . Gregory Peck."

So Jasper Pippin entertained them with tales of working with glamorous movie stars back in the day, and Janet busily scribbled notes while I studied the man, wondering if he'd been angry enough about losing his business to attack Olivia.

"I like to strip the leaves off the main buds and put the plumpest blossom in the middle. See?" he explained as he worked his magic with several vases filled with peonies. When he'd finished, the ladies cooed over his artistry. Jasper declared, "Okay, girls, enough of me! Now it's all about you. So come on up here, pick out your greens and your peonies, grab a pair of scissors, and make something pretty to take back to your boudoirs."

As Jasper's rapt audience got up out of their chairs and ambled toward the front of the room, Janet leaned over and said, "So he's the only one who gets a knife?"

"He's good with it, too, isn't he?" I remarked, and I squinted toward Mr. Pippin, trying to imagine him confronting Olivia in her office, snatching up the Tiffany cake knife and stabbing her in the throat before she knew what hit her. "He could have done it," I said, "if he caught Olivia by surprise."

Jasper's smile slipped as he glanced toward us. He brushed a stray leaf from the sleeve of his jacket. Then he tugged at his cuffs. My mother would have called him a dandy.

"I don't know, Andy," Janet whispered back. "He doesn't seem like the kind of guy who'd be okay with getting blood on his clothes."

I sighed. Yes, so it appeared that Jasper was rather meticulous. I'm sure a lot of killers were. It probably just made them a lot harder to catch.

We had to wait another half an hour before the class wrapped up and all the twittering ladies had left with their peony arrangements in hand.

It was only then that Janet stood and approached Belle Meade's resident floral technician. "Mr. Pippin, hello, I'm Janet Graham from the *Park Cities Press*," she said, extending her hand. "Did Madge tell you I was coming by?"

"She did, although I'm not sure I like the idea of talking to the media." Jasper didn't take her hand. He made a point of sticking his into his pocket. "Do you plan to take photographs?" he asked, jerking his chin my way.

It took a second before I remembered I was holding Jan's camera.

Apparently, Janet had forgotten, too. She glanced at me and nodded. "Oh, yes, Andy's helping me today," she said, "but we don't have to shoot you if you're shy."

I didn't get the idea that Jasper Pippin was a wallflower, but he didn't look happy when I raised the camera. Instead, he waved it off.

"I'd rather not, if you don't mind." He screwed up his face. "I don't want to be too firmly associated with my stint here. Perhaps you can photograph the arrangements instead."

"You make it sound as though you're leaving," Janet said.

Jasper smiled. "Nothing is forever, is it?"

"Hmm, I guess not." Janet pointed to the flowers on the table and said, "Take a few shots of the peonies, Kendricks."

"You're Andy Kendricks?" Jasper repeated, giving me a look. "Are you related to Cissy Blevins Kendricks?"

I glanced at Janet before I answered, "Sort of. I'm her daughter."

"Ah." He crossed his arms, tapping a finger to his chin. "You're the one who didn't debut and caused such a stir. I was doing the flowers for the White Glove Society's deb ball that year. They were very upset."

"Um, yes, that was me." Great. A dozen years later and I was still infamous for being the debutante dropout.

"So you ended up taking pictures for the *Park Cities Press*? Ah, well, *c'est la vie*," Jasper said with a sigh, which I took to imply, *I guess that's what happens to trust fund babies who run away from their debut.*

Janet clamped her mouth closed. Knowing her, she probably wanted to retort, *And what's so bad about working for the* Park Cities Press?

"Um, I'll just take pictures of the flowers since that's why I'm here, right?" I said, and Janet nodded.

"Wait, let me arrange them," Jasper said and

went to the table to place the three vases he'd done in a fashionable stagger.

I stood and turned on the camera. There weren't too many ways I could make vases of peonies interesting so I'd only clicked off a few shots before Janet tapped my arm.

"That should do, Andy, thanks."

I settled down into a chair in the front row to watch and listen.

Janet started with an easy lob. "What kind of response have you received to your classes at Belle Meade?"

"It's been inspiring," Jasper said, and his cheeks flushed. "The ladies seem to love it, and I enjoy teaching them what I've learned from my years in the business."

"You owned a shop in the Bishop Arts District for nearly thirty years," Janet said. "Do you miss it?"

"I miss the area, yes," Jasper replied, biting his lip. "It was such a great atmosphere. And I miss the customers, some of whom I'd known since I first opened my doors. Losing them was like a small death." He shrugged and dusted off his sleeves. "But like Lazarus, I've come back to life."

Janet cocked her head. "Do you have something up your sleeve you'd like to discuss?"

Where else would Jasper go if not Belle Meade? I wondered. I had a feeling he'd had few offers for employment after the smack-down on Olivia's show.

"My time at Belle Meade has been lovely and a wonderful opportunity to regroup," he said without giving anything away. "It was fortunate for me that they asked me to share my talents when I needed somewhere to go after—"

Olivia's hatchet job, I nearly shouted out to fill in the blank.

"After you sold off your shop," Janet said instead. "I'm sure that can't have been easy."

Jasper glanced toward the doorway then leaned nearer Janet. He fairly trembled with excitement, like he had a secret he just couldn't hold in. "Off the record—Miss Graham—"

"Yes?"

"Don't quote me on this, but I will be moving on soon."

"What's up?" Janet pressed him. "Do you have plans to open a new shop?"

He put a finger to his lips, tapping and thinking before he replied, "I'm not at liberty to share details just yet. But it won't be long. So leave your card, and I'll call you the moment I can toot my horn. Then you can do a proper interview."

Janet glanced at me, and I shrugged.

What was Jasper up to? Had he been biding his time until Olivia was dead, and now that she was, he had some great opportunity knocking on his door?

"Here you go," Janet said, pulling a business card from her bag and handing it over to him. "Can't you give me a hint?" she asked. "My readers would love to know what you're up to. I'm sure they'd be thrilled to hear you'll have a happy ending to your story after all."

"Well, they'll just have to wait." Jasper smiled.

"But it's going to be bigger than a mere flower shop." He looked at the open door again then lowered his voice. "Promise you won't breathe a word, especially not to Madge. She thinks I'm a permanent fixer already."

"My lips are sealed," Janet said, even pulling an imaginary zipper across them.

No one asked me to pinky swear that I wouldn't discuss Jasper's plans, thank God, so I wouldn't have to feel guilty when I made sure Malone put Jasper Pippin on his "prime suspects" list.

Jasper glanced at the clock on the wall above his head.

"Is there anything else?" he said. "I need to pick up flowers and do new arrangements for the dining room, and I'm creating a spray of lilies for a memorial service·this afternoon, a dear woman who still had so much life left in her."

Janet's chin jerked up. "You don't mean Olivia La Belle?" she asked, which was exactly what I was thinking because I had Olivia on the brain.

"God, no, not Olivia La Belle," Jasper moaned with a pinched expression. "Why would you ask such a thing?"

"You must have heard about her death," Janet said, intrepid reporter that she was. "She was killed in her office yesterday morning."

I sat on the edge of my chair, thinking, Yes, yes, finally! Go get him, Jan!

"Of course I heard. It's all over the news," he replied, glancing down to pluck at lint on his mustard jacket. He mumbled something that I couldn't make out, and apparently neither could Janet.

"Any thoughts you'd care to share?" my friend pressed.

I waited for Jasper to retort something along the lines of, *Nope, I've got nothing to say about that bitch.* But instead he squared his shoulders and uttered, "The world is such a cruel place, isn't it?"

"It certainly is," Janet said and scribbled on her notepad.

Those darned hairs at my nap prickled, and I squirmed in my chair. I cleared my throat, trying to get Jan's attention.

But she ignored me. "So the flowers you're doing for that memorial service, they aren't for Olivia?"

"Absolutely not," Jasper replied and fussed with his cravat. "They're for Grace Louise Fairchild. She was ninety-three and one of Belle Meade's queen bees. She survived five husbands and two children before she breathed her last. She lived here for twenty years, would you believe," he added with a shake of his head. "She was worth a hundred Olivia La Belles, and unlike Olivia she'll actually be missed," he remarked then checked the clock again. "Sorry, girls, but I've got to scoot. It's been nice chatting."

He took off like a rocket.

I got up from the chair to confront Janet. "Why didn't you ask where he was yesterday morning at eight?" I asked, frustrated. "Isn't that why we came? So we could grill him about Olivia's murder?"

"I'm not the police, Andy." Janet gave her glasses an impatient nudge. "I'm not sure he would have told us anything worthwhile besides. You asked me to find him, and I did. And if I can find him, the police can, too. *They* can ask him the tough questions." She tucked her pen and pad in her bag, shaking her hatted head. "Call me crazy, but he doesn't seem like a cold-blooded killer, and even if he was, he wasn't going to blurt out a confession."

"And this observation comes from all the experience you've had interviewing real cold-blooded killers?" I remarked and handed back her camera.

"He just isn't the type."

"Maybe not on the surface," I said. But I'd been around plenty of people who'd seemed entirely normal and did horrible things. "I don't trust him. I get this feeling he's hiding some big secret."

"Yeah, he has a secret all right," Janet said with a sigh. "Like he told us, he's got a new business venture in the works." She looked at me with squinty eyes. "I think you've been watching too much *Castle*. You suspect everyone and read too much into everything. FYI, writers don't get to interview suspects or collect evidence unless the cops don't want anything admissible in court."

"Thanks for the news flash," I grumbled. Yeesh.

"Maybe you should write mysteries instead of trying to create them."

"Hey, I didn't create this one, Olivia did!"

"But you can't leave well enough alone."

Would Nancy Drew have turned a blind eye and let the Cake Lady rot in jail? *Hell, no!* I wanted to say but didn't get a chance.

Janet stuffed the camera into her voluminous

carryall. Then she grabbed my arm. "Come on," she said, "let's go."

"By the way, I don't watch *Castle*," I said with a sniff, then added in a murmur, "much."

I didn't care that Janet thought I was tilting at windmills. Something funky was going on with Jasper Pippin, and it had to do with Olivia. Why else would he have said the words "the world is such a cruel place" in response to Janet's comment about Olivia's death? It was like a line he'd rehearsed to avoid saying what he really felt— that he was pleased as punch that Olivia was gone or that she'd gotten what she deserved—and it wasn't even original besides.

I'd already heard someone say something awfully similar yesterday: Terra Smith, who'd happened to be driving a borrowed car with a TSFA sticker on its bumper.

And I didn't believe in coincidence.

Chapter 24

When Janet dropped me back at my condo, it was just past ten o'clock. I didn't have much time to kill before I had to leave for Mother's house to pick her up. We were supposed to be downtown at the Market Center campus for Draco's bridal showcase at eleven, and the clock was ticking.

So I went inside just long enough to sit down at my laptop and do some belated digging into Jasper Pippin. First, I Googled TSFA and his name, and sure enough, he'd been on the board of directors of the Texas State Floral Association before his take-down by Olivia. Next, I dug into the archives of the *PCP* and *Dallas Morning News*, finding several small articles about Jasper selling off his shop in pieces. One even called it a "fire sale," which sounded awfully desperate. Janet had said he'd begun getting rid of his business *before* Olivia's show had aired—and the dates of the articles confirmed it—which made no sense.

Was there more to Jasper's story than met the eye?

Maybe Olivia hadn't destroyed his career glibly. If he'd been such a floral powerhouse, perhaps she would have found another target. Mother had mentioned Jasper's arrangements getting "fuddy-duddy." Had he been losing clientele well before the drama on *The Wedding Belle* had aired? What if his career was on the wane, and he'd been looking for a way out?

I couldn't help wondering if Jasper had been paid off somehow. Could the entire scenario between him and Queen Olivia have been scripted? What if his business had been in trouble already? Perhaps he'd viewed Olivia's show as his way out, his path to resurrecting a dead career?

But didn't it seem a bizarre way to save face when his reputation would suffer? Or had it truly been damaged? I'd wager that getting embarrassed by Olivia had generated an awful lot of sympathy, where simply going out of business would have branded him an out-and-out failure.

Which got me thinking about Terra Smith.

Had she been on her way out, too, at least where her gig with *The Wedding Belle* was concerned? Was it a fluke that she'd made her entrance on the final show of the season just as Jasper was exiting? Had Terra and Jasper banded together? Was her Planet Wedding idea the next big thing that Jasper had alluded to? What if they were going into business? Had they conspired to do away with Olivia to pave the way?

It was an interesting theory anyway, and one I mulled over plenty as I jumped in my Jeep and headed south to Highland Park.

When I reached Mother's house, I thought about pulling into her circular drive and honking. But sitting outside and laying on the horn wasn't something that sat well with Cissy (or any of her neighbors, for that matter). So I made myself park the car, get out, and ring the bell. I knew that she was alone, as Brian had taken Millie downtown to the ARGH offices bright and early.

When Mother didn't answer the door after I'd tapped my foot for at least a minute, I got worried. I pressed the bell again but the end result was the same. So I located the gold key on my ring and let myself in.

"Mother!" I hollered as I entered, and my heart pounded and my imagination wandered in a million directions. "Are you here?"

"For heaven's sake, there's no need to shout," she admonished as she came gliding down the stairs. "Just let me grab my bag, and we're off."

For Pete's sake.

I released a held breath.

"You're all gussied up," I said, figuring that was what had taken so long, not Olivia's deranged killer holding her hostage.

"This old thing?" she remarked and did a Vanna White with her hands to indicate her ensemble. "I figured you'd be wearing jeans with holes in them, so I didn't want to overdo."

"I decided not to go with holes today," I said dryly.

She was wearing her favorite pink Chanel suit with black trim, a triple strand of pearls, and black heels. She looked like she was ready for New York Fashion Week. I, on the other hand, had on a pair of khaki cropped pants, my slip-on sneakers, and a plain black T-shirt. Well, at least we were somewhat color-coordinated.

Mother ducked into the hall closet and emerged with a black Chanel bag. Before we'd even stepped outside, she tucked on her Jackie O sunglasses and pulled her keys from her purse.

"Whoa, put those away," I told her and jangled my keys. "I'm driving," I said, and she made a face.

"You want me to get into your Jeep in these heels?"

"Is there a problem?"

"Not if we take the Lexus," she replied then bit her lip. "Perhaps I should have called Fredrik and had him ready the Bentley."

I tried not to laugh. "Didn't Fredrik retire last year?"

My mother's longtime driver had to be at least eighty years old. She'd used him forever to take her to parties and teas and funerals, whenever she wanted to make an impression or just didn't feel like driving herself. The Bentley pretty much sat in the garage these days, gathering dust.

Cissy wrinkled her nose. "He said I could call him if it was an emergency."

"Well, it's not," I remarked and caught her arm. "Come on. Time's a'wastin'."

Reluctantly, she followed me outside and locked

up behind us. She frowned as she headed toward my car even though I opened up the passenger door and held it wide for her.

"You need a boost?" I asked.

She wasn't any taller than I was—five-five if I stood up very straight—and the step up was pretty steep with or without high heels.

"Should I get a footstool?" I asked when she stood and surveyed the situation.

"No," she said and flicked her bag onto the seat. "If I could get onto an elephant's back in a pair of strappy Jimmy Choos at that circus fund-raiser Mirabelle Braxton threw for the children's hospital, I can surely get into this rattletrap single-handedly," she announced. Then she hiked up her skirt a few inches and proceeded to climb her way in.

I was a little surprised she didn't just will herself inside.

"Are you okay?" I asked as she settled into the seat.

"Well, I didn't dislocate anything," she replied.

I shook my head, walking around the hood of the car to the driver's side. I opened the door just in time to hear my mother let out an inelegant grunt as she shut the passenger door. She brushed at a piece of hair that had come unglued from her perfect 'do and gave me a look that said, "Well?"

"You ready to go see some dresses?" I asked, pulling on my seat belt.

"I will be if I survive the drive," she said and smoothed her skirt before finding the seat belt. I heard it click before I started the engine. "So how am I supposed to act today?" she asked as I pulled away from the house. "Am I the good cop or the bad one?"

I bit the inside of my cheek and played it straight.

"You're the mother of the bride, remember?" I said, trying hard not to snicker. "So that must make you the bad cop."

She scowled. "Very funny."

I grinned and steered the Jeep onto Beverly Drive and away.

It took about twenty minutes to get downtown to the World Trade Center building, although I used the time to fill my mother in on what had happened that morning with Jasper Pippin. She mostly made *ah* and *um-hmm* sounds throughout, not offering much in the way of comments, which wasn't like her. She seemed distracted, and I thought I knew why.

After I parked and we'd exited the Jeep, I walked beside her toward the glass doors beneath the portico.

"Does Stephen get back this afternoon?"

"Yes, thank heavens," she said with a weighty sigh. "I'd hoped he'd come back sooner but he didn't want to cut out early on his chums."

I was actually surprised to hear that. "You told him what's going on, didn't you?"

"Of course I did!" She bobbed her blond head. "But he seems to think I should let the police do their job and stay out of Millie's troubles." She sniffed.

I felt an unfamiliar sense of solidarity. "He sounds just like Malone."

And Janet, for that matter, I mused. My very own George (or was it Bess?) didn't seem to be nearly as into this investigation as I was. Maybe she believed the police would entertain other suspects besides Millie but I had my doubts.

"If only Stephen had been here with Millie last night," my mother went on. "He wouldn't say that. He'd understand why she needs all the help and support she can get."

"Amen, sister," I said and scrambled to hold open the door.

Mother strode in before me, and I paused just inside the lofty atrium with the circular fountain bubbling ahead. My gaze immediately ascended each of the fifteen stories, taking in all the showrooms and their glass storefronts filled with color. Music swirled around us, and I smelled fresh-roasted coffee coming from one of the ground-floor restaurants.

"So where are we headed?" Mother asked, and I dug into my shoulder bag for the slip of paper on which Terra had jotted down Draco's suite number. "The fourteenth floor," I said and nudged Mother toward the glass elevators.

As I pushed the up button and waited for the elevator to descend, Cissy leaned nearer to whisper, "Maybe we'll get lucky and this Dracula fellow will blurt out a confession that he killed Olivia. Do the police know if he drank her blood?"

"No, he didn't drink her blood. He's not a vampire. He's a designer," I said, grateful for the *ping* as the elevator arrived and a pair of doors slid wide-open. I was about to remind her that his name wasn't Dracula when she piped up again.

"Oh, even better, maybe we'll actually find you a wedding gown!" she drawled happily. She had such an eager look on her face that I knew she was way more excited by that prospect than Draco confessing to Olivia's murder.

"We're not here to buy a dress," I said, thinking, *Not a chance in hell.*

"We'll see," Mother countered in a singsong voice and smiled.

I pressed 14, the elevator doors closed, and we went up.

Chapter 25

Terra was waiting for us outside the doors to Draco's showroom. She looked none too pleased, and I wanted to ask how her second interview had gone with the police, though I figured she hadn't talked much if they'd sprung her so quickly. And she'd been afraid she might be *très* late.

"I was beginning to think you weren't coming," she said and checked the clock on her phone. "You're late."

"We are?" Cissy piped up from behind me. "How can that be when Andrea drove like a bat out of hell?"

"Thank you, Mother," I said.

I glanced at the clock on Tara's phone. We were only five minutes behind schedule. Whoop-di-do. Then my eyes widened as I caught a glimpse of something else: the tattoo on Terra's ring finger, which I'd missed entirely yesterday. Mother was right. It looked like an inky wedding band. What else could it be?

So Terra was married? If she was, it certainly hadn't come out on the finale of *The Wedding Belle.* Terra played the show like she was single. That might be why she had the tattoo and no shiny rings on her finger. Could be it was part of the plot.

My gaze must have lingered on her hand, as Terra quickly stowed away her phone in her giant hobo bag and said, "We'd better hurry. Once the show starts, they'll shut the doors."

"Sorry," I apologized, "but it's been a busy morning."

"So I've heard," she snapped.

Wow.

I looked at Mother, who shrugged and mouthed, *PMS?*

Honestly, I didn't care about watching a parade of wedding gowns. I just wanted to meet Draco in the flesh and see if I could sound him out about his real relationship with Olivia. And maybe I'd ask Terra a question or two about Jasper Pippin.

"I saved us seats," Terra said, gesturing impatiently. "They're in the front row."

"Fab," I chirped, trying to act enthusiastic, though Mother didn't have to pretend at all.

"Oooh," she cooed, "I love VIP seats," and pranced giddily after Terra.

The minute we'd entered, a security guard did indeed shut the doors behind us, so Terra hadn't been lying.

The showroom had been staged with a raised runway jutting out between rows of white folding chairs. Giant screens at the rear displayed Draco's name in a burnished gold, the classic script nearly filling the entire space with "Fall Bridal Collection" in smaller black print just below it. En route to our chairs, we passed several dozen gowns worn by black velvet mannequins missing their heads. They were an eclectic mix of over-the-top satin ball gowns with flounces and rosettes and simple sleeveless A-lines. Draco was certainly a man of stark contrasts.

"This way," Terra said, indicating a trio of white chairs with RESERVED cards set across the seats. Thank goodness she'd saved them for us, as all the other chairs appeared to be filled with women holding clipboards with paper forms on their laps. The buzz of their voices sounded rather like a swarm of cicadas.

"My, oh, my, but Draco has a lot of fans," I remarked as Terra settled into the first available seat, and I took the next empty one. Mother settled in beside me.

"They're buyers from various department stores and bridal shops," Terra informed us. "They'll mark the gowns they like best and place orders with Draco."

"Are mothers of the bride allowed to place an order?" Cissy asked, leaning forward to look across me at Terra. "I particularly like bateau necklines on a princess cut gown. Something like that would look lovely on Andrea."

Dear Lord. I rolled my eyes.

"Don't worry, Mrs. Kendricks," Terra told her, "Draco and I have already pulled some gowns from his sample inventory specifically for Andy to try on after the show."

"Marvelous," my mother crowed.

Yep, she was doing a picture-perfect impression of a pain-in-the-ass mother of the bride, which definitely made her the bad cop.

Before I had a chance to join in that conversation, the lights went dim and music began to thump from unseen speakers. I couldn't say exactly what the tune was except that it wasn't anything from Vivaldi's *Four Seasons*. It sounded more like Japanese bubblegum pop.

I heard my mother murmur, "What in heaven's name is this? It sounds like cats in heat."

It made sense the moment a pair of models began to slink down the runway in Draco's gowns. They had Manga makeup: big eyes with even bigger faux eyelashes.

"They look like cartoons," Cissy whispered.

"Shush," I said, for all the good it would do.

She—and the weird makeup—had distracted me so that I didn't really see the first two dresses. But I did catch their bustle bows and winced. If that was an example of Draco's fall collection, I wondered how he was going to pay the bills.

Then all of a sudden there was the noise of a record scratching. The lights went dark again, and the audience began to murmur as a voice announced over the speakers, "Ha! Got you! Consider that a belated April Fools gift. Let the real show begin!"

I heard Terra sigh. "Mel has such a warped sense of humor."

"Mel?" my mother whispered and pinched my arm. "I thought his name was Dracula?"

"Shhh," I murmured and rubbed my skin, wondering why she couldn't read the giant letters of Draco's name printed on the background screens and get a clue. Sometimes I think she played dumb just to get my goat.

And it worked.

Abruptly, the spotlights went back on. They formed heart shapes as they zeroed in on the next model emerging from the wings on either side of the screens. Lovely, lilting music began to play what sounded like an Irish melody. I actually caught my breath as the first gown came into view, the model holding a ribbon-tied cluster of daisies. Her hair pulled back in a loose chignon and makeup subtle, she looked ethereal yet casual despite the long dress, its hem floating about her ankles. Her bare feet peeked out from beneath the swooshing fabric, and something about that earthiness tugged at my heartstrings. I could imagine a bride wearing that gown and walking through a field of clover.

"It's beautiful," I said of the dress that seemed so light and airy.

"It's far too plain," Cissy whispered.

Nope, I thought, we would never agree.

And so it went throughout the show, which had its share of simple dresses that appealed to me as well as full-blown princess gowns that had my mother patting my knee and nodding in approval. She was taking this way too seriously, especially when the gown that was the grand finale appeared. It was like an updated Princess Di affair with a lot of layers and lace. The elongated train went on for days, and I imagined a dozen doves holding it up with their tiny claws in a Disney flick.

"Oh, my word"—I could feel my mother tremble as she squeezed my thigh and panted in my ear—"now *that's* a dress!"

"No, that's a costume," I shot back. It was so not for me.

Before the lights turned up, the screens with Draco's name parted and a tall man emerged from between them. He was dressed all in black and had dark hair that skimmed his shoulders. He opened his arms, and the models appeared from the wings to take his hands and walk down the runway alongside him. The audience jumped up from their seats, dropping clipboards on their chairs, as Draco paused to bow before them. He could have been a rock star, for all their thunderous applause.

"That's him," I said, recognizing him from the episodes of *The Wedding Belle*. I noticed Terra's eyes watching his every move, like every other woman in the room.

"He's very handsome," my mother whispered, and she was right.

When the lights came up, Draco didn't leave the stage. Instead, he addressed the crowd via a microphone on his lapel. "Thank you so much for coming," he said in a throaty voice with a slight accent that I couldn't place, "as this particular show means more to me than most. I want to pay respects to the woman who helped bring my name to the spotlight." He tipped his face toward the ceiling. "Olivia, this was for you," he said then blew a kiss heavenward. "Rest in peace."

Terra made a sound like a cat with a fur ball caught in its throat.

"Are you all right?" I asked as Draco left the runway and we rose from our chairs.

"I'm fine. Let's go backstage. You can meet Draco and then try on the gowns we've pulled for you," she said with a stony expression.

Oh, yeah, she was clearly ticked off about something, and I didn't think it was because Mother and I had shown up five minutes late.

"I guess I could try on a few," I replied, though I didn't really want to play Bridal Barbie. I wanted to talk to Draco.

"Maybe you'll want to take a look, too, Mrs. Kendricks," Terra said to my mother, and I inwardly groaned.

"Oh, my dear, I can't wear an actual gown at my nuptials. I'm far too old," Cissy insisted. "But I do have a vintage Valentino suit that I've been saving for a special occasion. It's ivory and has the most gorgeous, one-of-a-kind crystal buttons."

"It sounds lovely," Terra said.

"Yes, it's lovely," I repeated, nudging Mother along. "Now let's go see the gowns, shall we? I have to meet Brian this afternoon so I can't be here for hours."

"You said Brian's a lawyer, right?" Terra remarked.

Had I? I hesitated, wrinkling my brow. I didn't recall mentioning that.

Mother stepped in to answer, "Yes, and he's brilliant." She touched my shoulder. "He's quite the catch."

"I'm a lucky girl," I said, and I got that funny tingling at the back of my neck. Something was up. I suddenly wondered if Terra had Googled me, just as I'd Googled her. That was an easy answer for how she'd found out about Brian's job. There was little privacy in the world anymore unless you lived off the grid.

"Let's head back," Terra said and started walking.

"To the gowns we go!" my mother chirped, like a rallying cry, and we followed Terra through the crush of women busy scribbling on their order pads, past a cluster of headless mannequins in wedding gowns, around the screens with Draco's name to the backstage area.

Terra ushered us through a door marked PRI-VATE into a quiet room staged like a giant dressing area with mirrors, hanging racks filled with at least a dozen gowns, and pink tufted and fringed settees that were round with elevated centers, like from an old-style hotel lobby. The walls appeared papered in pale pink silk wallpaper. Malone would have said, "It looks like a chick room," and it did.

"Why don't you both take a look at the gowns while I go off to fetch Draco," Terra said. "He's going to take a break from schmoozing the buyers to come back for a few minutes. So stay put," she instructed and quickly disappeared through the door, shutting it soundly behind her.

My mother dumped her handbag on the nearest round settee and headed to the racks first. She pulled out a princess-cut gown with wispy cap sleeves and embroidery on the satin skirt. "Oh, Andy, you have to try this one first."

"You do know we're not really here to find my dress," I told her as she hurried over to hold the gown up against my chest. "We're here to dig into Olivia's relationship with Draco. I think it was as staged as her show."

"Of course we're here to help poor Millie, but why not take advantage of the situation," Cissy said, swiveling so she could see my reflection in one of the many full-length mirrors. "It's beautiful, Andy. Go on"—she shoved me and the dress toward an enclosed dressing room— "do it for your dear old mother if for no other reason."

Hello, American Airlines? I'd like to book another guilt trip.

"For Pete's sake," I mumbled and snatched the hanger from her, shutting myself and the voluminous dress into the enclosed space that had several pink upholstered wing chairs bookending a tiny table, even a tiny oil painting of lilies of the valley on the wall.

Muttering all the while, I dropped my small cross-body bag onto a chair and began to systematically pile my things atop it: first, my T-shirt, then Capri pants. Standing in my bra and underwear—and slip-on sneakers—I unzipped the gown and stepped inside, wriggling my arms through the cap sleeves as I tugged it up.

I avoided looking into the mirror until I had the dress on and halfway zipped, which was as far as I could reach. But when I'd tucked my bra straps beneath the sleeves and lifted my chin, I bit my lower lip.

Oh, wow, I thought as my eyes got vaguely teary. It was the first time I'd seen myself in a white gown since the fitting for my debutante dress over a dozen years ago. *That* dress hadn't meant anything to me except to symbolize how Mother was twisting my arm into doing something I didn't want to do. *This* dress meant more than I could say, and I was struck by the fact that I looked like a real bride, not someone playing pretend. Suddenly, I had flashes of walking down the aisle to a waiting Brian and dancing in his arms at our reception, my gown swishing around my ankles.

Not that I wanted to say yes to this *particular* dress, but my knees felt a little shaky. I was so used to seeing myself in jeans or yoga pants that getting a glimpse of how I might look on my Big Day was a bit of a shocker.

"How's it going in there? You're so quiet," Cissy called through the door. "Do you need help zipping up?"

"I do," I said, which she took as an invitation to come bounding in.

The moment she entered the dressing room, I heard her breath catch, and a hand went to her throat. "Oh, Andrea," she sighed, "you look absolutely stunning."

As she came up behind me, her hand clasped my shoulder, and I smiled, still biting my lower lip. She nodded as her eyes welled, and I felt her fingers tremble as she struggled to finish zipping me up.

"There you are, and the fit is rather good for a sample," she said and patted my back. "This is really going to happen, isn't it?" she whispered. "You're getting married to Mr. Malone."

And I whispered back, "Yes, it's going to happen."

"This October?" she pressed.

"I don't know," I confessed, "but soon enough."

I heard my mother draw in a deep breath, and I did, too. It didn't matter that we were here at Draco's showroom to snoop. This was a special moment, one that neither of us seemed to believe in full.

Then Cissy added softly, "I only wish your father were here. How he would have loved to give you away. Loved it and hated it, too." She laughed and wiped at her eyes.

"I know," I told her and reached for her hand.

"Whatever you wear, you will look like an angel, and I will be so proud of you," she said and squeezed her fingers over mine.

"Thank you." I sniffled, thinking we had to stop talking like this or I very well could start bawling like a baby.

"No"—she let me go and brushed my tangled hair from my face—"thank you for being my daughter. I know I haven't been a perfect mother, and it hasn't been easy sometimes. But you've made my life far richer than I'd ever dreamed."

Oh, man! Was she trying to make me sob uncontrollably?

"Don't forget that I've made your life crazier, too," I remarked, because if I didn't say something to lighten the mood, we were both going to break down and Draco would find us here in the dressing room, weeping. I wonder if Starsky and Hutch had ever found themselves in such a situation.

"Yes, you have," Cissy said with a smile, "at least as crazy as I've made yours."

A sharp knock sounded at the door, and Mother brushed tears from her cheeks. I sniffed back the threat of tears of my own and said, "Yes?"

"Are you decent?" It was Terra's voice.

"I am," I told her.

"Then come out," she said, "and meet Draco."

Chapter 26

Mother was first to the dressing room door, and I turned around as she opened it.

"Here comes the bride," she trilled and stepped out ahead of me, all the while humming, *"Dum-dum-da-dum."*

I took a deep breath and gathered up the skirt of the dress before I plodded out on my tennis shoes less than gracefully. "Here's Mother's first pick," I said as I paused and let go of the fabric so the hem puddled on the floor. Despite the wealth of mirrors around me, I avoided looking at my reflection. Instead, I focused on the reactions of Terra and Draco.

She had her arms crossed and was frowning. Draco cocked his head, watching me, tapping a finger to his full bottom lip. He looked so dark and brooding amidst the delicate pinks and whites of the room. I imagined him peddling vodka or whiskey, not designing frothy white dresses for women.

"So what do you think?" I asked nervously, worried that I didn't do the gown justice. Why else would Terra be scowling and Draco squinting at me like I'd put it on backward?

"Well, you know what *I* think," Mother said when they didn't answer.

"Yes, I know," I replied under my breath.

After an extended pause, during which I listened to my stomach gurgle, Draco sighed and came toward me, his arms extended.

"My dearest Andrea," he said, pronouncing my name An-drey-ah, "you are a most magnificent flower. The dress becomes you."

There was that strange accent again. He sounded like a bad actor—albeit a good-looking one—trying to portray a man of mysterious origins. I thought I remembered Janet telling me that Melvin Mellon hailed from America's heartland. Well, it was very American to reinvent oneself, wasn't it? Or to pretend to be something one wasn't? Cissy and I were playing detective, although I had to admit we were far less proficient at it than Draco was at playing a male fashionista. His persona certainly didn't seem to hurt his business, considering how the female buyers in the bridal show audience had reacted. So I had to give him props for taking the Madonna Louise Ciccone approach and changing himself into exactly what the public wanted.

"Thank you for the compliment," I told him,

appreciating the flattery, phony accent notwith-standing. "It's a gorgeous gown."

"No, thank *you* for doing it justice," he said and took my hands, bending over to kiss them. "Terra has told me so much about you and your delightful mother. It's a pleasure to finally meet you both."

"The pleasure is all ours," Cissy said, blushing like a schoolgirl.

"Ditto," I replied, which might not be consid-ered the de rigueur response per my Little Miss Manners classes all those years ago, but that was all I had.

Draco smiled warmly—oh, yeah, he was good, I mused—and he let go of my hands, but not before I'd spotted the tattoo on his left ring finger. *Surprise, surprise.*

It looked exactly like Terra's.

"Oh, fudge," slipped from my mouth, and I wanted to bang my head against the powder pink wall. My mother had been right about Terra keep-ing secrets. This one was a whopper.

I was pretty bad at math, but I could put two and two together. Terra had told me she'd come to Dallas with a friend who knew Olivia and got her the job with the Wedding Belle. Terra had attended the Art Institute of Indianapolis, which was defi-nitely in the Midwest and was a design school for artists and designers of all stripes. Could that be where she and Draco had met before he'd done *Operation: Runway*? But if they were married to each other, why would Draco have feigned a rela-tionship with Olivia? Was it just for the publicity, as Janet had suggested? Had Terra taken the job as Olivia's sidekick to keep an eye on them? Either way, it seemed pretty weird.

I couldn't help wondering what the hell was going on.

"Andrea?" Draco saw my confused expression. "You're not pleased, I can tell," he remarked, "but I think I can fix that."

He snapped his fingers at Terra.

"It's not the dress," I said, but he didn't seem to listen.

"Fetch a veil for Andrea, would you?" he told Terra, and he nodded toward a round rack flush with headgear. "Grab the one with the seed pearls. And pull her hair off her face. We should give you the full effect, yes? It doesn't seem like you're happy, and I want to make you a happy bride."

"That's all right. I don't need a veil . . . really." I tried to nix that plan of action, for all the good it did.

Mother was practically jumping up and down. "Yes, bring on the veil," she drawled and clapped her hands.

Terra grabbed a floor-length model and returned. I winced as she roughly scraped back my unruly hair with the comb before tucking it onto my crown. Then she pulled the tulle forward so it covered my face. I felt like I was trapped behind mosquito netting, and I didn't like it.

"Um, I'd rather not," I said and flipped the netting right back over my head so I could see clearly again.

"Yes, of course, you don't have to wear it down,"

Draco insisted. "Why cover up such a lovely face, eh? Leave it pulled back so all your family and friends can see your bliss."

"I like the veil," my mother said, looking at me askance.

I wanted to pull her aside and tell her it wasn't the veil that was the problem.

But I didn't. Instead, I stared at Terra.

She'd hardly said two words in Draco's presence. She seemed überupset, and I wanted to know why. She kept stealing glances at him, and I wondered if she had gotten tired of the whole charade. Had she said anything to the cops?

"You're awfully uptight, Terra," I remarked, and her head snapped in my direction. "Did you have trouble at the police station? You said you had to go talk to them again this morning. Is anything wrong?"

"I don't know. Is it?" she asked, crossing her arms and looking defensive, hostile even. "A little bird told me you've been busy this morning, too, talking about Olivia."

Oh, boy, this was so not good.

I swallowed. "What's that supposed to mean?"

Terra glared. "Don't play dumb."

"Ladies, let's not squabble," Draco said, reaching out to squeeze Terra's shoulder. "Let's leave poor Olivia out of this, shall we? We're looking for Andrea's gown for her wedding—"

"Are we?" Terra replied, arching her eyebrows.

I glanced at my mother, but she pursed her lips. I could tell she wasn't going to be much help getting us out of this one.

"Maybe you should just say what you're thinking," I told Terra, "and stop with this whole passive-aggressive *shtick*."

"You want me to say what I'm thinking?" Terra frowned. "You might not want your mother to hear. Although she must be in on it or she wouldn't be here."

"I came to buy Andrea a gown," Cissy said, for all the good it did.

"Incredible." Terra chuffed. "So you've got her lying, too?"

"Mother's not lying," I returned the volley. "She does want to buy me a gown."

"But that's not what you're really after, is it, Andy?"

Ah, there she went again, trying to deflect her guilt onto me. Well, it wasn't going to work. I'd had a lot of practice with guilt, and I was pretty sure I could beat her at this game.

"What I'm after is a little honesty," I said, brushing my hands on the silky embroidered skirt. "I can't believe you don't want that, too. I'll bet it's been hard for you both, hasn't it, keeping such a huge secret for months," I pressed on, deciding someone had to get to the heart of the matter. If I waited for Terra or Draco to spill their guts, I might turn into Miss Havisham for real, wearing this wedding gown and sprouting cobwebs.

How had Terra kept mum for so long? I'm surprised she hadn't busted out with the truth on the finale of *The Wedding Belle*'s first season . . . unless she and Draco had signed a confidentiality agreement, which I'd bet was the case. Had they promised to stay apart as long as Olivia was alive and needed a beard?

Well, what about now that Olivia was dead? Could they finally stop pretending?

"I don't know what secret you're talking about," Terra said. She tightened her arms over her chest and pursed her lips. She wasn't going to be such an easy nut to crack.

"How about this one," I said and wet my lips, deciding to go ahead and take the plunge. "When you spoke with the Highland Park police, did you tell them that you're really Mrs. Melvin Mellon?" I asked, because I was sure no one would be more interested to hear about that than the po-po.

My mother sucked in her breath.

Terra fumed. Her face was so purple that I expected steam to rise out of her ears.

"An-drey-ah, Terra, please, don't be like this," Draco said, stepping between me and Terra. He lifted his hands in plea then realized I was staring at the tattooed ring so he dropped them to his sides. "Why can't we forget this nonsense and move on to another dress? It's so rare to fall in love with the first one you try on."

"Cut the crap, Draco, Melvin, whoever you are," I said testily. "Apparently, Terra's been doing some snooping—"

"I'm the one who's been snooping?" Terra cut me off, her eyes flashing fire. "Why don't *you* stop wasting our time and be honest, huh?"

"Me?" I blinked.

"Yes, you!" she insisted, clenching hands into fists. "How convenient that you didn't tell me yourself about being at Olivia's office right after Millie slashed her throat, and how convenient that you didn't spill that your fiancé happens to be the defense attorney who's representing the woman who killed Olivia!"

"How'd you find out about Brian?" I asked, because I was awfully sure at this point that I hadn't told her anything about Malone being a lawyer.

"Online," Terra said in a tone of voice that implied, *Duh.* "I saw an old engagement announcement in the *Park Cities Press* when I Googled his name. It said he worked at a big law firm downtown. So did the article from today's *Morning News* about him defending the killer cake baker." She turned her glare on Cissy. "I don't know what the two of you think you're going to find out with your Snoop Sisters routine—"

"Wait, you saw the engagement announcement in the *Park Cities Press*?" Cissy piped up, sounding pleased. "See, Andrea, I told you someone would notice."

Somehow, I refrained from hitting myself in the head with the heel of my hand.

"Speaking of the *Park Cities Press,* it's pretty popular with you Kendricks women, isn't it?" Terra paused to point at me. "Uncle Jas said that this one showed up at Belle Meade this morning with a reporter, nosing into his business and asking lots of questions about Olivia."

"Uncle Jas?" I squawked. "As in Jasper Pippin? The florist Olivia deflowered," I babbled on, then waved a hand. "You know what I mean."

When Terra said nothing, I knew I was right.

Oh, hell. Was he the relative she'd been living with since she came to town? Had Olivia known about their relationship? Was it part of this bizarre love/hate triangle—um, square—they'd cooked up to punch up the ratings for *The Wedding Belle*?

"Was that Jasper's car you borrowed yesterday when you came to the condo?" I asked. "I saw the TSFA bumper sticker and the one about honking for roses. He used to be on the TSFA board before Olivia humiliated him on national TV, and now he's got some big secret project in the works." I paused, cocking my head. "Funny, how it came along so quickly after Olivia's death."

Terra's gaze shifted over to Draco, but he didn't do anything at all except stand there and listen.

I gave it my best shot, asking, "That top secret project doesn't happen to be Planet Wedding, does it? Were you and Jasper and Draco plotting to put it together before Olivia was murdered?"

Terra clenched her jaw.

It was Draco who jumped in to answer. "You don't understand," he said, and Terra sighed, shaking her head as he spoke. "Salvo Productions has offered us a new show. Terra, Jasper, and I are all involved. If anyone was working behind Olivia's back, it was Sammi Garber and the other producers. They didn't want Olivia to know until the taping had gotten under way. They were afraid she'd be livid."

If my mouth fell open, it was with good reason.

That was even crazier than I'd imagined.

"Let me get this straight," I said, trying to wrap my head around the whole thing. "So you two were planning to jump Olivia's ship, and no one wanted to tell her? Did she find out and pitch a fit? Did one of you kill her and pin it on Millicent Draper since she was Olivia's latest target?" My gaze went from one to the other. "Which of you actually did it? Maybe it was Uncle Jasper? Or is it like one of those teen movies where the friends pinkie-swear to never tell?"

"No." Draco began shaking his head.

Terra's face pinched. "It wasn't any of us."

"Right," I replied. I suddenly felt like part of a reality show that wasn't reality at all, and I didn't know what to believe.

Draco reached out his hands like a beggar. "It's the God's honest truth," he said, dropping his accent. Without it, his voice had the flatness of a corn-fed Midwesterner, and he seemed a lot less mysterious. "We had nothing to do with Olivia's death. Why would we want her dead? As long as she was alive, she was money in the bank. Our careers would be nowhere without her and Salvo Productions."

"If you're so innocent, why haven't you publicly acknowledged that you're married? Did you at least tell the police?" I asked Terra, whose red cheeks turned milky pale. "I'll take that as a no," I said flatly. "If Mother and I noticed your matching wedding band tattoos, someone else will sooner or later. How long could you go on pretending, and why?" I stared at Terra.

She remained silent but I could see such sadness in her eyes. Sadness and anger.

"I can't believe you were okay with him living

with Olivia in the Turtle Creek penthouse and pretending to be her boy-toy . . ."

"No!" Tears sprang to her eyes. She swiped at them roughly. "I hated every second of it. It was a horrible way to live."

"But we couldn't tell anyone," Draco said. "We could have been sued. It would have been breaking our contracts." He ran a hand through his dark hair. "We signed confidentiality agreements with Salvo Productions," he explained, and Terra nodded. "We had to stay quiet. That was part of the deal. We shouldn't even be talking to you."

"Well, the police are going to find out soon enough," I said. "I'm seeing Brian at his office this afternoon. Once I tell him all of this, he's going to have to share that information with the DA."

"Andrea, you can't." Draco's dark eyes filled with panic. "We can't let you do that, not yet," he said, and he looked at Terra. "We need time to think. And I have to get back to the buyers first. I'm sorry. You'll have to sit tight for a while," he added, and he nodded at his wife.

Without warning, she came toward me and grabbed my arm, holding it in a death grip. "Hey," I said, unsure of what she was up to until I saw Draco put a tight squeeze around my mother all the while apologizing, "I'm sorry, ma'am, really I am."

"What are you doing?" I asked. "Let us go!"

"We're just going to keep you in the dressing room for a bit," Draco explained. "Consider it an intervention."

"You're locking us up?" I said as I stumbled forward in the gown, tripping over its hem as Terra proceeded to push me toward the open dressing room door. "That won't look good on your rap sheet, but I guess nothing's as bad as murder."

Terra shoved me into the small room.

"Are we being kidnapped? Is this a kidnapping?" my mother was saying as she came stumbling in behind me.

I grabbed for her, holding on as the door slammed shut.

"Don't do this!" I shouted, to no avail.

We heard the jab of a key in the door handle and then the click of the lock. I reached for the handle and jerked, but the door didn't budge.

"You're in over your heads!" I shouted and banged on the door as hard as I could. "You can't shut us up forever!"

Okay, I'd been in stickier situations before, I thought, glancing up. Clearly, the walls were too high to climb over without a ladder. I looked down and saw that the space beneath the door was far too slim to crawl under.

Rats.

I could still hear Draco and Terra somewhere in the room, arguing in low voices. That gave me hope. Maybe one of them had a conscience.

"Are you going to kill us with a cake knife and blame it on Millie?" I yelled, and my heart pounded because I wasn't at all sure they wouldn't. I didn't know who to trust, and they weren't giving me much ammunition to err toward the "not guilty" side of the fence.

I pressed my ear to the door and realized they'd

stopped arguing. I heard the retreating shuffle of their footsteps although I didn't hear the door open or close. What were they waiting for?

"Fantastic, we're locked in a stupid pink dressing room," I remarked to Mother, and I began to pace the small space like a caged cat.

"And I left my purse out there so I can't even powder my nose," Mother said and sighed as she settled onto one of the empty wing chairs. "Perhaps you could try on a few more dresses as long as we're stuck here."

I heard music coming from beneath my clothes on the other wing chair. It took a second for me to realize it was my ringtone for Malone. Mother's purse might be outside the locked door, but mine was inside.

Ha! Take that bumbling kidnappers!

I quickly dug for my phone beneath my pants and shirt.

Brian to the rescue! I thought as I picked up.

Except Draco and Terra must have heard the ringing phone, too, as suddenly their footsteps backtracked and Terra said, "Why didn't you grab her purse?"

Draco shot back, "Why didn't *you*?"

I had my phone out and hit the speaker button as they bumbled with the key in the lock.

"Brian!" I said, so he could hear everything going on. "Mother and I are"—*trapped*, I was about to tell him, but he ran right over me.

"I have news about Olivia's preliminary autopsy report," he said, his voice coming through loud and clear. "Someone in the DA's office must have leaked it to the press 'cause it's all over the media . . ."

The lock clicked, and the door handle turned.

I gasped.

Brian asked, "You still there, Andy?"

Draco pushed his way in and knocked the phone from my hand. With the grace of LeBron James, Mother snatched the cell out of the air before Draco could get at it.

And that was all the time we needed to catch the bombshell Malone dropped. And just in case we'd missed it, he repeated it for good measure.

"Did you get that, Andy? She was pregnant. Olivia La Belle was pregnant."

Chapter 27

The news hit Draco hard.

"No, that can't be true. It can't be," he mumbled, and he staggered away, out the dressing room door.

Terra followed on his heels.

"Andy? Andy, are you okay? Is something going on?" Malone was asking as I picked my phone up from the floor.

"I'm here," I said, breathing hard.

"Are you and Cissy all right?"

"Yeah," I told him as Mother caught hold of my arm, and we stuck our heads out of the dressing room. "We were tied up for a few minutes, but we're fine now."

"Someone posted a few seconds of video of Olivia and Millie from that wedding," he added, as Mother and I listened, my pulse thumping. "It's gone viral, like, a hundred thousand hits already."

He sounded perturbed, which was exactly how I felt. "It's one more thing for the police to use to build a case against Millie."

"Damn," I said, anger washing through my blood like hot oil. I was furious. "Can't anyone find that cameraman, Pete?"

"We're looking for him, Andy. No one at Salvo Productions knows who he is, and we've tracked down the wedding photographer through the Ryans. This Pete guy definitely wasn't part of their crew," Brian said, which is exactly what Janet had said, too. "Allie's taking Millie home now. She needs a break, and she's ready to deal with the mess left by the cops. Allie's going to stay and help her clean up."

Oh, yeah, that Allie's a saint, I wanted to say, but bit my cheek.

"I'm going to grab a sandwich, but feel free to come in sooner than two. I have something I want to show you."

"We'll be there soon," I told him. "I promise."

Draco was slumped on the round pink settee, and Terra stood in front of him, looking but not touching. I had a feeling she was wondering the same thing I was wondering: was he the father of Olivia's unborn baby?

Mother whispered, "Andrea, let's go. I don't want to find you a wedding dress *this* badly. We can always go to Neiman Marcus."

Call me stupid—and maybe I was—but I didn't feel threatened by Terra and Draco, not really, and I couldn't leave yet, not with so many questions burning in my brain.

I slogged toward Draco in the wedding gown until I was close enough to ask point-blank, "Was the baby yours?"

"No," he said without looking up. He dragged his fingers through his dark hair and stared at the floor. "No, it couldn't have been mine," he repeated, and he lifted his gaze to meet Terra's. "I never slept with Olivia. Even those nights I stayed at the penthouse and they taped those—" He stopped and swallowed hard. "—those bedroom scenes for the sake of the show. You believe me, don't you?"

Terra nodded. "Yes, I believe you."

Draco reached for her, and she took his hand. "I would never really cheat on you, not for fame, not for money."

No, you'd just sign some paperwork, pretend you're not married, and agree to live with a woman who wasn't your wife for fame and money, I thought, which in my eyes made him a greedy man-ho. But it didn't make him a killer.

"The other day," Draco went on, "Olivia said something about kicking up the ratings with a pregnancy scare. I thought she was joking. I told her that was going too far, and I wouldn't go along with it. I couldn't do that to Terra. Olivia was pretty upset."

"Maybe she already knew she was pregnant," I said.

He shrugged. "Olivia was complicated. She kept a lot to herself."

"Oh, Mel, you should've told me," Terra said to him, and he just held her hand and repeated, "I'm sorry, I'm sorry."

I didn't want to, but I believed him.

Olivia wouldn't have wanted Draco for a lover much less a baby-daddy. He was far too pretty, too up-and-coming, too ambitious, too young, and too poor (at least from her perspective). In other words, he wasn't remotely her type. So who had gotten her knocked up for real?

"So who was Olivia sleeping with?" I asked. When neither of them answered, I got angry. "If you don't speak up now, it's going to look even worse when the cops find out what you withheld from them. And they will find out, I promise you that."

I would make sure of it.

Draco hung onto Terra's hand, but they both remained tight-lipped.

"Come on," I pleaded, "you must have some answers. I knew Olivia way back when, and if she stuck to her old M.O., she was seeing someone older, someone with a big bankroll." Recalling Janet's gossip, I added, "Probably someone with a wife and kids."

I saw Draco's Adam's apple bob.

Terra wouldn't even meet my eyes.

Cissy tapped my back. "Darling, you should change," she said, "and we should go. *Now.*"

But I wasn't ready to quit.

"C'mon, people," I growled. "The police will assume you're the father, Draco. They'll hound you, and your charade will be exposed in the worst light. If you volunteer the information, you'll have some control of things."

Silence.

I threw up my hands and stomped around them in the wedding gown. "What if the real baby-daddy is the one who killed Olivia? What if he wanted to keep her from ruining his life? There's a murderer out there. Don't you want him to be caught? Or would you rather a sweet, little old lady who did nothing but bake a wedding cake go to prison and have that on your heads for the rest of your lives?"

I paused before them, staring daggers, like I was a Marvel Comics superhero who could summon confessions with the Evil Eye.

"We don't know who he is," Draco said, looking up at me. "I swear, Olivia never told us. She always met him somewhere private, not the penthouse and not at the office or anywhere else they might be seen or ratted out to the press by a doorman."

That wasn't what I'd wanted to hear.

"But you know *something*, don't you?" I said. "You two worked with her"—I looked at Draco—"you *lived* with her. Surely she dropped a few hints."

The Olivia I'd known was a braggart. She had a deep-seeded desire to feel superior, and she'd never been quiet about it.

Draco glanced at Terra, who stood stock-still. "She called him 'Frog' sometimes."

"Was he French?" I asked. "Olivia's parents live in Monte Carlo. Her father's an ambassador."

Draco shrugged. "Olivia made comments now and then, like, how he had people kissing his ass right and left. How he had women passing him their numbers on napkins, wanting to get him in bed. She got a kick out of the fact that she was the one who'd roped him in."

So Olivia's lover was in the public eye, too? I tried not to be disappointed by the lack of facts. "Anything else you can think of?"

"He must have paid for the penthouse," Draco said. "Olivia called it hush money for keeping her mouth shut. But she told me no one would know it was him because everything was handled through some dummy corporation."

"What dummy corporation?" I asked.

"I don't know. Something like Staypuff," he said.

"Like the Staypuff Marshmallow Man from *Ghostbusters*?" I asked.

Draco grimaced. "I'm sorry. That's all that comes to mind. I only heard her mention it, like, once. I didn't pay attention. It didn't matter to me what she did on her own time." He got up from the settee. "Look, I promise that we'll tell the police everything we've told you. But let us talk to our lawyer first. If we're violating our contracts with Salvo Productions, we need to know what our options are." He rubbed his hands on his dark black jeans. "But I don't want to stay silent and protect Olivia's killer."

"You almost sound as though you liked her," I said.

"I felt sorry for her," Draco replied. "She wanted things she couldn't have, and when she got them, it wasn't enough. I wondered if she would ever really know what it felt like to love and be loved unconditionally."

No, I thought, and she never would.

"One last thing," I said, looking at Terra, as she'd barely said a word. "Can you tell me how to reach Pete, the cameraman who was shooting footage at Penny Ryan's wedding? Olivia must have worked out some special arrangement with him. He wasn't with Salvo Productions or the official wedding photographer's crew."

Terra's eyes went round. "You mean the guy with all the tats?"

"Yeah, and the beard and black shirt," I said.

She looked confused. "He wasn't with the network?"

"No, the TV producers didn't send anyone to cover the wedding. Lester Dickens wouldn't allow it," I said without going into detail about how I knew that.

Terra and Draco exchanged glances.

"Sometimes," Draco began slowly, "Olivia would ask for help from her boyfriend. He seemed to be able to get things done when no one else could. If the Salvo people don't know the guy then that's probably what happened. He was probably a hired gun."

Hired gun, I thought, how apropos.

"Andrea, please," my mother whispered loudly from behind me. She'd stayed so quiet that I'd almost forgotten she was there. "It's time to leave before they decide to lock us up again."

"We're not locking you up again," Draco said flatly, and he gave us his saddest puppy dog eyes. "I apologize for panicking."

"You did go overboard," Mother scolded then

added under her breath, "I liked him better with the accent."

Terra suddenly came alive again. "Mel, get back to being Draco and go out to your buyers," she instructed and fairly pushed him out the door. "Go air-kiss them all so they double their orders. Then we'll call our attorney, okay?" She waited until Draco had gone before she snapped at me, "Are you happy now, Andy?"

"I'll be happy when Millie's off the hook," I said.

She flipped her skunk-hair and turned her back, reaching for the door.

"Oh, Andy"—she paused to aim one final salvo over her shoulder—"don't forget to leave the dress . . . unless your mother wants to buy it for you since that's the reason you came today, isn't it?"

She pulled the door shut with a *bang*, and I gritted my teeth. Yesterday, I'd actually begun to like Terra Smith; now, not so much.

"You were right, sweet pea," my mother drawled as she unzipped the gown and helped me out of it, "that girl is most definitely not Junior League material."

Chapter 28

After all the insanity, I was starving.

Cissy insisted on taking me to lunch after the Fashion Show from Hell, and I didn't fight her. We ended up at Dakota's, which wasn't far from Brian's office. I hadn't been there in a while since I didn't get downtown that often. I was instantly reminded of how much I loved the sleek black decor with the crisp white tablecloths and all the light coming through the huge windows. The food wasn't too shabby either, although Mother merely picked at her salmon and pasta salad—no wonder she was a size nothing. I demolished my jalapeño chicken mac and cheese with the fried onion crust, chasing down the spiciness with two tall glasses of tea, and I still had room for the chocolate mousse.

"Are you sure that you're not in the family way, sugar? You're eatin' enough for two," Cissy remarked, staring wide-eyed as she watched me suck down dessert.

"Oh, I'm sure," I said as I finished licking every smudge of mousse off my spoon. I wanted to remind her that Malone was a Boy Scout and was *always* prepared (elbow jab to the ribs and a hearty *yuk-yuk*). But I didn't think that was proper table talk, especially not with my own mother.

I felt like I was fueling up to do battle, and in a way I was. I couldn't wait to get to Abramawitz, Reynolds, Goldberg, and Hunt and share what I'd learned with Brian.

Though I told Mother I'd be happy to take her home first, Cissy insisted on going, too, if only to back me up. She was afraid he'd think I was making things up for Millie's sake. Even with Mother to stick up for me, I braced myself for the chastising that was sure to come—*I told you not to interfere in the investigation blah blah blah*—but Mother and I got our stories straight postmousse while we waited for the bill. We both agreed we wouldn't lie but merely stretch the truth, telling Brian that we were at the bridal show hunting for a gown and had overheard a private conversation between Terra and Draco. One thing led to another. How could we have not gotten involved?

Malone knew I was a magnet for crazy people. So I hoped he'd find the whole thing plausible, at least enough to follow-up on everything. And if he wouldn't, I'm sure the police would.

We were about to step into the elevators of the building where Abramawitz, Reynolds, Goldberg, and Hunt dominated a floor when my phone rang.

It was Janet. So I moved away from the elevator doors and Mother followed.

"What'd you find out?" I asked.

."You're not going to tell me you miss me this time?"

"No," I said, not in the mood for jokes.

"All righty, then I'll get straight to the skinny." She sniffed. "I talked to Sammi at Salvo about Olivia's beef with Millie at Penny Ryan's wedding. She wouldn't confirm that it was scripted, but she did say Olivia had lots of input on preparing scenes. Olivia discussed different options with the producers before they filmed and sometimes they shot things a couple different ways so they could use whatever had the biggest impact."

"That sure sounds scripted to me," I remarked as Mother tried to listen in.

"Sammi said they're going to use what footage they have so far for the second season and cobble together a few episodes," Janet went on. "She predicts the ratings will go through the roof."

"Wow, making money off a dead woman," I said and got a horrible taste in my mouth, "that's pretty sick."

"That's reality TV, kid." Janet sighed, telling me, "I've got to run," and hung up.

I shook my head as I put away my phone.

When we reached the floor with the ARGH offices, Malone was hanging out at the reception desk, waiting for us.

He looked relieved when we appeared.

"Hold my calls, Sarah," he told the woman with

the headset, who nodded and said, "Of course, Mr. Malone."

"I'm glad you're here." He kissed my mother's cheek then planted a quick one on my lips. "I've got a video to show you. This might take a while, Cissy. Can I get you settled in my office with some magazines and a cup of coffee?"

"Andrea?" Mother started to say.

"She's coming with me," I told Brian. "We both need to talk to you. We have some vital information about Terra Smith, Olivia's assistant, and Melvin Mellon—um, Draco—the designer Olivia was living with in the Turtle Creek penthouse."

"And don't forget Uncle Jasper," Mother reminded me.

"Right," I said. "And Jasper Pippin, the florist that Olivia supposedly drove out of business."

Brian's wide blue eyes blinked hard behind his glasses. "Andy," he said in a tone of voice that wasn't happy, "what have you been up to?"

"Mother and I went to a fashion show, like I told you," I said, my heart pounding, though that wasn't a lie. "But we stumbled upon some incredible tidbits about Olivia's inner circle that the police will want to hear." I summoned up a hopeful smile. "It might even be enough to keep them from arresting Millie."

"You just stumbled upon this vital information, huh?" he said and hooked a finger beneath his collar. "Did you break any laws that I should know about?"

Almost in tandem, Mother and I replied, "No!"

Malone let out a slow breath. "Okay, let's get started."

Without further ado, he ushered us through a hallway and past his office. We ended up in a conference room that had a table filled with paperwork, photographs, a large bottle of Tums, and what appeared to be a tiny camera and microphone for recording. The TV had been angled away from the wall, and I could see something on the screen that had been paused.

I saw a glass of melting ice cubes with red lipstick on the rim, and my stomach clenched for a moment. I was grateful for Allie's absence. It was going to be tricky enough telling Brian what I'd found out without his ex-girlfriend staring me down.

He pulled out a chair for Mother, and I'm sure he would have done the same for me but I beat him to it, sitting down where I could see the TV.

"What were you looking at?" I asked as Malone settled into a position nearest the open files. "Is it unaired footage from Olivia's show?"

"No." He picked up a remote and pressed a button so the screen began to move, tracking back. "It's surveillance video from the Highland Park Village parking lot," he said. "We went over it a dozen times with Millie, trying to find something the police might have missed."

"Did she tell you about the thumping noise?" I asked.

He nodded. "We didn't see anyone else exiting the building after she went in, and that includes anyone on the roof or climbing down. If someone was up there, they parked somewhere else and managed to avoid the cameras."

That didn't sound good for Millie.

"I want you to take a look," Brian said. "There are multiple views from different cameras, but this gives us the best view of Olivia's building."

"Okay," I said, because I hadn't arrived long after Millie. Maybe I'd notice something that she hadn't.

Brian nodded. "We'll start it when Olivia arrives, about fifteen minutes before Millie."

I'd spent most of yesterday watching all the episodes of Olivia's show, so my eyes felt a little bleary. I realized a parking lot surveillance video was not going to be nearly as dramatic as *The Wedding Belle*, but I had to be way more focused on the details.

I squinted at the TV screen and said, "I'm ready. Let her rip."

The quality of the video was much better than I'd expected, and it was in color, too. For some reason, I'd thought it would be grainy black and white like so many of the "Have you seen this person" videos of bank robbers on the evening news. But there it was: the parking lot at HPV, nearly empty early on a Sunday morning.

I remembered the sky being so blue and the clouds very wispy with the barest hint of a breeze. I watched as various store owners arrived and left their cars, heading to their respective shops.

A dark BMW four-door pulled up in front of Olivia's building, and she got out. There was no big white Escalade and no driver, like on her show, but I realized now that much of what happened on *The Wedding Belle* was less reality than fiction. She glanced around before she went inside and paused for a moment to grab hold of her hair, which began to blow, as did the potted plants on the sidewalk. As suddenly, the gale stopped, and she went inside.

Nothing happened for a while, at least not at her building. I didn't see a single other human being park nearby or wander in from outside the frame. The potted plants remained still. Minutes passed before I saw Millie's white Acura SUV pull up with the distinctive hot pink lettering. She didn't emerge for another five minutes. I could only imagine that she was sitting there, deciding whether or not to actually go in and confront Olivia. When she left her car and walked toward the building, her shoulders looked slumped. Her whole demeanor was reluctant. She certainly didn't appear to be in any kind of murderous rage.

As she opened the glass doors to the building, there was another gust like the one that had whipped up Olivia's hair. The flowers in their pots waved again, and Millie seemed hardly able to shut the doors against the gusty wind.

I said aloud what I was thinking. "But it wasn't gusty that morning. There was barely a breeze."

Something weird was in the air. That was for sure. I just had to figure out what it was.

I didn't say anything to Brian, watching silently as my Jeep drove into view and parked. No gust of wind greeted me as I went inside Olivia's building. Within moments the ambulance and cop car pulled up.

"That's all she wrote," Brian said and hit pause.

"Can I see it again?" I asked, because there was something about the video that reminded me of one of Olivia's episodes of *The Wedding Belle*. But I needed to be sure I wasn't wrong.

But by the second time, I was even more convinced that the killer had not arrived by car. He hadn't parked in the parking lot. The way he'd come and gone made him virtually unseen, at least by the surveillance cameras.

"On one of Olivia's shows," I said, "a bride arrived by helicopter. She made everyone's hair a mess and blew decorations around."

Brian tensed. "You think the killer flew to Highland Park Village?"

"Yes," I said, even though I knew it sounded kooky as hell.

"Where did he land?"

"On the rooftop," I suggested.

Brian shook his head. "There's no helipad on any of the HPV buildings, Andy. They're old, sit too low, and they're not equipped for it."

"Then he landed somewhere close," I said. "Millie heard a thumping sound. What if it wasn't footsteps? What if it was the helicopter blades? Who even notices helicopters these days? Those stupid news copters are everywhere, morning, noon, and night. It's like white noise."

Brian sighed and removed his glasses, rubbing at the bridge of his nose before he plunked them back on.

Why wasn't he taking me seriously? Did he think I was just blowing smoke?

"Call the FAA or whoever you call to find

out about flight plans," I said, getting ticked off. "Wouldn't a pilot have to file one?"

"You think some hit man dropped out of a helicopter to kill Olivia, stole her laptop and phone, and then disappeared into the clouds like Batman?" Brian offered.

"Yeah," I said, because it was the twenty-first century. Stuff like that wasn't science fiction; it was real and doable if you had the money.

"I'll have someone look into it," he said, but I only half believed him. "Why don't you and Cissy fill me in on that important information you stumbled onto," he prompted. He had a pained look on his face, like he was afraid of what was coming. "Should I chew some Tums now or after?" he asked as he leaned back in the chair and loosened his necktie so he could unbutton his collar.

"Now would be good," I said and looked at Cissy.

Mother nodded at me. "Go on, Andrea," she encouraged. "Tell him about that handsome vampire's fake accent and the tattooed wedding bands and how those two nutty fruitcakes locked us in the dressing room."

"Oh, God," Malone sighed and reached for the big Tums bottle. He popped the cap and shook a few out, chewing on them as I started to talk.

I took a deep breath before pitching headfirst into my monologue about being at Draco's show, going backstage for some personal pampering and then "eavesdropping" on an argument between Terra and Draco about Olivia. I explained about their tattooed ring fingers and how Mother had noticed Terra's first. Then I filled him in on Jasper Pippin and his connection to Terra, and how Draco said that Salvo Productions was planning to spin them all off in a new show minus Olivia.

"Jasper Pippin, Draco aka Melvin Mellon, and Terra Smith . . . they're all tied together, don't you see? They were all tangled up in Olivia's web of lies," I said as Brian sat back in his chair, staring stupefied at me. "They could have plotted to kill Olivia," I offered halfheartedly, "only I don't know which one of them actually did the deed."

"My vote is Jasper," Mother volunteered. "He can't be as inept as the other two at criminal activity."

I thought of Jasper carving up peony stems with the paring knife and nodded. "You could be right. Janet thinks he's too prissy to be a killer."

Malone squeaked, "Janet's involved in this?"

"Hmm, she might have something there," my mother agreed. "If he could do the flowers for the White Glove Society's deb ball with Dorothea Amherst breathing down his neck for twenty years without killing *her*, then perhaps he doesn't have it in him."

"What about Terra?" I suggested. "She sure turned into Super Bitch in the blink of an eye, didn't she?"

"Yes, she did," Mother replied.

"Damn," I said, thinking that all three suddenly seemed like lame suspects to me. I wasn't sure I could see any one of them confronting Olivia in her office, grabbing a cake knife, and stabbing her to death.

"Ladies, can we move on, please." Brian leaned forward, his arms on the conference table. "I'll pass along all those insights to our investigator. Anything else you'd care to share?"

"Yes," I said, perking up. "Draco and Terra both knew about Olivia's real boyfriend, who is probably married and who definitely bought her silence by getting her the Turtle Creek penthouse. Only he used a dummy corporation to buy it so no one would be the wiser." I looked at Mother. "Draco thought the name was something like Staypuff."

"Yes, that's what he said." Cissy nodded.

"Staypuff?" Malone repeated, and I knew he was thinking of the Marshmallow Man, too. "While you were, um, eavesdropping, did you get the boyfriend's name, by chance?"

"No, sorry, Draco and Terra didn't know," I admitted. "But Olivia bragged that he had lots of people kissing his ass and lots of women who wanted to sleep with him." I leaned my elbows on the table. "If this rich and powerful boyfriend was really married, I'm sure he freaked at the news of Olivia's bun in the oven. Draco said that just a couple of days before she died, Olivia suggested playing out a pregnancy scare on the show, only he wouldn't agree."

"But she *was* pregnant," Malone said, and I saw a vein bulge on his forehead. "She didn't have to fake it."

"Yeah, but Draco didn't know that at the time." I sat up straighter as a couple of giant *what ifs* came to mind. "What if Olivia wanted this baby to happen? And what if her boyfriend didn't? What if the baby was his worst nightmare?"

"It's despicable"—Cissy clicked tongue against teeth—"the lengths that some men will go to, to avoid taking responsibility for their actions."

"Or to protect their social standing," I said.

"Hmm." Brian made a noise and started shuffling through some paperwork. He withdrew a page and squinted at it. "We do have the name of the corporation listed on the property tax records for the purchase of the Turtle Creek penthouse," he said. "It's called Stayman, Inc."

So Draco hadn't been too far off the mark after all.

"Someone named Stayman also posted the video of Millie threatening Olivia at the wedding," Brian said and glanced up. "We're looking into who operates that YouTube account, and we're also looking into ownership of the company, but it might take a while to get answers."

"So much of Olivia's life was a mystery," I said.

"Excuse me." My mother cleared her throat and raised her hand, like a child in a classroom. "But I have a question."

Brian turned to face her. "Shoot."

"You said Stayman, did you not?" Cissy asked.

"That's right, Stayman." He pushed at his glasses.

I wrinkled my brow. "Have you heard of it?"

"Well, it could just be coincidence," Cissy murmured, fingering her pearls, "but Stayman is a bridge term . . ."

"So?" I said, because I wasn't sure how that mattered. Lots of people knew bridge terms. "It also could be someone's name."

"Oh, it's that, too," she told me and stopped playing with her pearls. She clasped her hands on the conference table, focused on Brian. "It was the name of one of my best bridge partner's beloved cocker spaniels many moons ago," she explained.

"Stayman was a dog?" Brian remarked.

Mother nodded. "He belonged to my friend Adelaide, bless her heart, when she was married to Lester Dickens."

Chapter 29

We left Brian's office about an hour later, after Allie had returned, of course, and grilled me even harder than the police about Olivia La Belle. By the time Mother and I escaped, went down the elevator, and exited the doors of the downtown high-rise, I was exhausted and tense and more convinced than ever that Millie had been set up. Not by a trio of bumbling amateurs, but by someone with a big wad of cash, enough to have bought and paid for a professional hit.

Someone like Lester Dickens.

At first I'd wondered if Olivia was having an affair with the oilman. But why would Dickens need to kill a pregnant girlfriend? Why not just write her a check and dispense with her relatively quietly, as he had multiple wives? No, it made more sense that he was protecting someone else, a man who had way more to lose than a marriage or a reputation if word got out that he'd knocked up his mistress.

A man like Vernon Ryan.

When I'd suggested to Allie and Brian that they have the firm's PI investigate Lester Dickens's and Senator Ryan's ties to Olivia, they'd looked at each other and then at me like I was a lunatic.

My mother hadn't appeared any too happy either. "You think Vernon was sleepin' with Olivia?" She'd frowned, though her brow stayed smooth as silk. "I hope you're wrong, Andrea. That would break Shelby's heart. They've been together since high school, and she spent a lot of time alone raising Penny when Vern was in the Navy. She's put up with a lot for him."

"Sorry, Andy, but I'm with your mother"—Allie McSqueal had jumped right on the Bash Andy Bandwagon—"that theory's six kinds of crazy. We can't go around accusing Senator Ryan of being involved with Olivia La Belle without some pretty solid evidence."

I didn't have evidence. But I did have a hunch that Lester Dickens had orchestrated Olivia's murder and implicated Millie in her death.

It fit like a kidskin glove.

"Who else could have pulled it off?" I'd said.

"All you have is a bunch of hearsay," Allie had insisted. "Forget Senator Ryan for a moment. You do know who Lester Dickens is?" she'd asked, like I was some brainless bumpkin. "He's not just the biggest oil tycoon in the state, but he's a political heavy hitter, like a wannabe Koch brother. And he comes with his own goon squad. They're probably armed better than the Dallas Metro Police."

"So that makes them off-limits," I'd replied, "even if Senator Ryan's the reason Olivia's dead and Dickens is the one who had her killed?"

"It's not our job to identify or prosecute the guilty parties," Allie had retorted, giving Brian a look, like, *Why are you with this chick?* "We don't even have to prove Millie's innocence, just that she's not guilty and someone else had the opportunity to do it."

"So you're not going to look into Dickens?" I'd asked, because that was the feeling I had gotten despite Malone's promises.

"We have to tread lightly, Andy," Brian had said. "We can't just bulldoze our way into his business and his private life. We'd need evidence, something concrete, something we could take to the police, like emails or voice mails, some kind of trail."

"But that's why he took Olivia's laptop and her phone!" I'd said, throwing up my hands. "He had to be sure no one found his footprints. He had to protect himself and Vernon Ryan."

"You don't know for sure that she was sleeping with the senator," Allie had shot back, shaking her head. "That's a huge accusation, and not one we can throw around without something to back it up."

"Why don't you tell the DA to check for a DNA match between Olivia's unborn baby and the senator," I'd said, shaking with frustration. "That should give the police enough to start digging into Vernon Ryan's connection to Olivia."

"I've had enough," Cissy had said and put an arm around my shoulders, quietly telling me, "You've done all you can, Andrea. It's time to let go."

And she was right.

I didn't know what else I could do to help Millie except sit back and wait for the chips to fall where they may. I was pretty sure that Terra Smith would never speak to me again much less help plan my wedding (not that I'd want her to). Ditto Draco and Jasper Pippin. At least I'd given Brian and Allie a ton of food for thought—and more suspects to consider—and I had to believe that the truth would win out, despite Millie looking as guilty as ever with that carefully edited video playing on YouTube showing her telling Olivia, "One day, you'll get what's coming to you, and it won't be any too soon!"

As I got behind the wheel of the Jeep and started the engine, I told myself, *Hang it up, Nancy Drew.* I'd given sleuthing my best shot, and I'd failed.

The drive back to my mother's house was a fairly silent one until Mother's phone trilled. "Stephen!" I heard her say, and her voice joyfully rose. I quickly gathered from the conversation that he'd landed ahead of schedule and was already at Beverly Drive, waiting to see her. "Oh, sweetheart," she cooed, "I've missed you, too!"

Hearing the affection in her tone gave me such bittersweet emotions. Though I wished to God every day that I still had my father, I figured Stephen wouldn't be a half-bad stepdad. He was kind and smart, and he was manly without being macho. He made my mother happy—and softer somehow—and that was worth scads.

When Mother hung up with her beau, she turned to me and said, "Step on it, would you? My man is back!"

Um, hello, wasn't I the woman who drove like a bat out of hell?

But I gave the Jeep more gas regardless, making the engine *vroom*, which made Mother's smile even wider. Maybe all wasn't quite right with the world, but you wouldn't have known it by looking at Cissy in that moment.

I offered to drop her off in front so as not to crash their reunion. But Mother insisted I come inside.

"Nonsense," she said once I'd pulled into the driveway, "Stephen will want to see you and hear all about us being locked in the dressing room at the World Trade Center."

I wasn't so sure that I wanted to tell that story again, considering the reception it had gotten from my own fiancé, but what else did I have to do but go back to the condo, work on clients' Web sites, and wallow in self-pity? And, admittedly, my mind was not on Web design at the moment.

"Sure, I'll come in for a few minutes." I caved, turning off the ignition and getting out. Mother had already climbed down from her seat by the time I came around the hood, and she was smoothing down her skirt when I saw the front door open.

"Sweetie!" she cried as Stephen appeared.

"Cecelia!" he called to her and started down the steps, his arms opened wide.

She scooted across the cobbled driveway like a gazelle in three-inch heels.

Cecelia?

Wow. I hadn't heard that name uttered in eons, not since I was about ten and my great-grandmother had been on her way out of this life. We'd visited her in the nursing home when she had late stage dementia and thought I was my mother. "Cecelia," she'd said, "your nails look filthy. Don't you ever wash your hands?" I remembered my mother explaining to me that Cecelia was her given name but no one ever used it. She'd always been Cissy to everyone, including me and my father.

Except for Stephen, I mused, but I thought I understood. Since neither Daddy nor I had ever called her Cecelia, maybe that was why she didn't mind Stephen doing it. It made him separate from us and what we'd had. It could be her way of starting fresh.

"Hey, lovebirds," I said and cleared my throat to get their attention. "Maybe I should duck out and leave you alone."

They stopped hugging the lights out of each other, and Mother swiveled in Stephen's arms so I could see her pink cheeks.

"You'll do no such thing!" she called. "Stephen said he has pictures from Augusta to show us!"

Yeeha.

I should have slipped away while I'd had the chance.

Unable to extricate myself gracefully, I followed them up the steps, across the porch, and inside.

"It's so good to have you back," Cissy told her beau, squeezing him around the waist. "Do you need a drink?"

Good thing I wasn't thirsty 'cause she didn't even ask.

"I've already got a cold beer in the living room," he said.

"Then let's head in and rest our feet," Mother suggested.

"Sounds good to me," I replied, though, again, nobody asked.

I sunk down into an easy chair while Cissy kicked off her heels and dumped her suit jacket on the back of the sofa. She looked so cool and crisp in her pink dress and pearls as she tucked her stocking feet beneath her. Stephen settled down at her side, an open bottle of Peroni propped on a coaster on the coffee table, easily within arm's reach.

"Let me see the pictures," Cissy said, sticking a hand in his jacket pocket.

Stephen laughed, batting her fingers away and withdrawing a paper packet. He slid photographs from the sleeve and handed them to my mother.

"Have at it," he said.

"Oh, you look like you were having fun," she murmured as she began to flip through the stack of them. "Ah, there's the Eisenhower tree . . . and the Big Oak."

My mother had gone with my father to Augusta more than once when I was little and Sandy had babysat me. I was sure she knew each landmark well.

"So Andy," Stephen said while Mother continued to admire his pictures. He had his hand on Cissy's knee, and she didn't seem to mind. "I've heard you've had quite a time while I've been gone. Your mother said you lost a classmate in a pretty rough fashion."

"Yes, Olivia La Belle," I said, slumping against the pillows at my back. "She was a bitch and a half. But murder is a harsh way to go."

"It definitely is." He raised his eyebrows, which were cinnamon tinged with white, like his hair. "You didn't like her?"

"No, she was awful," I admitted, squirming. "But I didn't know she was having a baby. Maybe she wanted to change. I'd like to think so, anyway."

I rubbed my eyes, thinking of something Olivia had said to me. I had thought she was about to apologize. Perhaps, in a way, she was.

I can't always do what's right and I can't always please everyone, can I? I have to look out for myself and sometimes that makes me a little too—

Dead, I thought, and I sighed.

"So the police haven't arrested anyone yet?" Stephen asked, and I shook my head.

"No, not yet, but Brian said they're building their case against Millie. I'm sure Mother already told you that I'm part of the reason Millie's in trouble, because I walked into Olivia's office and saw her with the body. But she didn't do it," I said, more certain than ever. "You know she stayed here last night?"

"So your mother mentioned," Stephen replied and nodded at Cissy. "I wanted to fly back sooner but she wouldn't let me. She didn't want Millie to feel unwelcome, and I trusted her instincts."

"Really?" It was my turn to be surprised. I glanced at Mother, but she still had her head down as she went through the photos. "I thought she'd have begged you to come home and set things to right."

He smiled. "Well, I'm here now. Any way I can help? Though I know Millie's in great hands with Brian on the case."

"I don't know if there's anything else we can do except support her," I said, resigned to the fact that I had to sit on the sidelines.

"And we will support her to the fullest," my mother chirped, glancing up. She tapped the photos together on the coffee table then passed them across to me. "Have a look, Andrea. See what fun a vacation can be? Seems to me you haven't taken one in a long time. Though I guess your next one will be your honeymoon, *n'cest pas*?"

"I guess you're right," I said and took the photos.

She turned to her beau and they started chatting about his trip, the weather in Augusta, how much golf he'd played, and what he'd scored.

It was as though a murder hadn't happened and everything was hunky-dory.

I tuned them out and halfheartedly shuffled through the pictures. Ah, there was Stephen with his buddies on the golf course. There they were drinking beer after golf. There were the obligatory sunsets, a giant loblolly pine, a pretty bridge, and an older dude standing in front of a fountain with his arms hooked over the shaft of a golf club.

I peered more closely and noticed that those arms happened to sport tattoo sleeves that looked an awful lot like roses and thorns. I couldn't help but think of Pete the Cameraman, and my heart skipped a beat.

"Who's this?" I asked Stephen, interrupting him and Mother as I handed the photo back.

He shot me a toothy grin. "That's an old Navy buddy of mine. His name's Bill McGill. Handicap's twelve, but he's got a hell of a chip shot."

"So are the tattoos military?"

"They can be," Stephen said with a nod. "They are for Bill. The thorns represent every tour he did. The roses are for his wife and kids. He got a bone frog on his ass after he retired, but I don't have a picture of that, thank God."

"Oh, you!" Cissy giggled.

"A bone frog?" I said.

"It's a skeleton frog," Stephen explained, "for Navy special ops. You don't want a thing like that on your body while you're serving, in case you run into trouble and have to wiggle out. In my day, only a few of the guys had tats, but all the young ones do it now. The old-timers waited to get ink until they mustered out."

I knew I'd seen a tattoo like that somewhere. But my brain was too filled with other stuff to remember where. But the rose and thorn tattoos I could never forget.

So who was Pete the Cameraman really?

He's not just the biggest oil tycoon in the state, but he's a political heavy hitter, kind of like a wannabe Koch brother. And he comes with his own goon squad.

They're probably armed better than the Dallas Metro Police.

I'd bet Dickens's goon squad was made up of military vets who'd gone into private security. I had no doubt that Pete the Cameraman wasn't a cameraman at all. He was former military with the tats to prove it. Did he work on Lester Dickens's crew? There were an awful lot of dots to connect, but I could see the picture they were painting pretty clearly already.

Why couldn't Allie and Brian see it, too?

I squeezed my eyes shut, recalling a remark Lester Dickens had made about Vernon Ryan at Penny's wedding reception: *Damned fool . . . a man can't reach his full potential when he's distracted by women and babies.*

He hadn't been referring to Penny's baby, as I'd thought then, not entirely. He was talking about Olivia's pregnancy, too. Maybe Vernon Ryan's affair with the wedding planner alone wouldn't have kept Lester's candidate from aiming for the White House, but a baby born of that affair surely would have put an end to any presidential dreams. Once Olivia had given birth—even if they'd stopped sleeping together—that child would have been a constant reminder of the conservative politician's indiscretions.

And Lester couldn't have that hanging over Vernon Ryan's head.

Lester Dickens had Olivia killed. Of course, he hadn't gotten blood on his own hands. That was what guys like Pete were for.

Ugh.

I dropped my head into my hands, feeling sick to my stomach.

"Andrea," my mother said, leaning forward, "what is it? You look nauseous. Is it morning sickness? You can have it any time of the day, you know."

"Morning sickness," Stephen repeated. "Andy, are you—"

"No," I said as my phone started playing AC/DC. I reached for my bag, which hung low on my hip. I didn't recognize the number but answered anyway.

"Oh, thank God!" I heard a voice that seemed vaguely familiar. "You have to help me. Terra told me to call if something went wrong."

"Draco?" I said, recognizing the flat Midwestern twang interspersed with the mangled European accent, like he wasn't sure which one to use at the moment. "What's going on?"

So much for figuring I'd never hear from him again.

"It's Terra," he said, and he sounded on the verge of tears. "She's missing."

Chapter 30

"Right after you and your mother left the showroom, she started acting weird," he began to explain before I'd even asked. "She seemed really nervous and said she had somewhere to go. When I asked where, she just kissed me hard and said that it was time to play the big money card. After that, we'd be set for life."

"Set for life, huh?"

I got a big knot in my belly, sure now that Terra had known who Olivia's lover was all along. But instead of telling the police, she was going to get herself killed trying to scam a boatload of money from good ol' Lester Dickens. And I'd thought she was smart.

Hmph.

"You should call the cops," I told Draco, wondering what he thought I was going to do about it. "You need to talk to them anyway."

"I did call them!" he said. "They won't lift a finger, not until she's been gone at least forty-eight hours. She gave me your number before she took off and said if anything went wrong I should call you."

Why? Did Terra think I could do something the police couldn't?

"Have you tried her cell?"

"I've called and texted at least a dozen times in the last four hours. All the calls go straight to voice mail. My texts don't get answered."

"Did you mention to the cops that she was Olivia La Belle's assistant?" I asked, getting up from the chair while Mother and Stephen looked on with concern. "Have they forgotten what happened to Olivia?"

"They think I'm overreacting." He snorted. "They said she probably went shopping or out for a drink with some girlfriends, but she didn't. Terra hated shopping for herself, and she didn't have any real girlfriends here. She just had me."

Considering how she'd treated me and Mother and her penchant for fashion circa 1980, I was convinced.

"Have you checked with Uncle Jasper?" I asked dryly.

"He hasn't seen or heard from her either, and he's worried, too. She borrowed his car again, and it doesn't have OnStar." Draco paused, and I could hear him breathing heavily. I hoped he had a paper bag handy in case he started to hyperventilate. "I think she's in serious trouble, Andrea. I think she's meeting with Olivia's boyfriend."

"What's his name, Draco?" I asked, tired of being jerked around, though I was pretty sure I knew who it was already.

"I don't know any more than what I already told you. I heard Olivia call him Frog, and Terra did, too. I figure she had something of Olivia's the police didn't find, something that incriminates the guy."

"Ya think so?" I replied, unable to keep the sarcasm from my voice. "Was she the one who stole Olivia's laptop and phone?" I asked. "Did she have them this whole time?"

"No, she would have told me," Draco insisted. "She even turned her office laptop over to the police. She's only had her old laptop these past few days. It was one she didn't use for business."

Ah, yes, Terra's spare laptop, I thought, wanting to tear out my hair.

It's my insurance policy, she'd told me, and I'd figured at the time she just meant it was her backup in case the office laptop crashed. I suddenly remembered where I'd seen that photo of the bone frog tattoo: in a file on Terra's computer labeled "Big Money Shot."

I had a feeling that butt wasn't Draco's.

"You don't have a frog tattooed on your ass, do you?" I asked, only to get a befuddled, "What?" in response.

"Oh, man, that's it," I moaned as the light went on in my brain, and, like Eliza Doolittle, I think I finally got it. Senator Ryan had been in the Navy. I'd wager it was his butt with the tat and the brown mole in the photograph. I was pretty sure that a forensics expert could compare the photo and the actual ass to confirm it.

Was that the evidence Terra had? Or was there more to it? Maybe she had emails or texts or sexts. Who knew? Technology was making it too damned easy to keep anything private anymore, and she'd worked closely with Olivia for months.

No wonder Terra had been so silent when I grilled her and Draco about Olivia's lover. It wasn't because she didn't know who he was. She just hadn't wanted to share. She'd been gearing up for a big blackmail attempt.

"Did she take that spare laptop with her?" I asked Draco.

He paused. "Yeah, I saw her carry it out. It's hard to miss with that stupid pink sticker."

"If you know where she went, you'd better tell me now," I demanded, and my face got hot. "Olivia's killer doesn't care about Terra. He'd just as soon get rid of her, too."

"She said the meeting was at Alva's, but I don't know who that is, I swear." He paused to sob then got ahold of himself. "I guess we'd both been keeping secrets."

"Yeah, you've got a great marriage there, Melvin," I murmured.

"Please, don't let anything happen to her. Can't you call your lawyer boyfriend?" he asked. "Can't you get him to do something if the police won't? Can't they ping her phone or the laptop and find her like they do on TV?"

"Does she have tracking software on the computer?"

"Does she need it?"

"Yeah," I said through gritted teeth. "And if her phone's turned off, it wouldn't do any good to try to track it." She wasn't answering his calls or texts. So that was probably the case.

"You have to do something," Draco whined. "Nothing I have means anything without Terra, and I can't go anywhere. I don't even have a car."

Oh, boy.

What was I supposed to do? Call Brian and tell him that Terra Smith had been gone a few hours and that her husband—aka Olivia's phony-baloney live-in lover—was afraid she was blackmailing Olivia's potentially homicidal baby-daddy?

That would go over big, I was sure.

Brian and Allie had all but rolled their eyes earlier when I suggested Olivia was in bed with the oil tycoon and the senator.

So who did that leave? I mused, and my gaze settled across the coffee table on Stephen and Cissy.

"Please, Andrea," Draco begged. "If anything happens to her—"

Yeah, yeah. I'd heard that part already.

He started to cry for real, and my chest clenched.

"Okay, okay," I said, giving in.

Mother must have been right about my getting involved in other people's problems being a compulsion. Or else I just couldn't stand to hear a grown man sob.

"I'll see what I can do," I told Draco. "In the meantime, call me if you hear from her."

I hung up and met the stares of my mother and Stephen.

"Hey," I said, tucking my cell back in my purse, "are you two doing anything special tonight? If not, could you possibly go on a rescue mission with me?"

"Oh, Andrea, no," Cissy drawled, and started shaking her head. "Stephen just got back. I was thinking I'd order in dinner and we could relax."

"We can order dinner later," my future step-father said, and he rubbed his hands together. "Who needs saving this time? At least I know it's not Malone or your mother."

Hmm, I thought. It might not be bad having a stepdad who was a former Navy SEAL and ex-IRS.

"It's Terra Smith," I told him. "She was Olivia La Belle's assistant."

"But she's the one who locked us in the dressing room," Cissy declared with a frown. "I don't know if I like her well enough to save her."

"*Mother,*" I said in my best shame-on-you voice. "She left Draco to meet with someone, and she's been gone for four hours. I just need you to make one little phone call."

"To whom?" she asked, eyeing me suspiciously.

I drew in a deep breath then let it out again.

"Lester Dickens," I said. Draco was mistaken. Terra hadn't gone to Alva's to meet someone. She'd gone to the house on Alva Court.

"He told you to call if you wanted a private showing of his Preston Hollow mansion, right?" I said, putting the pressure on. "And now's as good a time as any."

Mother waved her hand dismissively. "No, no, no, I'm not going over to Lester's house alone. You think he had a hand in Olivia's death. Why would I put myself in danger?"

"I'll go with you," I said, "and Stephen can come along, too. I'll make sure Lester keeps his hand off your butt."

"*Andrea,*" my mother scolded.

"Keeps his hands off your what?" Stephen asked none too happily.

"It was years ago at a party," Cissy said, unfurling her legs from beneath her. "He'd had too much to drink, and he acted like a clod."

"I'll clod him," her beau grumbled, rising to his feet.

Mother blushed.

"Do you still have Fredrik's cap?" I asked, figuring Stephen could play chauffeur, wait outside, and call the police if things got dicey. "Is the Bentley gassed up?"

"Yes and yes," Cissy said, scrambling up from the sofa.

"Will you do it?" I asked. I had a sinking feeling in my chest. "We have to get there before he does anything to Terra, even if we just distract him long enough for Stephen to convince the cops to come. If we don't, she's as good as dead."

Chapter 31

I don't know what my mother said to him, but Lester Dickens agreed we could come by the house on Alva Court for a very quick private showing. Apparently, he was impatient to fly off to his cabin in the Hill Country by nightfall.

Maybe I should write a mystery, like Janet had suggested, because I thought the Hill Country sounded like a very good place to bury a body.

Stupid, greedy Terra.

"What are we looking for, Andrea?" Mother asked as Stephen pulled the Bentley up to the gates and we were buzzed through.

"It doesn't matter," I said, "we're just going in for a few minutes, long enough for Stephen to call the cops and tell them something's wrong. We need to get them out here to look around, and I don't think anything else will do it."

"If they've got her locked up in a closet, it would serve her right," Mother murmured.

I sighed, thinking maybe we should just turn around. I wasn't sure if we were the A-Team or the Three Stooges. I just hoped we wouldn't need rescuing ourselves.

"I'll give you five minutes," Stephen remarked over his shoulder as he drove the Bentley onto the grounds. "Then I'll dial 911 and tell them I heard screaming."

"Fine," I said and gazed out the window as we headed up the long drive toward the sprawling villa.

"I should have called Shelby," Mother said, "and just asked outright if that husband of hers had been diddling the wedding planner. Sometimes the wife isn't the last to know. She's found a fair share of lipstick on his collar for the past twenty years since he entered politics, all explained away innocently, I might add."

"No doubt," I said. Excuses were the one thing that politicians did best.

Ahead I saw the sun setting behind Lester Dickens's Mediterranean villa, silhouetting the massive home. It seemed almost an island unto itself. I felt as if we were driving down a country road, far away from the city. It would have been a perfect setting for two lovers to meet, I decided. The Alva Court mansion fit all the criteria for a love shack. There was no doorman. No one was living there permanently although I was sure Lester came and went. The nearest neighbor was a few acres—and one tall gated privacy fence—

away. What more could a cheating senator and his mistress have asked for?

"I'll bet they came here," I said, voicing my thoughts out loud. "It's the perfect spot for a rendezvous."

"I hate to think you're right about Vernon," my mother said. "I'd like to believe that there are some good men left in the world and perhaps one honest politician."

Stephen cleared his throat, and I caught his eyes in the rearview mirror.

"Yes, my darlin', you're one of the good ones," Mother cooed from the backseat.

"Thank you, ma'am," he said and tipped his hat.

As we neared the house, I looked for Terra's borrowed car, but I didn't spy the old Mercedes wagon with the TSFA sticker. I didn't see anything suspicious, including Lester Dickens's private security hanging around either, not until we pulled into the circle around the fountain and the front door opened wide.

Out strolled a pair of Black Suits, one of whom stayed near the door. The other came forward to lean in the window as Stephen rolled it open.

"You can wait out here," the Black Suit told him, glancing into the back where Mother and I sat. "I'll escort the two of you inside. Mr. Dickens is waiting."

Cissy seemed reluctant to leave the Bentley. I nudged her, and she scooted out as the Black Suit came around and waited for us to emerge. He escorted us to the house, where a second Black Suit manned the front door.

I looked hard at the second man as we approached. Something about him seemed familiar. It wasn't until I'd passed him, stepping into the foyer, that I realized it was Pete, only he was clean-cut and shaved. What a difference that made.

"Hey—" I started to say but quickly clamped my lips shut.

I must have stared, as he gave me a look and not a friendly one either.

"This way," he said and took over as our escort from that point forward.

Why did I feel like this was a very bad idea? The knot in my stomach tightened, and I reached for my mother's hand.

Only I didn't hold it for long.

As we stepped into the two-story living area with the folding doors that opened to the patio, Lester Dickens rose from a chair and opened his arms. "Cissy, darlin'," he said, like they were long lost pals. "You look as pretty as ever."

"Lester," my mother said stiffly, turning her head when he tried to plant a kiss on her lips. He caught her cheek instead. "I know you don't have long so let's get started. Andrea's anxious to see more of the place."

"That's right, you were here for the wedding, weren't you?" he remarked, giving me a squinty-eyed stare.

"Yes," I replied and wished he didn't give me the heebie-jeebies.

"You sure you're interested in my place?" he asked and took a step away. "It's eight thousand square feet so we could be here all night. Is there somethin' specific you're looking for?" he asked, wandering over near a big round marble coffee table. "Something like this," he said, and he practically pointed down at a laptop with a hot pink smiley face sticker.

My heart nearly jumped from my chest. I knew instantly the computer belonged to Terra Smith.

She's here, I thought and looked at my mother. She was here, and Lester knew that was why we'd come. Oh, man, we were so screwed.

"Something wrong, ladies?" Lester asked, smirking the way Olivia used to when she was sure she'd bested me.

I hoped to hell that Stephen had called the police already 'cause Plan A had gone out the window, and we didn't have a Plan B.

"You know, on second thought," I said, trying hard not to panic, "this place is way too big. It's not really what I'm looking for at all."

"Are you sure? Because I could swear I've got what you're after. Hold on a sec," Lester remarked, and nodded at the clean-shaven Pete. He disappeared for a few minutes only to return carrying a woman in his arms. Her head hung slack, her two-toned hair swaying. I could see her hands were bound behind her back and her mouth was duct-taped.

Pete deposited her on one of the plush sofas.

It was Terra Smith.

And she wasn't moving.

"Good Lord, Lester!" Mother said. "What have you done? Is she dead?"

"Not yet," Dickens said. "She's still breathing for now. When she realized I wasn't gonna go for her tricks, she told us you'd be coming. She also spilled quite a bit of detail about how you've been sniffing around trying to save that cake baker's neck." He shook his head, rubbing his jaw. "This low-life girl who was so desperate for money she would've given up her own mama."

"What's wrong with you, Lester?" Cissy said, and her voice shook. "Are you just going to keep hurting people until there's no one left?"

"If I have to," he replied, walking up to my mother, his hands on his hips. "I really hate to do this, Cissy, 'cause I like you. I truly do. But you should have left well enough alone."

"You're out of your mind." Mother turned to me, her pale eyes scared. "Andrea," she said, "we should go."

"No, ma'am, you should stay," Lester said and grabbed her arm. "In fact, I insist."

"Andrea, go!" my mother shouted, and I turned to run.

I raced like a bat out of hell through the foyer and got to the front door, only to fling it wide and find a Black Suit on the other side. Before I knew what hit me, he grabbed me and put me in a chokehold I couldn't break.

I couldn't breathe. I clawed at his arms, struggling for air, but his grip didn't ease. What would Nancy Drew do? I wondered, but my mind was going black. I started to pray, and my last thought was: *Dear God, don't let me die and leave Brian to Allie.*

Then nothing.

When I came to, I heard their voices even before I could force my eyes into slits.

"Cissy, darlin', I had no choice," Dickens was saying, his Texas twang sounding mournful. "My back was against the wall."

My mother sounded way too calm. "We always have a choice, Lester, and you've got more than most."

My cheek pressed into the floor and my mouth was so dry I couldn't have gotten a word out, even if my lips weren't wearing duct tape. I tried to wriggle my hands, but the tape around them was wrapped so tightly. I quickly realized my ankles were bound, too.

Lester sighed and walked across the room. I could just see his cowboy boots and a little of his cuffs. "I didn't do it just for me, or even for Vernon. I did it for the country, *my* country," he said and then turned around. He sounded chockful of self-righteousness. "We're going to hell in a handbasket here, if you haven't noticed, and I want to do something about it. If I can get Vernon in the White House where he belongs—"

"You killed a girl," my mother interrupted. "You murdered her in cold blood, and you're going to kill another."

"For God's sake, Cissy, *I* didn't do the killing."

"No, you hid behind your money," she told him, and her voice trembled, not with fear but with fury. "You had one of your goons do it for you, just like a mobster, and you framed a lovely, kindhearted woman so you wouldn't get caught."

"It's called collateral damage," Dickens insisted, and those cowboy boots turned around and headed back to the chair where my mother sat. "It's a by-product of war. Ask any vet who's ever served."

If I rolled my head slightly back, I could see him get down on his haunches to look her in the eye. Her ankles were bound to the chair legs with duct tape, and I'd wager her arms were bound, too.

"Oh, Lester, you've never been in the military," my mother scolded in the same tone she'd used when I'd done something to disappoint her. "This isn't a war you're fighting, not one for this country anyway. You were doing this for yourself. You were protecting Vernon from his own weaknesses. He cheated on Shelby and got Olivia pregnant—"

"And she was going to blab it on her damned show!" Lester sprang to his feet, and I winced as he pounded a fist against the wall. "She was going to blow everything to smithereens so she could get more press. That damned girl didn't care about anything but herself. Why else would she have used her wiles on Vern to get him in the sack?"

My mother sniffed. "Oh, yes, I'm sure it was all her doing," she said.

"You're not seein' the big picture here, Cissy!"

"Oh, I see it just fine."

And so could I, even with my brain still half foggy and my throat aching like someone had karate-chopped it.

If Olivia had made her affair with Senator Ryan public knowledge—if she'd gone through with the pregnancy—the senator would never have survived the scandal. Maybe Shelby would have stood by her man, but his party would have forced him to bow out of the election. And Lester Dickens could kiss his chance at getting a president in the White House good-bye.

"It's going to all come out anyway," Mother said. "They're going to use DNA to find the baby's father. They can do that stuff, you know. It's not just made up for *Law & Order*."

"We'll see about that," Lester chuffed. "I have friends in high places, darlin'. Reports can be changed. Lab results can be fabricated."

I tried to squirm like an inchworm but I hardly moved. It was more like the futile flapping of a dying fish. The best I could do was angle my head to better see them.

My mother kept talking. "Are you just going to keep murdering anyone who gets in the way of your grand scheme, Lester? Shame on you! If Adelaide were still alive, she'd be appalled at the man you've become."

"Don't you bring Adelaide into this," Dickens said, and he came away from the window to bend low over my mother.

"You already did," Cissy said in her *I'm so disgusted* voice, "when you used Stayman to mask your dirty deeds. You know how Adelaide loved that pup, and now you've sullied his name, too."

"I did what needed doing," Lester said, "and I'd do it again. In fact, I think I'd better see if we can fit two more bodies on the heli to Austin tonight—"

The door came open and Lester Dickens froze.

I tried to turn my head to see who'd come in, praying like heck it was the cops. But I could only see a pair of legs in dark denim and a pair of tailored loafers with tassels. They looked like the Bruno Maglis my father used to wear on weekends.

"Les, you have to let them go," a man said, and I realized it was Vernon Ryan.

I closed my eyes and thought, *Thank God*.

"I mean it," the senator said, taking a few more steps in. "This has to stop now."

"Get out of here, boy," Lester railed at him. "You've made a mess enough, and I'm just trying to clean it up. Let me handle things—"

"I called the police," Vern announced, and he walked over to the chair that held my mother. "I'm going to tell them everything about me and Olivia, about the baby, about you. I can't keep pretending I don't know what's going on, Les."

"You called the cops? Son of a bitch!" Lester fumed, and his cowboy boots stomped straight up to Vernon Ryan. They had to be standing nose-to-nose. "What the hell'd you go and do that for?"

I heard a soft grunt. Lester must have pushed hard as the senator fell back into a standing lamp, knocking it over. It clattered to the floor near my head, and I winced.

Ryan bent to pick it up, and he saw me watching. He gave me a vague nod, as though to reassure me everything would be okay.

Slowly, he righted the lamp and then he stood.

"It's time I did the right thing," the senator said, raising his voice, "and it's about time I stood up to you, Les. I don't want the Oval Office nearly as much as you do. It's not worth it." His voice broke. "It's not worth killing for."

"You're a fool, Vernon," Lester told him and spit at the floor. "You stay and wait for the cops. You explain it all away and see if they buy your bullshit. I'm getting the hell out," he said. Then he stomped across the den and threw open the door.

When he was gone, the senator drew in a deep breath and let it out.

"I'm sorry, Cissy, so damned sorry," he said, and he went to my mother, crouching low beside her chair. He pulled out a penknife and began to cut the duct tape that bound her ankles.

"Thank you, Vernon," my mother said, looking over at me with tears in her eyes. "Andrea, are you all right?" she asked.

"Um-hum," was all I could croak with the tape on my mouth.

I heard the wail of sirens getting louder, and I realized the senator hadn't lied. He'd called the cops, and just in time. Or perhaps Stephen had done it, but I didn't care which.

Oh, yes, there were more than a few good guys left in the world, I thought as Vernon Ryan crouched beside me, sawing the duct tape with his penknife to set me free.

At the moment I knew of three.

Chapter 32

Not twenty-four hours after Lester Dickens had been arrested for murder and attempted murder—along with several members of his goon squad—Senator Ryan called a press conference and announced his retirement from politics.

It didn't look like Shelby was leaving him, though. Mother had talked to her, and Shelby claimed they were going overseas for a much needed vacation and they weren't saying where. "They have to get away from the press if they're going to work things out," Cissy explained, and I couldn't blame them.

I understood about working things out. Malone had been pretty pissed at me when he found out what Mother and I had done. "You could have gotten yourselves killed. How could you do something so reckless? Why didn't you call me first so I could talk you out of it," he'd ranted, saying plenty of things I'd already said to myself.

Reminding him that Stephen had been along for the ride—heck, he'd driven—and had called the police once we'd gone inside hadn't seemed to help, at least not for the first few days after.

But once Vernon Ryan had spilled his guts to the police and a warrant was issued for Lester Dickens's arrest, along with a few of his henchmen, Brian eased up on me.

He even apologized for not taking me seriously when I'd suggested that Lester Dickens had been involved in Olivia's death.

But no apologies were necessary, not once I knew Millie was off the hook. Mother even threw a dinner party to celebrate (only she had the beef Wellington catered).

It was good to see Millie so happy and talking about opening up that restaurant for real. "Your mother wants to invest, can you believe?" she'd confessed, and I told her that I'd be pleased as punch to contribute to such a worthy cause, too.

"Only if you let me bake the cake for your wedding," she'd told me with tears in her eyes. "And it's on the house."

"I'll let you know," I promised, "when we set the wedding date."

Millie had glanced from me to Mother, a puzzled look in her eyes. "But I thought Cissy said October sixteenth . . ."

I'd assured Millie that date wasn't for real, that it had just been a part of the ruse Mother and I used when we were snooping.

Only I'd begun to realize that maybe my mother didn't think it was a joke. Particularly when, the very next day, the doorbell rang and who should I find on my doorstep but the wedding planner.

"Ta-da!" Terra Smith held out a garment bag emblazoned with *Draco* in gold. The bag was far bigger than she was. I could barely see her two-toned head behind it.

"What is that?" I asked, reluctant to let her in after all the trouble she'd caused. I couldn't even believe she had the nerve to show up at my place. "Is it a peace offering? If that's the case, you should have brought a puppy."

"No, it's your dress, silly," she told me and pushed her way inside.

"It can't be mine," I insisted as I closed the door and followed her in. "I didn't order a dress. There must have been some mistake."

"Ah, but it is yours," she insisted and deposited the puffy bag on my sofa. The zipper made a zzzzz, as she tugged it open. "Your mother picked it out from Draco's fall collection. She said it's exactly what you would have wanted, so it's been bought and paid for. We used measurements Cissy had left over from the deb dress you never wore, and we added about an inch or so to account for gaining a few pounds through the years. Don't worry," she added when she saw my horrified expression, "if it doesn't fit perfectly, we've still got time for alterations."

Good Lord. I nearly asked if she was kidding, but I could tell that she wasn't. I was about to say, *Well, you'll have to return it,* when Terra opened her mouth again.

"Cissy also had me book the Highland Park Presbyterian Church for your ceremony, and we're set with the Dallas Country Club for the reception. It'll be a sit-down dinner, of course. And Uncle Jas is doing the flowers—"

"Of course," I repeated, though barely any sound emerged. My mouth was drier than the Mojave Desert. "I thought Cissy didn't like you."

"We made up." She shrugged. "Okay, I think she just really wanted the dress and Draco wouldn't give it to her unless she used me."

"Ah-ha." Now that made sense.

"Anyway, everything's set for October sixteenth, just like you'd planned," she said, and she pulled the gown from the bag.

"But October sixteenth was just for show," I tried to say, only my protest was lost in the swish and swoosh of endless yards of fabric.

For a brief instant my heart pitter-pattered, and I had hopes I might see the delicate dress that the model had worn with bare feet and daisies. It would have been lovely to think that Cissy had actually listened to me and paid attention to my feelings.

But that pitter-patter soon turned to a clunk.

"So," Terra said and held the gown up before her, "what do you think?"

It wasn't the ethereal dress that had floated across the runway. It was the finale gown, or at least a toned-down version of it, all flounces and poofs with a train that required at least a dozen doves to carry it.

Lord have mercy.

I wet my lips. "So Cissy has everything worked out down to the appetizers, does she?"

"Yep, you don't have to lift a finger," Terra said and looked around for a hook to hang the dress. She ended up catching the hanger over the top of my TV armoire. "Just enjoy being a bride," she rattled on as she backtracked toward the door. "You're good to go. I've got all the details covered. All you have to do is show up at the church!" she remarked with a wave and a "Ta-ta!"

Then she was gone.

I stared at the Princess Di gown that filled my tiny living room, and I felt surprised and confused and ticked off all at once.

Okay, ticked off most of all.

So I was getting married on October sixteenth, was I?

Funny, how the bride was the last to know.

I felt my blood pressure rising, and I tipped my head to the heavens, doing my best Captain Kirk impression—or was it my Olivia La Belle impression?—as I hollered, *"Muuuuther!"*

I felt wrath all right, and I curled my fingers to fists. Bravo, Cissy, I thought. She'd turned me back into my insecure eighteen-year-old self, reliving the horror at getting railroaded into a cotillion.

It was what I'd feared most, and it had happened.

Cissy had planned my wedding without me, and it was everything she wanted and nothing that I wanted. It was my debutante ball all over again.

Déjà poo.

Only I was a grown woman now. I could do as I pleased. I just had to find a way to stay true to myself without Breaking My Mother's Heart, Part Deux.

And I thought I knew just how to do it.

Epilogue

 October 16
2:00 P.M.
Wedding Day

I put the phone to my ear as it dialed Cissy's cell, and I waited through one ring and then two.

She picked up with a breathless-sounding, "Andrea?" *Stay strong,* I told myself. Giving in was not an option, even though I cringed as she asked, "Where the devil are you?"

I glanced at Malone, seated in the chair right beside me. He squeezed my shoulder and whispered, "You can do this. Go on."

"I'm at Love," I told her bluntly.

"You're in love? Well, of course, you are," she said, and I caught the strains of a string quartet in the background and the noisy hum of voices. "Do you know there are four hundred people waiting inside the church for you to appear?"

I steeled myself and blurted out, "I'm at Love Field, Mother. I'm not coming. So I'm not going to make it to the church on time or late even . . ." I paused, and Malone squeezed my arm again, urging me on. "I told you to leave the wedding up to me and Brian, and you couldn't do it."

"But I sent a car for you," she insisted. "You should have been here an hour ago."

"We took a cab to the airport," I said, and my pulse bounced around like a pinball. "We're waiting on our flight."

"What flight?"

"We're eloping," I confessed, holding the phone away from my ear as she cried, "Nooooo!"

Her usually smooth-as-silk voice shook like a rattle. "You can't do this to me, Andrea! You ran away from your deb ball. You can't run away from your wedding, too!"

Oh, couldn't I?

"I didn't want a big wedding any more than I wanted to debut," I reminded her, refusing to let myself feel awful, or like I'd abandoned her. This wedding was her Frankenstein's monster, not mine. "It's what you wanted, Mother. This was all for you, not for me."

"So what am I supposed to do?" Cissy said tearfully. "There are four hundred people filling the pews, glancing at their watches and whispering about why the bride is late—"

"Get married," I told her, because it seemed the most logical thing in the world. "You're engaged to Stephen. You wanted this wedding. So now you can have it, everything you've always dreamed of. Don't think about it. Just do it."

Her reply was a miffed-sounding, "Andrea, you stop this nonsense and get back here right this minute! I was in labor with you for twelve hours while your father passed out cigars in the hospital lobby. It was too late for an epidural, and I didn't take so much as an aspirin. I have never been in such pain in my life," she said, starting in on the tired, old spiel that was supposed to make me drop everything—a spiel I had memorized—and I looked at Brian, shaking my head.

"Now boarding, United Airlines Flight 1459 to Las Vegas," I heard over the loudspeaker, and Malone tapped my hand as he got to his feet.

"Mother, I've got to go," I interrupted her tirade. "I love you very much. Have a wonderful ceremony, okay?" I said in a rush. "And don't forget to email pictures!"

Then I hung up.

I sucked in a deep breath, my emotions bittersweet.

"Can you do this?" Brian asked. "Will you be okay?"

"I'll be fine." I nodded. "But I don't know about Cissy."

Brian must have seen my legs wobble as I got up to stand in line to board, as he took my carry-on bag from me. Then he leaned over to whisper, "Good-bye, Dallas, and, hello, Vegas. Pastor Elvis, here we come!"

I kissed him hard.

God, I loved that man.

"As God is my witness, I will not let ten thousand dendrobium orchids and four hundred plates of coq au vin go to waste," Cissy said under her breath, and she snatched the bridal bouquet from Terra Smith's hands. Grabbing her tuxedo-clad beau, she whispered, "Plans have changed, darlin'. It looks like Andrea isn't coming."

"Andy's not coming?" Stephen's wide brow wrinkled and he scratched his faded ginger hair. "What the hell's going on? Where is she?"

Cissy sighed. How could she possibly explain that phone call from Andrea, who had clearly gone insane? There were no words. And worst of all, perhaps Andy was right.

"Cecelia?" Stephen said softly.

"I screwed up," she whispered and frowned. Maybe she'd overstepped her bounds the tiniest bit. But she had done it all with the very best intentions. Every detail had been planned with love and affection. She only wanted the best for her child. Couldn't Andrea see that?

"Sweetheart, talk to me," Stephen pleaded.

Cissy bit her lip. "You know how we'd discussed going to Paris to marry, and I'd wear my lovely cream silk Valentino suit?"

"Yes?"

"Well, scrub that. We're getting married now."

"We are?" Stephen looked at her as if she'd gone as mad as Andrea; although, oddly enough, she had never felt saner.

"You love me, don't you?" Cissy asked him, because that was all she needed to know.

"I do," he said, "more than anything in the world."

"You said 'I do,'" she remarked with a smile. "Those were exactly the words I wanted to hear. Just say them one more time when the minister asks, and we'll pull this thing off without a hitch."

"I do," he said again, as though practicing to get it right. Then he gave her his arm and quietly sang, "Here comes the bride."

"Oh, you!" Cissy scolded, but her heart swelled in her chest.

"Mrs. Kendricks?"

Terra Smith stood by the vestibule doors, looking hesitant, and Cissy nodded. As if reading her mind, the girl pulled the doors wide, and Cissy heard the string quartet begin to play the Wedding March for real.

She gripped Stephen's arm tightly with one hand and the bouquet with the other. "Let's do this," she said, and she took a deep breath.

He squeezed her hand and replied, "Yes, let's."

Cissy held her head high and smiled at Stephen. As the wedding guests rose from their seats and four hundred pairs of curious eyes turned upon them, they began to walk down the aisle together.